Praise for Kinley MacGregor's
MASTER OF DESIRE

"*Master of Desire* proves once again that
humor and passion are the trademarks
of any Kinley MacGregor book."

Christina Dodd, author of *Rules of Attraction*

"Warm, witty and wonderful, Kinley MacGregor
weaves a magical minstrel's tale."

Stephanie Laurens, author of *All About Love*

"*Master of Desire* was the perfect mix of passion
and pageantry, tenderness and humor.
Every page was a pleasure!
The witty and talented Kinley MacGregor
just shot to the top of my 'must read' list."

Teresa Medeiros, author of *The Bride and the Beast*

"I love Kinley MacGregor's books! They brim with
laughter and love. *Master of Desire* is her best yet!"

Cathy Maxwell, author of The *Marriage Contract*

Books by
Kinley MacGregor

A PIRATE OF HER OWN
MASTER OF SEDUCTION
MASTER OF DESIRE
CLAIMING THE HIGHLANDER
BORN IN SIN
TAMING THE SCOTSMAN

Kinley MacGregor

Master of Desire

AVON BOOKS
An Imprint of HarperCollins*Publishers*

This is a work of fiction. Names, characters, places, and incidents are products of the author's imagination or are used fictitiously and are not to be construed as real. Any resemblance to actual events, locales, organizations, or persons, living or dead, is entirely coincidental.

AVON BOOKS
An Imprint of HarperCollins*Publishers*
10 East 53rd Street
New York, New York 10022-5299

First Avon Books paperback printing: February 2001

Avon Trademark Reg. U.S. Pat. Off. and in Other Countries, Marca Registrada, Hecho en U.S.A.
HarperCollins® is a trademark of HarperCollins Publishers Inc.

Printed in the U.S.A.

10 9 8 7 6 5

For the four most important men in my life—Ken, Madaug, Cabal, and Ian.

For Monique in appreciation of all the hard work you do, your keen insights, and the never-ending laughter you give (and for being a sane voice on the phone when I need a good pick-me-up)—you're the greatest and I adore you! For Nancy who is a wealth of encouragement and sage advice, and who is just plain wonderful through and through!

For my dearest friends without whom I would be forever lost: Rickey, Deb, Cathy, Laura, Diana, and Rebecca. And a special thank-you to Varlerie Walton at IEI.

And of course there's my most wonderful mom to whom I owe the greatest debt of all. Thanks, Mom, I love you.

I am truly blessed to have all of you in my life!

Prologue

"He is the devil!"

Draven de Montague, the fourth earl of Ravenswood, snorted aloud at the conviction in Hugh's voice as they stood before the throne of King Henry II, while Draven's brother and one of Hugh's men stood a few feet behind them. 'Twas an epitaph he'd heard more times than he could count.

His lip curling in wry amusement, Draven quickly agreed. "Spawned of hell and suckled on the teat of a demon. I make no claims to anything else." It was, after all, his reputation they spoke of. And in this land of chaos, Draven was the undisputed champion.

Two guards, who stood as still as statues, flanked the throne where the king sat. Dressed in a dark mulberry with his gold crown shining in the torchlight, Henry looked less than pleased as he darted his gaze between his two noblemen. Even though

1

Draven had shed his own blood, and spilled even more to secure Henry's crown, he knew the limits of his monarch's tolerance, and at this point, the king had been pushed too far.

Hugh took a careless step toward Henry's throne. "I want him to leave my lands alone, Majesty. Surely he has enough land to pacify himself with that he can leave off Warwick."

Henry Plantagenet was not a man one approached recklessly. He was a man made by his own determination and raw courage, a man who had much in common with Draven, and better still, he was a man indebted to Draven.

The look on Henry's face was one of hell wrath and brimstone.

Finding a moment of sanity, Hugh stepped back and cast his gaze to the cobbled floor.

Henry looked to Draven and sighed. "We do not understand how this conflict started. Draven, you say he attacked you, and Hugh, you say he attacked you, and neither of you claims to have instigated the matter. This reminds us of two ill-bred children fighting over a toy while they both scream injustice. We particularly expect better from you, Draven."

Draven did his best not to show the anger coiling through him. He had served Henry faithfully for more than half his life. Even so, he was no man's fool or pawn, and he answered to no one save himself. Henry had long ago learned that fact, and it was what made Draven such a valuable ally to him. Their alliance had been forged in battle and in blood.

His rage simmering, Draven dared to meet the king's gaze as an equal. "As you well know, my liege, I do not cower, nor will I bow down before this man as he attacks my peasants and raids my fields. If Hugh wants a war, then by God, I am definitely the one to deliver it to him."

Henry looked upward as if seeking the holy saints to aid him. "We grow weary of our lords battling amongst themselves. We realize the years under Stephen were lax, but those days are gone. 'Tis I, Henry, who rules this land, and we shall have peace in it." He looked straight at Draven. "Do you understand?"

"Aye, my liege."

Henry's look then turned to Hugh, whose gaze still examined the floor at his feet. "And you?"

"Aye, sire."

Henry's stern features relaxed a degree. " 'Tis good then. But since we know better than to trust two mice left afield while the cat is occupied elsewhere, we must set this deal in a more permanent fashion."

A sick feeling of dread settled in Draven's gullet. He knew Henry well enough to realize this would not be to his liking.

Henry continued, "Since neither of you seems wont to admit who attacked first, we shall implore the wisdom of Solomon. If you both have possession of something the other cherishes, then mayhap you'll think twice before committing any further hostilities."

"Majesty?" Hugh asked, his voice carrying the weight of his own trepidation.

Henry stroked his auburn beard. "You have a daughter, do you not, Hugh?"

"Aye, sire, I have three still living."

Henry nodded, then looked to Draven, who met his gaze with impertinent directness.

"And what of you, Draven?"

"I have a wastrel brother I have longed to be rid of for years."

Said brother sputtered in indignation from ten paces behind him, but wisely kept his silence before his king.

His face perplexed, Henry thought the matter over. "Tell us, Simon," he directed to Draven's younger brother, "what does your brother hold dearest on this earth?"

Draven turned slightly to see Simon squirming beneath the attention of his king. With his head sedately bowed, Simon spoke, "In truth, Your Majesty, 'tis his honor only that he treasures. He would die to protect it."

"Aye," Henry said thoughtfully. "We have seen the limits to which he would go to see his honor held. Very well, we demand Draven swear on his honor that he will not raid or harass Hugh, and Hugh is to hand one of his daughters over as pledge for his good conduct."

"What!" Hugh bellowed so loudly that Draven half expected the rafters to fall down around them. "You cannot be serious."

Henry directed a heated glare at Hugh. "Sir, you forget yourself. 'Tis your king you address and treasonous ground you tread upon."

Hugh's face was redder than the crimson surcoat

Draven wore over his armor. "Your Majesty, I beg you, do not ask this of me. My daughters are gentle creatures unused to hardship or the company of men. My eldest is to marry a few weeks hence, and her sister is a nun sworn to St. Anne's. Surely you cannot demand that they relinquish their oaths to be held hostage for an indefinite term?"

"You spoke of a third daughter?"

Complete and utter horror was etched on Hugh's long, withered face. "Sire, Emily is the gentlest of all my daughters. She quivers at the slightest scare. An hour with Ravenswood and she would die from her fear. I beg you, please do not demand this."

Henry narrowed his eyes. "We wish the two of you had left us with a choice. But alas, we grow weary of the constant complaints and accusations of our lords. Indeed, on the morrow I am bound to Hexham to settle yet another matter between two barons who can't seem to mind their own lands. All we want is peace!" Henry bellowed.

The king's glare intensified. "Hugh, you are the one who beseeched the crown to intervene in this matter. We have given you our solution, so let it be done, and pity to the reckless soul who dares cross this crown."

Henry appeared to calm a degree. "The Lady Emily is to be handed over to Draven for safekeeping."

A lady in his home! Draven could feel his lip starting to curl at the thought. It was on his tongue to tell Henry to forget the whole matter, but one look and he knew better than to question the king's dictates.

Then the most incredible thing happened. Hugh went down on his knees before Henry's throne. His yellow and white surcoat billowed around him in a puddle as he bowed down and touched his forehead on the stone floor.

"Please, Majesty," Hugh begged, his voice quivering. "You cannot take my daughter and then ask only for Ravenswood's oath. I beg you. Emily is . . . she is my life. You may have my lands, but please leave my daughter be."

For an instant Draven almost felt sorry for the man, until he recalled the village that had been burned in the dead of night. The women who had been raped and butchered in their beds.

Had it not been for Henry's summons, he would have besieged Hugh's castle over the deed and seen the earl's walls torn asunder.

But the king owed a blood debt to Hugh's father, and as the king's champion, Draven had been bound not to harm Hugh without royal decree.

Like it or not, Draven knew that only the presence of Hugh's daughter in his home would guarantee Hugh's benevolent behavior toward Draven's people. And as always, he would protect his people and do as his king bade him.

Henry stroked his beard in thought as he listened to Hugh continue to implore his mercy. "On your feet, Hugh."

Hugh stood, his eyes shining bright from unshed tears.

"We hear your plea, and we can assure you Draven takes his oaths most seriously. We have seen him execute his duty to us with acts of unquestionable loyalty. However, since you have been known to recant your oath, we must ensure that this time peace is kept."

The king referred to the fact that Hugh had once promised to support Henry's claim to the throne, only to turn around two months later and join King Stephen's forces.

Hugh was not one to be trusted. Ever.

"If Your Majesty so doubts my loyalty, then why do I still have my lands?" Hugh asked.

Henry's nostrils flared. "You have your father to thank for that, and rather than ask our motives, you should be grateful for our continued mercy and should act with appropriate gratitude. Draven shall hold her for one year. If in that time you have shown yourself honorable, she shall be returned to you."

Hugh's face turned to granite. "You act as if I am the one who instigated this matter," he muttered. "Why am I to be punished while he—"

"Silence!" Henry roared. "Another insolent word from you and I shall see you stripped of all you hold dearest."

Hugh wisely held his tongue, but his eyes glowed with pure malice.

Henry motioned for his scribe to write down his decree. "Should you attack Draven or any of his people or lands in the coming year, your daughter will be his to do with as he pleases."

Hugh slid his gaze to Draven. "And if he should harm or shame her, sire?"

Henry's face hardened. "As the right hand of the crown, Draven knows firsthand what we do to traitors. We have trusted our life to Draven, and we will accept his pledge on the bones of St. Peter that he will not harm her. To allay your fears, Hugh, I shall send one of my personal physicians to inspect your daughter now and again in one year to ensure she is returned to you in the same condition in which she leaves your protection."

Then to Draven Henry said, "Lady Emily will be considered our ward. Any harm done her will be done to us. We trust you will guard her accordingly?"

"Aye, Your Majesty. I shall guard her with my life."

" 'Tis good then. Now go and make preparations. Draven, seek out our priest and make your oath."

Henry directed his gaze to Hugh, then spoke ominously, "Draven will ride home with you to secure your daughter. Should our royal messengers return from Ravenswood with news she is not there, we will not be pleased."

Simultaneously, they bowed and walked backward from the throne room.

Once the heavy wooden doors were closed behind them, Hugh whirled on Draven. "One way or another, I shall see you dead over this," he hissed.

"Is that a threat?" Draven asked with a hint of amusement in his voice. The last thing under heaven Draven feared was death; indeed it would come as a welcome relief.

Simon grabbed Draven and pulled him back from Hugh. "The king lies within hearing," he whispered furiously. "Does either of you wish for another conference with him?"

Hugh's eyes flared, and then he spun on his heel and stalked off.

"Fear not, Hugh. I shall make your daughter most welcome."

A curse echoed in the hallway, but Hugh never looked around, and it was only after the earl was out of his sight that Draven allowed his face to show just how ill he felt inside.

No lady had been inside Ravenswood in almost a score of years. Closing his eyes to blot the memory, Draven wished he could also block out the screams of terror and pleas for mercy that echoed through his head.

And now another lady was coming.

"It's only for one year," Simon whispered.

Draven locked gazes with him. "Need I remind you, brother, of the curse?"

"You are not your father."

He arched a brow. "You think not? Am I not his equal in speed and battle? Does not everyone remark that I am truly his image?"

"You are not your father," Simon repeated.

But Draven didn't hear it that time either. For he knew the truth. He was his father's son, and unlike Simon, the curse of that man's fetid blood beat through his veins.

To bring a well-born woman to Ravenswood was to sign the order for her execution, and Draven was about to swear his holy honor on a lady's welfare.

Fate was indeed a cruel bitch, and she was laughing mightily at him this day.

Chapter 1

"All a woman ever needs know about men is that they are creatures of their codpieces. Appeal to their chausses and you will have complete control of them, for when their male piece is in control, their brain is not."

Emily sat on her bed beside her sister Joanne, trying not to offend Alys by cracking a smile at her proclamation. She pressed her fist to her lips to hold back her mirth.

Then Emily made the unfortunate mistake of looking at Joanne, and the two of them burst out laughing.

Who wouldn't laugh? Especially given the image in her mind of the overexaggerated codpiece Joanne's betrothed wore.

Why, Niles paraded around like the god Priapus at a virgin festival.

Her maid, Alys, however, didn't look so pleased

by their merriment. Clearing her throat, Emily pressed her lips together and did her best to sober.

Alys set her hands on her hips and grimaced at them. At barely five feet in height, the maid was hardly one to intimidate. Still, they had been the ones to ask after the matter. The least they could do was listen without laughing.

"I thought my ladies were serious about this?" Alys asked.

"Forgive us," Emily said, clearing her throat and folding her hands primly in her lap. "We shall behave."

Indeed, they had no choice for they were conspiring to gain Emily a husband, and since neither sister had any idea how to seduce a man to marriage, Alys had been the only woman at the castle they dare ask. Any other would have made straight for their father with the news.

But luckily, the earthy and often corruptible Alys could be counted on to remain loyal to the ladies she served.

Alys flipped her black braid over her shoulder and shrugged. "Well, as Lady Joanne can attest, the seduction part be easy enough. 'Tis the keeping part that is difficult."

Joanne's face flushed deep red, highlighting her blue eyes. "I did naught but enter the room. Niles was the one who seduced me."

Alys raised her hand, palm upward, in triumph. "As I said, the seduction—"

"But what if he doesn't want to be seduced?" Emily asked, interrupting her.

Alys returned her hand to her hip. Though Alys

was in fact two years younger than Emily, she had been around all sorts of men and was considered by all the young women in the shire an expert.

"Milady," Alys said, her face one of studied patience. "I had my flower plucked when I was scarce more than a girl, and I can assure you there's not a man born who isn't randy. The only reason you've never had to fight them off is because of His Lordship's sharp sword."

Emily couldn't argue that. Her father kept watch over his daughters as if they were his most prized falcons, and he dared any man to look.

And if one dared to touch . . .

Well . . .

She was quite surprised Niles had anything left beneath his codpiece.

Another thought struck her. "But what if I want him and he wants another?" Emily asked.

Alys sighed. "Lady Emily, you are always so full of *what ifs*, and *ands*, and *buts*. Let us say for argument that he might have interest elsewhere. All you must do is keep yourself in his presence. Flash him a little smile, a little ankle, a—"

"An ankle!" Emily gasped. "I should be mortified."

"Better mortified than an old maid."

Perhaps there was some truth to that, and at this point in her life she was becoming quite desperate. Her father wouldn't listen to reason, and if she had any hope of finding herself a husband, then she'd best be on with it.

"A little ankle," Emily repeated, her face growing hot at the mere thought. "Anything else?"

"Always make him wait," Alys said. "Anticipation makes a man appreciate you all the more."

Emily nodded.

Joanne folded her arms over her chest. "Now, the next question is where do we find this man?"

Emily frowned in frustration. "Aye, that would seem to be the crux of the whole seduction thing, wouldn't it? How can I make a man marry me when there's no desirable man to be found?"

"Well," Alys said. "My mother always says you'll find your rose where and when you least expect it."

Later that day, Emily left the kitchens and headed back to the donjon. She'd no more than taken two steps when she found her way blocked by Theodore, the cousin of her sister's betrothed, and the man they had disaffectionately dubbed the "demon from the devil's most odoriferous pit."

They must have inadvertently summoned him with their words that morning, for Alys had no sooner finished her lecture than Niles and Theodore had shown up on their doorstep.

A great big bear of a man, Niles had rudely taken Joanne off on a picnic and left his cousin behind. From the moment her sister and Niles had vanished, Theodore had done nothing save make a nuisance of himself as he hung about her skirts while trying his best to get beneath them.

Emily's patience had long worn thin, and all she wanted was peace from her pestilence.

If Theodore be the rose Alys had referred to earlier, then Emily decided spinsterhood had great possibilities.

He rushed to her side and immediately reached for her hand, sending a wave of revulsion up her spine.

Why could he not leave her in peace?

The man might be considered passably handsome, if a woman were desperate enough. And Emily prayed she never became *that* desperate.

But he lacked basic hygiene. If it was true cleanliness was next to godliness, then this man had to be a heathen through and through, for his balding blond hair looked as if it seldom saw a comb and had never known soap. His clothes were eternally rumpled as if he slept in them, and by the stains marring the fabric she would say he cleaned them about as often as he did his hair.

"Are you ready to give me my kiss now?" he asked.

"Um, nay," she said, trying to step around him. "I fear I have many, *many* chores to do."

"Chores? Surely my company is far more desirable than any chore."

Personally, she'd rather clean the cesspit.

He stepped in front of her, cutting off her escape. "Come now, sweet Emily. I know how lonely you are here. Surely you dream of a man to come and claim you for his own?"

Aye, she did, but the key word was *man*. Since she barely classified Theodore as a bedbug, he would never be the one she dreamed of at night.

He reached out and touched her veil to the side of her face in a familiar gesture that made her cock her brow in censure. He disregarded her look. "You're fast passing your prime, milady. Perhaps you should consider doing as your sister did in order to gain yourself a husband."

Emily didn't know what part of that offended her more. The insult to her age or the reminder of her sister's shame at being caught abed with Theodore's cousin.

"I can find my own husband, thank you," she said icily. "And without any help from you."

Anger darkened his gaze.

"I *will* have you." He wound his fist in her veil.

Emily clenched her teeth in expectation of pain as she jerked out of his hold. The pins that secured the veil to her head tugged at her hair before popping free and allowing her to escape.

She rushed across the bailey, hoping to reach the crowded donjon before he caught her again.

She was not so lucky.

Theodore tossed her veil to the ground and this time grabbed her arm to pull her to a stop.

Emily winced at the way his fingers dug into her upper arm as she tried to pull away. Scared and angry, she wished her father home. No man ever dared such insolence while looking at his fierce countenance, and wherever Emily went, her father's watchful gaze always followed.

"I *will* have a kiss, wench."

She would sooner kiss a leprous mule! Panicking, Emily looked about for some way to escape him.

A flock of chickens rushed out just then, gathering about their feet. As Theodore kicked at them, she was suddenly hit by inspiration.

She turned to face her pestilence with a charming smile as she recalled Alys's earlier advice.

"Theodore?" she said in her softest voice.

It worked. The anger left his face and he released her arm to take her hand. He placed a slimy kiss on her palm.

"Ah, Emily, you've no idea how many nights I've lain abed dreaming of you and your soft sighs. Tell me, how much longer must I wait before I sample the fruit of your succulent thighs?"

Until the devil's throne turned into icicles.

Emily barely caught the words before they escaped. She couldn't believe her luck, she finally found a man to whisper poetry to her and it was the most offensively obscene poetry she could imagine, and came from a man who was only one step up from a warted troll.

On second thought, he wasn't even a full step.

She forced herself not to let her distaste show on her face as she wrested her hand from his cloying grip.

She heard horses approach. Assuming they were her men-at-arms returning from patrol, she didn't even bother to look behind her as they entered the bailey.

Instead, she coyly wiped her hand off on her skirt. "At last you have won me over, milord."

The arrogance on his face was unbelievable as he postured before her like some molting peacock. "I knew you wouldn't be able to resist me, milady. No woman ever has."

He must make it his habit to stay in the company of women who'd lost their ability to see, their ability to judge, and, most of all, their ability to smell.

"Close your eyes, Theodore, and I shall give you what your tenacity deserves."

A sly smile curved his lips as he closed his eyes and leaned forward with what she assumed he thought was a seductive pucker.

Wrinkling her nose at the awful face he made, she seized one of the red hens at her feet and lifted it to his lips.

Theodore gave a loud smooch as he kissed its neck.

Then it must have dawned on him that his lips were against feathers and not flesh, for he opened his eyes and met the curious gaze of the hen.

His eyes widening, he gave a mighty shriek of surprise.

The frightened hen squawked back in reprisal. It raised its wings and flapped about in Emily's hands as it fought for freedom. Emily let go, only to have it launch itself at Theodore, who raised his arm to ward it off as its sister hens joined the fray. The hen pecked at his head, leaving tufts of his thin, greasy hair sticking straight up while the other hens gathered about his feet, tripping him.

Chickens and man tumbled backward in a cacophony of curses and clucks.

With a curse to shame all others, Theodore stumbled into a water trough where he landed on his backside. Water splashed up all around him, and Emily had to step back to keep from being doused. The chicken screeched, then shot to the edge of the trough, where it buried its head in its feathers in an effort to smooth the damage Theodore had done.

As Theodore came sputtering up from the water, the chicken moved to rest upon his head.

Emily burst into laughter.

"The gentlest maid on earth? Hugh, your lies know no bounds."

That deep, resonate baritone was not the voice of one of her men-at-arms. Her laughter dying in her throat, Emily turned about to see her father in a company of fifteen men.

By his face, she could tell the depth of her father's displeasure.

Still, relief overwhelmed her at his presence. At last she would have to tolerate Theodore no more.

As she took a step in his direction, her gaze went to the left of her father. On the back of the whitest stallion she had ever seen sat a knight wearing a bloodred surcoat emblazoned with a black raven. Even though she couldn't see the man's face, she could feel his gaze upon her like a blistering touch.

She stopped dead in her tracks.

Never had she seen his like. He sat tall in the saddle as if he and the horse were one creature united in power and in form.

His mail armor draped most sinuously over a body rock hard from years of training, and he wore his armor with the ease of a second skin. His broad shoulders were thrown back with pride, and the mail only emphasized the breadth of them.

The huge, powerful charger shifted nervously, but he brought it instantly under control with a squeeze from his powerful thighs and one taut jerk at the reins.

Still she felt his gaze on her, hot, powerful.

Disturbing.

This was a man who commanded attention. A man used to control and authority. It bled from every part of him.

And as she watched him, her gaze unwavering, he reached up and removed his great helm.

Her heart stopped beating an instant before it began to pound furiously. Never in her life had she seen a man so handsome. Eyes so light a blue they seemed to glow stared out from a chiseled face surrounded by his silver chain mail coif. The black brows that slashed above his eyes told her his hair must be the color of a raven's wing.

There was something mesmerizing in his gaze. Deep intelligence shone there along with a guarded look that kept his emotions well hidden. She had the impression that nothing escaped his attention. Ever.

For all his handsomeness, though, there was a hardness to his sculpted features that told her a smile was all but alien to those lips.

He raked her with a bold, assessing stare that set fire to her blood as he cradled his helm beneath his arm. She couldn't tell what he thought of her, but as his gaze paused over her bosom, she felt her breasts tighten in response to the searing heat of his stare.

"What goes here?" her father demanded as he dismounted and moved to her side.

She jumped at his thundering tone, grateful for the distraction from the strange things the knight's gaze had done to her.

Theodore shooed the chicken from his head and climbed out of the trough while trying to look dignified.

He failed miserably.

"I think you should ask your daughter if it is always her habit to attack any man who annoys her with a chicken," the handsome knight said with a hint of amusement in his voice. His face, however, showed nothing.

"Silence, Ravenswood," her father snarled. "You know nothing of my daughter, or her habits."

"That will change soon enough."

Emily cocked a brow at the comment. Whatever did he mean by that?

She wouldn't have thought it possible, but her father's face turned even redder, his eyes darker. It was only then she caught the handsome knight's name.

Surely he wasn't *the* Draven de Montague, earl of Ravenswood; the man her father had gone to the king to have Henry censure?

Why on earth would they be riding together? Given her father's hatred of the earl, she couldn't imagine it.

Something odd was afoot here, and she couldn't wait to get her father alone to find out just what was going on.

Her father's eyes softened as he looked at her. "Did Theodore hurt you, Em?"

Theodore stiffened. "I would never harm a lady." His eyes, however, told another story. She could see pure malice there, and she silently vowed to make sure he never caught her alone again.

Still, Emily was never one to be intimidated. She could handle him well enough, with or without a chicken.

"I am fine, Father," she assured him.

" 'Tis the chicken he terrified," the earl said wryly.

Emily bit her lip to keep from laughing again as she looked past her father's shoulder to see that the earl's face bore no trace of humor.

Her father's nostrils flared.

Emily threw her arms around her father and hugged him tightly. The last thing she wanted was for him to be angry the instant he came home. He'd spent far too much time brooding and being miserable. Besides, she hated to see anyone unhappy. "I'm so glad you're home. Did you have a pleasant journey?"

"A journey to hell would have been more pleasurable," he muttered.

Her father cast a feral glare back to the knights on horseback. "You might as well stay the night. You can leave first thing on the morrow."

The earl of Ravenswood narrowed his gaze on her father. "I make it my habit not to lie down with my enemies. We shall camp outside your walls." His gaze turned even icier. "We will leave at first light. I would counsel you to have everything in order."

And with that mysterious warning, the earl wheeled his massive warhorse about and led all but two royal messengers and her father's three knights from the bailey.

Theodore excused himself and made a dripping trail toward the stable.

Emily looked to her father. Something wasn't right about any of this. "Father?"

He sighed and draped a weary arm around her shoulders. "Come, my precious Em. I needs speak with you alone."

Draven and his men found a small clearing just beyond the castle's gate where a small stream provided fresh water. Left alone as was his preference, he brushed his horse while his men prepared tents and his brother, Simon, started a fire.

Still, he couldn't get the sight of Hugh's daughter from his mind. All he had to do was close his eyes and he could see her as plainly as he had when she'd stood before them, her face alight and smiling, and her dark green eyes shining in mischief.

And the chicken. . . .

He almost laughed. Until her smiling face drifted before him again and tormented him with a fiery groin.

Grinding his teeth, he tightened his grip on the brush.

The Lady Emily wasn't the typical beauty milksops sighed over. She held a strange exotic quality to her that almost defied his abilities to name her essence or her charms.

But what had held his attention most were her large, catlike eyes that burned mischievously while they took in the world with an astounding boldness.

She was slender with a wealth of curly blond hair that fell to her hips. He doubted if the very angels in heaven had a face that was so soft and alluring. No wonder Hugh had balked at the thought of letting her go. A treasure so priceless should be guarded with care, and in spite of himself, he felt a tiny degree of respect for a man who would try to protect his child.

Goliath reared his head and snorted.

"Sorry, boy," he said as he realized he'd been brushing the same spot far too long. Draven gave a gentle pat to the horse's flank to soothe his thoughtlessness. It wasn't like him to be careless with his animals, and he hoped he hadn't caused a sore spot with his daydreaming.

Pushing the girl from his thoughts, he continued his chores.

He was adding oats to his horse's feed sack when Simon approached.

"Not what you expected?" his brother asked.

"The feed sack?" he responded in a deliberate effort to keep his brother from broaching a most disturbing subject. " 'Tis the same as it ever was."

Simon rolled his eyes. "I have no interest in the sack as well you know. 'Tis the lady I speak of. Can you believe the daughter of Lord Big Nose was so comely? I can't recall the last time I saw a lady so well formed."

"She is the daughter of my enemy."

"And the woman you've sworn to protect."

Draven looped the sack over the horse's head. "Why do you bother me with trivial facts I already know?"

Simon had a devilish look about him, and if it were any man save Simon, that teasing quality of his would have been laid to rest long ago. But for all the annoyance, Draven loved his younger brother.

Simon grinned at him. "You know, I so seldom

get to see you squirm that I rather enjoy the novelty of it. It makes you seem almost human."

Draven stroked Goliath's forehead, then moved to retrieve his saddle and saddlebags from the ground before heading back to his men.

He paused by Simon's side. "Whatever humanity ever existed in me, I can assure you it was beaten out long ago. You of all men should know that. I will protect her because my king ordered it. Beyond that, she will not exist for me."

"As you say."

Draven narrowed his gaze. "It is as I say." He headed toward the fire.

"One day, I hope you learn, brother, that you are not a monster born of hell."

Draven ignored Simon's words. In truth, he envied his brother's optimism. It was a rare gift their mother had given her younger son. But he had not been so lucky, and fate had never been kind to him. Holding on to dreams and hopes only emphasized just how vacant his life had always been. He wasn't a fool to think anything would change.

It never had and it surely never would. This was his lot, and he would survive it just as he had always survived every blow dealt him.

Chapter 2

The wee hours of the morn found Emily alone in her bower with her sister as they finished packing Emily's things. Disbelief still filled her—at long last, and for the first time in her life, she was leaving home.

"I can't believe you'll be gone in just a few hours," Joanne whispered, her voice filled with tears.

"Nor I," Emily breathed. "I know I should be afraid, but—"

"You're excited," Joanne finished for her. "I would be too. Imagine"—she glanced around the tapestried walls surrounding them— "leaving this place for an entire year. I know how much you've always wanted to."

Emily nodded, her heart pounding at the thought. "I had always hoped it would be my husband who led me away. But I fear I lacked your courage to force Father's hand."

Joanne's face became a mask of horror. "You should be grateful for your good sense. I daresay I thought Father would kill the two of us after he found us."

Emily knew her words for fact. Their mother and two elder sisters had all died in childbirth, and since her sister Anna had died nine years past, her father had sworn that no man would take the life of another of his girls.

From that day forward, he had locked his gate against any man who would play suitor to them, forcing her sister Judith to join a convent to escape his watchful care.

Niles had been allowed inside only because their father had assumed she and Joanne would never find the baron attractive. In truth, Emily didn't know why Joanne had taken a fancy to him, other than the fact he wasn't married.

Niles was a bear of a man with a cruel tilt to his mouth, who seemed to enjoy bullying those around him. Many times she had confided in Joanne her thoughts, but Joanne dismissed her as foolish, saying that Niles treated her with only the greatest regard.

Still, Emily couldn't shake her misgivings about the man.

Not that it mattered. Joanne was determined to have a husband, and Niles seemed determined to have Joanne's dower property, which bordered his own outside York.

Joanne reached out and touched her hand. "I

know Father is difficult. But it is only his love for us that makes him so protective."

"Loves us so that we are treated like the birds in his mews. Forever kept locked in a cage without hope of freedom."

Joanne squeezed her hand. "He is a harsh, unyielding man, but his heart is good. You can't fault him for that."

Emily cocked an eyebrow at her sister's words. "This from the woman who railed against him just weeks ago when he refused Niles's offer for your hand?"

Joanne smiled sheepishly. "You are right. I hated him then, for I knew if Niles got away, there would be no other man to offer for me. I am long past a marriageable age."

"And I am fast passing it myself. How many men would have a bride at a score and two years?"

"Not many," Joanne agreed.

"Aye, not many."

They sat in silence for several minutes while they finished packing her last trunk. Emily allowed her thoughts to drift.

All her life she'd had but one dream—to be a wife and mother. Her father's adamant refusal to see her wed had long vexed her. But for the coming year, she would be out of her father's direct control, and if she—

"What?" Joanne asked, her voice thick with apprehension.

Emily blinked at the intrusion on her thoughts. "What what?" she repeated.

"What were you thinking?" Joanne asked. "By

the look on your face, I would say 'tis not something you should have been thinking."

"Meaning?"

"I know that look, Em, 'tis the same one you had just before you locked poor Godfried in the garderobe."

"He deserved it," she said defensively, even though she took pride in the memory of the deed. Her cousin Godfried had been in residence only a sennight when they had declared war on each other. In those days, she hadn't cared much for him, and to have him fostered at her home where he had been free to mock her at will . . .

Well, his two-hour stint in the garderobe had taught him well she wasn't one to be picked on with impunity. He had treated her much more kindly from that day forward.

" 'Tis also the same look you had just before you set father's prized gyrfalcon free."

Now that had not turned out so well. No older than five at the time, she still swore she could feel the sting of her father's hand across her backside. He had not been happy when he learned she had felt sorry for his caged falcon and set it loose.

"Every time I have seen that look upon your face, mischief always followed. I can only shudder at what it heralds now."

Emily dismissed Joanne's words with a wave of her hand. "Perhaps it heralds a way to have what I have always wanted."

"And that is?"

Emily looked askance at her. "Do you think the earl of Ravenswood is as evil as Father claims?"

Joanne frowned. "What are you thinking?"

Emily shrugged away her concern. "I was thinking that Lord Draven might be the rose I've been seeking."

"Oh, sister, please I beg you. Do not think that which I know you are thinking. You have heard the stories same as I. They say he killed his own father just for pleasure."

"Perhaps that is just a rumor, like the one calling Father a barbarous traitor. You said yourself that Father is a harsh man with a kind heart."

"Harsh, aye, but I have heard the earl of Ravenswood is mad. You have heard such tales yourself. That he is a demon who never sleeps. They say the devil himself has cleared a spot to the right hand of his throne in expectation of the day Lord Draven will join him."

Emily felt her hopes deflate as she considered it further. "Nay, you are right. 'Tis a foolish idea. I shall spend a year with a madman, then return here to finish out my life in solitary company."

A single tear fled down her cheek.

Joanne reached out and brushed the tear away. "Don't cry, Em. Someday your rose will come for you on the back of his white charger. He'll face Father's wrath and triumph, then take you away from here just as Niles is doing with me."

"But I want children," she whispered. "If he waits much longer, I shall be too old to enjoy them, or else see them grown. It's so unfair!"

Joanne pulled her into a tight hug. "I know, little sister. I wish I could spend the year in your place. But the time will pass, and I promise when it does I shall beg Father to let you come stay with me for a time. We will find you a husband then. I promise you."

Emily hugged her sister tightly. "Just promise me it won't be Theodore."

Joanne laughed softly.

They sat in silence for several minutes, until Emily heard footsteps shuffling outside. "I will kill him, if it is the last thing I do! I shall gouge out his eyes and grind them to dust. No man shall have my Em!

"By God's right arm, she is all I have left and I will not see her gone. Do you hear me?" he shouted angrily. "No one will take my youngest babe from me! Never!"

Emily's throat grew tight as her father made his way to the garderobe.

Closing her eyes, Emily realized how futile it would be to hope her father would wait out the year. There was no way under heaven he would ever leave her in the clutches of his enemy with nothing more than that man's oath to secure her welfare. He loved her too much and trusted Draven too little.

They locked concerned gazes.

"What are we to do?" Joanne asked fearfully.

Emily bit her lip as she tried to think of something. "I will have to find some way to get Lord Draven to marry me before Father attacks him," she said slowly.

"You can't do that!"

"I have to."

"But Emily—"

"But nothing, Joanne. If Father attacks, he'll lose everything. Including your dowry."

Joanne covered her mouth with her hand as the full horror dawned on her. "We'll be outcasts," she whispered. "Niles will cast me aside without my dower lands."

"Aye, and we'll have no one to shelter us. Already the king hates Father for what he did under King Stephen's reign. I should think he'd like nothing better than to see us all out on our ears."

"Oh, Lord, Emily. This is too frightening to contemplate. You can't marry a madman."

"What choice have I?"

Joanne shook her head. "There must be another way. Besides, why would Lord Draven want you?"

Emily dropped her jaw, offended to her very core at her sister's words.

"I didn't mean it that way," Joanne said quickly as she folded Emily's underkirtle. "But you know what father says of him. The man has never married, and to my knowledge no woman has ever caught his eye. It does bear mentioning that he may not be bent to feminine company, that he prefers other men. Indeed it could be that very reason that King Henry didn't order him to marry you as opposed to just being his ward."

Emily shook her head. "Nay, I don't think so. Not from the look he gave me this afternoon. Besides, Father said the king refused the marriage solution lest it cause more war between them. Henry tried that settlement last year between two other nobles and it was disastrous."

"Which brings up my next point; you are the

daughter of his enemy," Joanne continued. "Not to mention that if Lord Draven touches you the king will have his head for it."

Emily considered it for a moment. "Do you believe the king would kill him for touching me?"

"Why should I doubt it? Henry is a man of his word."

"Perhaps, but would he dare take the life of one of his champions over a mere dalliance? Father betrayed him far worse than that, and the king did nothing more than fine him and confiscate part of his holdings. Do you not think Lord Draven could petition the king for my hand and be forgiven?"

"The king did more to Father than just a little fine and confiscation, Em."

"I know, but the point is, the king didn't kill Father for his actions. Or harm him beyond repair."

Joanne sat back on her heels as she thought the matter over. "I don't know if the king would forgive him. 'Tis possible, perhaps."

"What choice do we have?" Emily asked.

"But Em, do you understand the full impact of what you're thinking? Lord Draven is an enemy to Father. To the father who has sworn he'll never allow you to marry and leave him."

"Aye, I understand. But I want a husband and I want children."

"And if Lord Draven wants no wife?"

"Then I will make him want one."

Joanne gave a short laugh. "You are so very stubborn. I pity Lord Draven for having to contend with you. But promise me one thing?"

"Aye?"

Joanne's face grew taut and serious. "If you see he is cruel, then I beg you rethink this scheme. I know how much you want children, but the last thing I would have is you married to a man who beats you. Better I should be thrown to the streets of London than see you sacrificed to a monster."

Emily nodded gravely. "I promise."

Dawn came all too soon to Emily, who met it with a mixture of tiredness, hidden tears, and excitement for the unknown. She entered the great hall where her father waited still awake. Drunk, but awake.

'Twas the first time in her life she had seen him in his cups. At this moment, his face bore all the traces of a man who had lived a warrior's hard life.

She approached his chair, where he sat on the raised dais. "I'll kill him!" he slurred as he focused a bloodshot gaze on her. The stench of ale over-whelmed her. "If it's the last thing I ever do I will tear down his walls and hang him from the tallest tree I can find. I'll carve his heart out and feed it to the . . . the wolves . . . or maybe mice."

He hiccupped and looked at his favorite hound, whose head rested in his lap. "What would hurt more? A mouse or a wolf? If a wolf—"

"You need to get some sleep," she said, inter-rupting him.

"I won't sleep until you return to me where I can keep you safe."

He reached out a gentle hand to touch her face,

and she saw the tears spring into his eyes. "I can't lose you, Em. You look just like your mother-fair." He touched her hair and his eyes grew even mistier. " 'Twould be like losing Marian all over again, and I could never survive that. Had it not been for you girls, I wouldn't have survived her passing."

"I know," she whispered. Never in her life had she doubted the fact that her father loved his daughters, or the fact that he would die to protect them. She just wished he had learned to let them go.

Joanne entered the room from the small door to the right of the table. She held a large basket in her hands, and her eyes were red and bright from her tears. None of them had slept, and Emily wondered if her own eyes had the same purple ring beneath them.

"I know 'tis only a day's ride, but still I packed you something to eat for the trip."

Emily smiled at Joanne's kindness as she took the basket from her. She was quite sure her sister had shown her usual diligence and prepared enough food to feed a small army. "I shall miss you terribly."

Joanne hugged her close as Emily held on to her. She and Joanne had never been apart before. They were closer than just sisters, they were best friends.

"It will be all right, Joanne, I swear it. You shall see, in a year we will laugh over this."

"I hope so," Joanne breathed. "It won't be the same without you here."

Tears stung the back of her eyes, but Emily refused to let them fall anymore. She must be strong for her family. Though the youngest, she was the one who had always been strong for them all.

"Just think," she said in an effort to cheer Joanne, "in a few weeks you won't even be here to miss me. You'll have your own household to run. Now, please, make Father go to bed."

Joanne nodded, then pulled back. Tears streamed down her face again, and she could tell her sister had passed the point of being able to speak.

Her own throat tight, Emily brushed a stray tendril of blond hair off Joanne's temple. "May God watch over you while I'm gone."

Joanne grabbed her hand and sobbed as if her heart were breaking. Wishing she could give such rein to her emotions, Emily kissed her sister's cheek, then gently extracted her hand. "All shall be fine, you will see."

She turned to wish her father well, only to discover he had finally passed out. Approaching his chair again, she touched his whiskered face.

"I know you love me, Father. I never doubted it. But we are grown women and you must let us live our lives for ourselves," she whispered. "Please forgive me for what I do. I'd never do anything to hurt you, and I pray one day you'll understand." She brushed her lips across his forehead, then turned about and left the hall.

With a deep breath to fortify her courage, Emily took one last look at the only home she had ever known, then made her way to the door and down the stairs, where her entourage waited.

One of the king's messengers came forward to help her mount her horse.

Thanking him for the kindness, she watched as

her maid, Alys, climbed aboard the first wagon and took a seat.

The messenger returned to his horse, and once he mounted, they were on their way.

Lord Draven and his men were waiting for them on the other side of the gate. His helm was in place and she found it disturbing that she couldn't see his face.

She could, however, hear his muffled curse as he spied the three wagons behind her.

"Did you pack the entire castle?" he demanded.

"I packed what was necessary."

Laughter rang out from the knight to the right of Lord Draven. His black surcoat bore a golden raven that was only slightly different from Lord Draven's.

"Shut up, Simon, before I run you through," Lord Draven snapped.

The one called Simon removed his helm and cast a glowing smile in her direction. He was every bit as handsome as Lord Draven, but his looks were entirely different and he lacked that raw, primal charisma that his brother seemed to excrete from every pore. Simon's red hair was just a shade darker than a pumpkin and his blue eyes twinkled in easygoing friendship. He wore a small, well-trimmed beard.

Kicking his horse forward, he paused by her side. "Allow me to present myself, milady," he said charmingly. "I am Simon of Ravenswood, brother to the ogre, and your most fervent protector for this journey."

"Wonderful," Lord Draven said dryly. "And pray tell who will protect her from your drooling?

Should I have my squire fetch rags now, or should I wait until she starts to drown?"

Simon leaned forward ever so slightly, then spoke in a low tone for her ears alone. "His bite is nowhere near as bad as his bark."

She cast a quick glance to the man whose name was synonymous with death. "That is not what I have heard."

"Aye, but you've heard from those who have faced him in battle. There, he is a champion to be feared like a charging lion. But away from battle he is a fair man with naught but a loud bellow."

"And a sharp sword for those who pester me," Draven said in that bellow Simon had just mentioned.

Lord Draven turned to his men and ordered them to start the journey.

His men rode to the front and back of her while Draven took the lead. Simon kept apace with her, and Alys followed in the wagons.

Emily tried to study the man she had vowed to marry, and was unsure now if she could truly carry the deed off. She'd heard much of Draven de Montague from her father and others who had visited her home.

He was a man known for unequaled prowess in battle and tourney. No one had ever defeated him, and he had once saved the king's life. The few ladies she had met who had seen him had not lied about his good looks. He truly was handsome and fierce.

No wonder maids sighed at the mention of his name.

He sat straight in his saddle and moved in rhythm with the horse. Anyone could tell that Lord Draven felt at home on horseback, and from what she'd heard, he had spent much of his life on campaigns.

Yet it was strange to look at him now, knowing that he might one day be her husband. That they might share a bed together where he would see her as no man had, touch her in places no one had.

And kiss her in the wee hours of the night.

Heat crept over her face. She'd never thought of a real man that way before. After Alys had been with her first man, they had talked at great lengths about what went on between men and women in country matters.

How it felt when a man claimed a woman with his body.

Since then, Emily had imagined a fair-haired man with humor in his eyes and laughter always on his tongue. She had let her fantasies loose at night where no one could see the blush that was currently blistering her cheeks.

As a girl, she'd naturally assumed her first would be the husband her father chose. And only in her wildest imaginings had she dreamed she would love the man who took her virginity. At best, she had hoped to be fond of him.

Now, the moment would soon be at hand, and Lord Draven would be the one . . .

She trembled at the very thought of the fierce warrior claiming her with his body. Of his mouth taking hers in her very first kiss.

Would he be tender, or would he ravish her?

Alys had warned her a woman could never tell simply by looking at a man how he would treat her in the privacy of their bedroom.

"Is it true your brother earned his spurs before he first shaved?" she asked Simon.

Pride shone in his eyes. "Aye. He was my father's squire in King Henry's army. When my father died in battle, he seized his sword, then protected Henry's back. He was knighted on the battlefield by Henry Plantagenet himself."

"How lucky for him that Henry became king."

"With my brother by his side, he couldn't lose, milady."

It gave her hope that a man who appeared as kind as Simon idolized his brother so much. From the tales she'd heard, she half expected Lord Draven to be a monster with horns who ate small children for pleasure.

Surely such a monstrous man wouldn't tolerate his brother's teasing, any more than said brother would idolize a beast.

Nay, there was much more to Draven than she'd been told. At least she hoped that was true. It would be much easier to give her future over to a man who could be kind than it would to a cruel man.

They rode in silence until late morning when Lord Draven decided to stop for a rest. Simon helped her down.

She followed him to a shaded spot while Draven and his men tended the horses.

Simon spread a cloak out for her to sit on the

ground beneath a large oak tree. "Would you care to share what my sister packed for my journey?" she asked as she sank to the ground.

Simon looked as if she had just offered him ambrosia. "Aye, milady. I have grown so ill of dried beef and cheese that I could just . . ." He smiled. "I truly appreciate your offer."

As he poured the wine and she cut the bread and mincemeat pie, Lord Draven returned from the stream. He'd removed his helm and coif, and his hair was damp as if he'd washed his face in the stream, then raked his hand through the sleek ebony tresses.

Never had she seen a man so handsome.

His features were more relaxed now than they'd been yesterday, and his face held an almost boyish charm to it. Except for his eyes. They remained stern and sharp and unyielding.

Unlike Simon, whose hair was clipped short in the latest fashion, Lord Draven had allowed his to grow just past his shoulders. The red of his surcoat heightened the dark tan of his skin, and she wondered how much of the breadth of his chest was padding from his aketon and how much of it was the man.

"Draven," Simon called to him. "Would you care to join us?"

He paused, glanced at her, then shook his head in declination. "I doubt your guest would care for my presence while she eats."

"I harbor no hatred of you, milord." She couldn't afford to, not if she were to succeed with her plans.

She smiled. "There is plenty enough to share."

"Hear that," Simon added. "Come and eat something before you waste away."

She arched a brow at Simon's words. Draven was a large man, at least six-foot-four with a sturdy frame. It would take him quite some time to waste down to even Simon's more conservative size.

Lord Draven approached, and for some reason she couldn't fathom, her heart raced at his nearness.

With his coif removed, she saw a long, jagged scar that ran from below his left ear and disappeared beneath his armor. It looked as though someone had once tried to cut his throat.

Was it from battle?

The rigidness returned to his face as he studied the ground by Simon's side. After a moment's hesitation, he knelt down slowly, then sat.

She caught Simon's concern as he watched his brother. "Is your leg stiff again?"

"My leg is fine," Draven snapped in a fierce tone that frightened her.

Simon, on the other hand, appeared unperturbed by Draven's rancor.

For the first time, she met Draven's gaze. Something warm and wicked flickered in his eyes an instant before a veil fell over the pale blue, turning his eyes icy.

Emily's lips parted slightly as an unexpected thrill shot through her. She'd never had the presence of a man affect her like this. Her hand actually shook as she prepared him a small meal of her bread, roasted chicken, and mincemeat pie.

She wanted something witty to say to him, something to mayhap bring a smile to those well-shaped lips of his. But for some reason, she couldn't think of anything. All she could do was watch the way his strong, masculine hand curved around his goblet, then lifted it to his mouth.

She couldn't imagine why he had never taken a bride. He appeared to be a score and five years, and had been landed since his teens. Usually such men were eager to secure their holdings by making a strategic marriage and begetting heirs.

She could think of only one reason why he hadn't married.

Coyly, she smiled at Lord Draven. "Tell me, milord, is there a lady somewhere you have sworn your heart to?"

"Why would you ask me that?" His tone made the cold look in his eyes appear like a hot summer's day.

That had obviously not been a good question, she realized too late. Though why such an innocuous question would cause such a heated response, she had no idea.

It was something he had no wish to discuss, and she quickly sought to lighten his mood. "It was just passing conversation, milord. I had no intention of angering you with it."

But it wasn't anger she saw in his eyes. It was something else, something she couldn't define or understand.

They ate in silence a few minutes more, each apparently lost in his thoughts.

"Lady Emily is a brave woman, don't you agree, Draven?" Simon asked at last.

A wave of fear swept through Emily that perhaps

Simon had somehow divined her scheme to seduce Lord Draven to marriage. If the earl thought she was laying a trap for him, there was no telling what he might do, especially given his reaction to her question.

"Brave?" she asked, noting the unusually high pitch of her voice.

"Aye." Simon nodded. "To be dragged from your home by your father's enemy and not shed a tear. I can't think of one other woman I've met who would have your fortitude."

Emily tried not to let her relief show, and it took her a minute to think of something to say. "I would be lying if I said I wasn't homesick already. I've never been away from my family before, but the king's men told me I could trust in Lord Draven's oath to protect me."

Draven gave a snort that she thought might be his form of a laugh. "You're a fool, lady, to believe in any man's oath."

Her heart stopped. Did he intend to harm her?

"He's just trying to scare you," Simon said. "I'm afraid my brother is a bit morbid. You'll get used to it in time."

A bit morbid, indeed. His words had come close to terrifying her.

She studied Draven, who kept his gaze locked on her face. How she wished she could read his emotions as easily as she could Simon's. It was so disturbing not to know where she stood with him.

Her intuition warned her that this was a most dangerous man. One used to taking what he wanted and damning the consequences.

Still, she knew better than to let her fears rule her. If her father had taught her anything in life, it was to stand strong and confront matters. Fears faced were seldom as bad as the mind made them.

"You'll have to do better, milord," she said to Draven. "You'll find I don't scare easily."

Draven looked away then, and she caught the flash of sadness on his face. "If you'll excuse me, I must see to my men." As he rose to his feet, she noted that he favored his right leg, and his gait had a very subtle limp to it.

When she looked back at Simon, she saw that his happiness had also fled.

"You'll have to forgive my brother, milady. He's a hard man to get to know."

"And why is that?"

She could see the war inside him as he chewed his food, then swallowed. He offered her a tentative smile. "I would never betray my brother's secrets. Suffice it to say he has had a very hard life."

Emily frowned. "A hard life? He is a hero to those loyal to the king. His legend is recounted in at least twenty chansons that I know off the top of my head. How can one so revered—"

"Draven is a man, milady, not a myth. He stands strong in battle because that is all he knows."

It dawned on her what he meant. Emily looked to where Draven stood beside his horse. She knew the type of man Simon referred to. One who was trained from the cradle for battle. Most noblemen, like her father and obviously Simon, were sheltered as children, then handed over around the age of six or seven to family friends or overlords to be trained first as gentlemen pages and then as soldiers. Their life was a mixture of courtly graces balanced by training for war.

But some fathers expected more of their sons. Those sons were never shown anything save war, and now she understood why Lord Draven was withdrawn. He had lived his life on the battlefield, in the company of enemies and soldiers.

"You do not share the same father?" she asked as she remembered Simon speaking of his father falling in battle.

"Nay, milady. My father was more minstrel than knight. He was reliable in battle, but never the best."

"And Draven's father?"

Simon fell silent. She looked to his face and there encountered a look of hatred so strong that it set her back. "He was undefeated in battle. I am told that some armies would merely see his pennant and immediately surrender."

She had heard those tales as well. Harold of Ravenswood was a man of renowned cruelty. "Why do you hate him?"

"I doubt you would believe me if I told you."

And before she could question him further, Draven announced it was time for them to renew their journey.

No more words were spoken as they packed up their meals and remounted their horses.

Emily remained lost in thought as she sifted through old memories of what she knew about Draven's father. He had died almost twelve summers back, not long before her mother. She knew that only because she recalled her father speaking about it to her mother over supper.

"I heard the devil claimed Harold of Ravenswood a sennight ago," her father had said.

"Harold is dead?" her mother had asked.

"Aye, and by the hand of his own son I am told."

Emily had been terrified by his words. She couldn't imagine anyone killing his own father. And at that time it had been the most horrific thing she had ever heard.

Had it simply been for the lands as she had been told, or was there more to the story?

Though Lord Draven was indeed terrifying and dangerous, there was still something about him that didn't seem in keeping with all the stories of cold brutality she had heard.

Nay, Niles and Theodore she could believe such tales about. There was a coldness to their eyes that appeared malevolent and cruel. But the iciness of Lord Draven's stare was nothing like theirs. It was different. As if the coldness was more internal and focused on himself rather than others.

Of course, she could just be fooling herself by seeing in Draven's eyes what she wanted to see. Just as Joanne had done.

"But I am not so foolish," she breathed. "At least I hope I'm not."

Chapter 3

Just before dusk, they entered the bailey of Ravenswood. Emily had always known Ravenswood bordered her father's property just to the south, but never had she realized how close they actually were.

But physical closeness was the only thing they had in common, for never had she seen a more dismal place.

Of course, her ability to compare was rather limited since the only castle she'd ever seen was her father's. Even so, she doubted if any place on earth could be less inviting than the foreboding hall in front of her.

Looking up at the bleak, dark donjon, Emily reined her horse to a stop. Stark, unappealing misery surrounded her at all angles.

The yard unkempt, it held no flowers or shrubs

anywhere. Weeds were the only thing that seemed to be in abundance.

A handful of scrawny chickens pecked at the bleak earth and squawked while dogs milled on the outskirts of the yard.

At this early evening hour only a handful of men lolled about. And none offered a greeting to their lord. They went about their business of pulling water out of the well, fetching horses, and baling hay as if they feared even to look upon their lord. And in truth, she had seen dead lice move at a faster pace than what any of them showed.

Emily frowned, then turned about in her saddle to scan the inner bailey.

"Milady?" Simon asked. "What do you seek?"

"A marker announcing this as the gate to Hades," she said before she realized it.

Horrified by her slip of tongue, she pressed her fist to her lips.

Simon tilted his head back and gave a great peal of laughter. "Keep your sense of humor, milady," he said as he sobered. "You're going to need it."

Simon dismounted and handed his horse over to his squire. "And have no fear of offending me. I assure you I have the hide of a boar."

"And the thick head to match," Draven muttered as he dismounted and handed his reins over to a young stableboy.

"Very true," Simon said, looking to his brother. "But 'tis why you love me so."

Draven removed his helm, coif, and arming cap and handed them to his squire, who then dashed off with them. "There is one thing I love about you."

"And that is?"

"Your absence."

Simon took it in stride and smiled up at her. "Now you know why I have thick skin."

Emily returned his smile as he helped her dismount.

Such bantering between Niles and Theodore had always made her uncomfortable, but it bothered her not when Simon and Draven did it. Perhaps because unlike Niles and Theodore, there appeared no real animosity between them. 'Twas almost as if the verbal sparring was a good-natured competition between them to see who could get the last word.

"I'm afraid you'll find Ravenswood far different from Warwick," Draven said as Simon set her down in front of him.

She thanked Simon as her gaze trailed up the old, dark gray stone steps to the thick wooden door. There was nothing inviting or warm about his home. Nothing at all.

No wonder the man was morbid.

"I can make do, milord. Just show me to your housekeeper and I—"

"There is no housekeeper," he interrupted.

"I beg your pardon?"

Draven shrugged. "I have only a handful of servants. You'll find I am not a man to waste time on frivolities."

If not for the fact she knew he employed twelve knights, had won numerous tourneys on the mainland, and been rewarded most handsomely by King Henry, she would have questioned his solvency. But

Lord Draven was a wealthy man with assets purportedly greater than even those of the crown.

Deciding criticism would not endear her to the man she hoped to seduce, she sighed. "Very well, milord. I shall make do," she repeated.

Draven ordered Simon to find someone to unload her wagons. "I shall show you to your chambers," he said to her, then turned and walked up the steps.

Stunned, Emily took a full minute before she followed. She couldn't believe the man hadn't even offered her his arm! No one had ever given her such a slight before.

At least he had the good grace to hold the door open for her.

Gathering her skirts, she entered his hall, then stopped dead in her tracks.

There was an indescribable odor to his home, something between rotted wood, smoke, and other things too foul to contemplate. The fading sunlight sliced through the slits of closed wooden shutters, showing her a wealth of rotted rushes, an unlit hearth, and only three dilapidated trestle tables set in the middle of the hall. Five dogs ran about, scavenging in the rushes, while the tops of the tables looked as if they had never known even a semblance of cleaning.

No matter how hard she tried, she couldn't keep her nose from wrinkling in distaste. She covered her nose with her hand in an effort not to choke on the stench.

Skimming the hall with her gaze, she noted the

lack of a dais and lord's table. "Where is your table, milord?"

"I don't have one," he said as he walked past her and headed toward the stairs.

Had that been a catch in his voice? She wasn't sure and he didn't pause in his journey.

Hurrying to keep up, she ascended the drafty stairs. At least up here, the odor abated to where she could breathe normally.

He stopped at the top of the stairway and pushed open a door. He stood back for her to enter, with one hand splayed on the door and the other on the hilt of his sword.

Emily swallowed hard as she walked past him. So close to him she could hear his breathing, feel the warmth of it fall against her skin.

Overwhelmed by his presence, 'twas all she could do not to pause and inhale the raw, pleasant, untamed scent of leather and spice.

Never in her life had she felt this way. So breathless. So titillated.

So very alive and alert.

Again an image of a charging black lion came to her mind, for the earl was every bit as wild and unpredictable. Deadly and disconcerting. She held little doubt he could take her in an instant and do anything he wanted with her. She would be powerless to stop him.

The fact that he didn't move toward her only added to her curiosity about him. And his appeal to her.

Seeking to distract herself from him, she stopped

and stared at a plain room that would rival a monastery for its spartan quality.

All her tender thoughts of him evaporated.

"This will not do at all," she said, horrified at the very idea of spending a night in this uninviting room.

"You said you could make do."

She looked at him in disbelief. "I assumed you had a home, sirrah, not a dungeon." Emily regretted the words as soon as they were out, but he showed no sign of anger, or anything else for that matter.

He just stood in the doorway, reserved. The fading sunlight caught in the reddish highlights of his hair, and reflected in the icy blue of his eyes.

He kept his spine ramrod stiff, his left hand on his sword hilt, and looked at her as if assessing her mettle. "I'm afraid Henry didn't give me time to make more suitable preparations for your stay. I shall send Edmond up to change the mattress and fetch new linens."

"Milord," she said, knowing she should remain silent on this issue, but too repulsed not to speak out. "I hope you won't take this the wrong way, but your home is dreadful and hardly fit for human habitation."

"Tell me, milady, is there a *right* way to take that statement?"

"Nay," she admitted. "But I will not stay here unless changes are made."

His gaze hardened. "You will stay here regardless."

"I most certainly will not."

Anger flared in his eyes, so intense that she took

an involuntary step back from it. Still, she refused to cower completely.

"You will do as you are told, *lady*."

Now that got her dander up. She knew her place as a lady, but with that station came certain rights, and this man was quickly violating every one of them. "I am not one of your men to be dictated to, nor am I your wife."

"True, you are my hostage."

"Nay, I am the king's ward. Is that not what he said?"

If she didn't know better, she'd swear she saw a light of humor in those icy depths.

"And my father told me the king said anything done to me would be done to him. Is that not correct, also, milord?"

"It is."

"Then I ask you, would you expect His Royal Majesty to sleep in this room?"

Draven didn't know what surprised him more: that she had the temerity to stand up to him or that she made such sense with her arguments. In truth, he knew his home was nothing more than a fetid sty to be endured. His life revolved around war, not country life.

He had never been able to stand Ravenswood and would gladly be gone from here forever, or see the donjon fall down in disrepair. 'Twas only his duty to the king that kept him here. Ravenswood was one of the corner pieces of the kingdom. Strategically placed between the north and the south, it needed someone loyal to the king to maintain it.

Even so, he couldn't very well expect a well-born

lady to suffer in his home. Such things had been his father's specialty. "Very well, milady. I shall give notice to my steward to approve any accommodations you wish to make."

"Does that include a housekeeper?"

"If it is necessary . . ."

"It is."

Draven nodded and did his best to ignore the sweet floral scent of her flaxen hair. If memory served, 'twas honeysuckle. It had been more years than he could count since he last stood this close to a lady. But one thing he was sure of: no other woman had ever made him long so much to touch the creamy softness of her cheeks.

There was something about the Lady Emily that reached out to him in a most unsettling way.

Indeed, he could barely stand here and not lean over to capture her lips with his own. Would they be as sweet and soft as they appeared?

His need to know bordered on desperation.

What was it about this woman that appealed to him?

But then he knew. She was as fair of form as any he'd ever beheld, and she had courage to rival any man. And courage was the one thing he valued most in others.

"I leave it in your hands," he said quietly as he tried not to notice the fact that the top of her head reached just below his chin. She was a tall woman, and a perfect size for his aching, hungry body.

By St. Peter's hairy toes, he had to get away from her. Anon.

Why, all he could think of was the bed that

waited just a few feet away from them. A bed he had seldom used, but one he wanted desperately to take advantage of while he had her in his room.

Aye, even with his eyes wide open, he could see himself laying her down on that bed, stripping her clothes from her body, and sampling for himself the wealth of her milk-white skin, the taste of her sweet flesh.

Burying himself deep within the hot moistness between her thighs.

His entire body flared with need.

"I shall send Edmond to see to you," he said, then turned to leave while he still could.

She reached out and touched his arm. Draven froze at her hesitant touch. Such gentleness was unknown to him, and few if any ever touched him physically unless it was a deliberate act to wound him in some fashion.

He couldn't speak as he glanced down at the tiny feminine hand resting innocently on his forearm. Those fingers, so long, slender, and gracefully tapered, her nails well manicured. It was all he could do not to take them in his hand, lift them to his mouth, and sample the sweet, delicate tips of them.

Did she have any idea how such a careless caress scorched him from the inside and out?

"Forgive me for my brashness, milord. I'm not normally so outspoken."

He lifted his gaze from her hand to those exotic, dark green eyes of hers that reminded him of a perfect summer's meadow. "Your father described you as the gentlest maid ever born."

A becoming shade of pink stained her cheeks,

making him long to brush his lips against her high cheekbones and long eyelashes. To taste her breath on his tongue.

Not that he would ever find out how she tasted, he reminded himself. Women such as this carried death with them, and he would never lose control of himself. Never surrender his body to the urges that were blistering his loins.

"My father often exaggerates my virtues, milord."

"But he didn't exaggerate your beauty," he whispered.

How had that escaped his control?

Her blush deepened, and the look of pleasure on her face almost undid him.

Unconsciously, he moved toward her, wanting to inhale more of her sweet, intoxicating, feminine scent, wanting to feel her arms wrap about him as he . . .

Retreat! his mind roared before he lost any more control over himself.

Without another word, Draven did what he had never done before in his life.

He withdrew from the conflict.

Not once did he look back as he left his room, descended the stairs, and entered his decaying hall. His entire body trembled from the pent-up lust she had awakened within him, and he shook forcibly with need.

He couldn't even remember the last time he'd had a woman, but it had been primitive and basic and quick, as were all his encounters with the fairer sex. Never once had he wanted to spend any more time with a woman than what was absolutely necessary to pacify his body.

Yet Emily was different. He couldn't imagine anything more wondrous than to spend an entire night making love to her, slowly, methodically. Touching every inch of her with his hands, his lips, his tongue.

Why he felt this way for her, he knew not. They had only just met, and yet . . .

It made no sense to him whatsoever.

Closing his eyes, he leaned back against the cold stone wall. It must be the fact he had sworn not to touch her.

Aye, that must be it.

She was his forbidden fruit, and though she might tempt him mercilessly, he would have none of it. He had sworn on the finger bones of St. Peter and on his very honor that he wouldn't lay a hand to her in anger or in lust. And he would abide by his oath even if it drove him insane!

Alone in her chambers, Emily sat at the small table before the open window, picking at her food. In truth, she was scared to eat any of it. Given how filthy the hall was, she could only imagine how much worse the kitchens must be.

Edmond, an older youth in his late teens, had changed the straw in her mattress and given her new linens. Her maid, Alys, had swept the old rushes from the room and cleaned the soot from the fireplace. It was still a dismal room lit only by a wall sconce of two tallow candles, but at least it was clean. For that reason she had told Alys to make a pallet for herself in this room until they could see to the rest of the donjon.

As she took a sip of her bitter wine, the door to her room swung open.

"Draven, I . . ." Simon's voice trailed off as he saw her sitting by the window.

Emily frowned at his intrusion and set her goblet back on the table.

His brows knitted, he looked about. "Where's Draven?"

"I know not, milord. Why would you seek him here?"

"This is his room."

Emily felt her jaw slacken at his news. With renewed interest, she glanced around the plain bed and austere wooden chairs. Why would Draven give her his bower?

"He told me I was to stay here."

Simon looked even more puzzled. "Forgive me, milady, for the intrusion."

And then he was gone. Emily stared at the closed door. Why on earth would Draven have done such a thing? If she didn't know better, she'd think he had a more lascivious reason for his charity, but the man seemed oblivious of her.

Nay, his actions made no sense whatsoever.

Sighing, she pushed those thoughts out of her mind and prepared a mental list of what she needed to do on the morrow to make this place suitable to live in.

An hour later Alys rejoined her and told her all her belongings had been unloaded and would be brought upstairs on the morrow. The two of them made ready for bed, then went to sleep with the candles still burning lest something more frightening than bedbugs were waiting to scavenge in the dark.

Emily spent a fretful night tossing and turning. Her body wasn't used to such a hard, unscented mattress, and since she'd never spent a night outside her own room, she couldn't quite adjust to the new sounds and smells of the donjon.

And if that wasn't bad enough, what little sleep she managed was haunted by dreams of a darkly handsome, enigmatic man. A man both beguiling and terrifying.

She'd never met anyone like Draven, and she was at a loss as to how to deal with him. An aura of danger and strength clung to him, warning her that if he chose, he could be truly terrifying.

If he chose . . .

He had been kind thus far, but so many people feared him, including her father, that it gave her pause.

Her thoughts turned to Niles and Joanne. Niles appeared to treat Joanne respectfully, but Emily had caught him beating his horse over a broken spur. And when his squire had accidentally dropped his sword, she had seen the extreme backhand Niles had dealt the boy.

If her father could respect such a man and call

him ally and son, then what of the man her father called enemy?

Was the earl of Ravenswood the ogre of legend?

How would she ever know?

When morning came, Emily welcomed it and the release it gave her from those haunting thoughts. She dressed with Alys's help in her light blue kirtle and white veil, then went below to break her fast.

Emily paused in the doorway as she surveyed the empty hall. Where was everyone?

Surely she hadn't missed the meal? Had she?

Puzzled, she walked out the front door of the donjon. Draven's men were already training in the list. And from the look of them, they had been at it for some time.

Off to the side of the field, Simon sat on the ground, leaning back against an apple tree in repose while he urged two of the knights on in their swordplay.

She saw Draven nowhere. Gathering her skirts, she descended the steps and headed across the yard to where the men trained.

As she rounded the side of the keep, she spotted Draven easily enough. The tallest of the men, he seemed to be training much more seriously than the others. The early morning light dappled against the black-colored mail and flashed across his black shield.

A group of four men surrounded him and he was doing a remarkable job of fending them off as they attacked him almost simultaneously. Never before had she witnessed such agility or speed. No wonder people sang his praises, she thought as he twirled his sword from one attacker to meet the blow of the man behind him.

Why, she hadn't known a man so large could move with such grace and ease. She doubted if even Mars or Ares could fight better.

In awe, she watched as he deflected each blow with astounding precision while whirling in a macabre dance to meet the next assault and drive his assailant back on his heels.

And in that instant she knew he could easily defeat her father in battle. In spite of her father's incredible strength, she had seen him train enough times to know he was no equal for Lord Draven's skill.

The thought made her nauseated.

"Good day, fair Emily!" Simon called in greeting to her.

At her name, Draven turned in her direction and paused in his fighting. As soon as he stopped, one of his men hit him across the head from the side.

Draven cursed loudly as he whirled on the man and raised his sword.

Emily, who had rushed toward him when he'd been hit, hesitated at the fierce battle cry. Never had she heard such rage. She couldn't imagine having to face the brunt of Draven's sword.

The man who had hit Draven dropped his sword, fell to his knees in terror, and raised his shield over his head in expectation of the oncoming blow. The other three knights hurriedly withdrew from the exercise.

Draven's sword arced toward the cowering man, and just as she was certain he would have the man's head, he stopped the blade a fraction of an inch from the man's raised shield.

Everything seemed frozen in time as the sword just hung there. So close, and yet not quite touching.

Draven stood as still as a statue. She had no idea how he had managed to bring the massive blow under control before he shattered the poor knight's shield and arm.

After a pregnant pause, Draven planted his sword in the ground before the cowering knight.

Emily approached them at a slower pace, amazed that Draven wasn't even breathing heavily from the exercise.

"On your feet, Geoffrey," he said in a calm voice. "I realize you are new to my company, but you should know I would never strike you for a well-placed blow just because I was distracted. I turned on you only because I thought you would strike again."

The knight lowered his shield, then removed his helm. He wiped his arm over his sweat-covered brow. "Forgive me, milord. My last trainer was not so understanding."

Draven extended his arm and helped him to his feet. "Go on and break your fast."

Geoffrey quickly did as he bade.

Emily frowned as Simon paused by her side. Lord Draven didn't appear harmed and yet the force of the blow had been significant.

"Are you all right, milord?" she asked.

"I fear the worst of it is the ringing in my ears," Draven said as he pulled his helm from his head.

Emily gasped as she saw the blood trailing down his temple. "Nay, milord, I fear the worst of it is the gash upon your brow."

Her father's enemy or not, she wasn't about to stand still in the face of an open wound and do nothing. She turned to Simon. "My maid is upstairs in my chambers. Please ask her to fetch my sewing kit and a cup of wine."

With a nod, Simon obeyed.

Emily took Lord Draven's hand to lead him toward a shaded spot, but when she stepped forward, he didn't budge.

Confused, she turned back to face him.

He gave her a suspicious frown. "Why do you touch me?" he asked.

Emily looked down at their joined hands in surprise. She immediately let go. "I didn't mean to offend you, milord. I was only thinking that I could better tend your wound if you were seated."

"My squire can tend my wound."

She lifted her brow at him. "Milord, if the scar on your neck is a testament of the boy's handiwork, then I beg you please allow me to stitch your forehead. I shudder to think of the scar he would leave there."

As if hearing his name, his squire appeared from the side of the donjon. He had a stool in his right hand, a bowl in his left, and a linen towel draped over his shoulder.

"Lord Simon told me to fetch this for you, milord," he said to Draven. "I also brought a cloth and water."

Lord Draven stood a moment as if debating with himself, then he finally spoke. "Where would milady like the stool placed?"

For some reason Emily felt as though she'd won a skirmish with him.

"Over there, please," she said, pointing to the spot where Simon had been resting earlier.

The boy ran to obey her.

She led the way with Draven no more than a step behind. As she walked, she could feel his gaze on her like a gentle caress. She sensed that he wanted to touch her and yet the very idea seemed ridiculous, especially given the tone of his voice when he asked why she'd touched him to begin with.

His squire placed the stool where she told him, then quickly ran off to fetch his master's sword and helm from the training field.

Draven settled himself on the stool while Emily dipped one corner of the towel in water.

No sooner had he removed his mail gauntlets and balanced them on his thigh than Alys came with her basket and wine.

"Thank you, Alys," she said, taking them from her and placing them on the ground next to the bowl of water.

To her consternation, Alys, who stood directly behind Draven, looked at the back of his head, then met Emily's gaze and patted her chest to indicate her heart raced the way Emily's did. If that wasn't bad enough, Alys balled her hand into a fist and bit her forefinger as her lustful, hungry stare followed the length of his body.

Heat stung Emily's cheeks at her maid's pantomimed expressions.

At that moment, Draven looked up at Emily, and seeing where her gaze was directed, he turned about to catch Alys still biting her hand.

Alys's smile faded and she took her hand out of her mouth and shook it. "Darn fleas. Bit me something silly last night."

Lord Draven looked less than convinced as he turned back to Emily.

Alys locked gazes with her and lifted her brows several times. "Milady has all she requires?" Alys asked in a tone that meant *I'll gladly leave the two of you alone.*

"Aye, Alys, thank you."

"Should milady have any further need of me for *anything*"—Emily cringed at the way Alys stressed the word—"please don't hesitate to call."

"I won't, Alys." Emily gave her a pointed glare. "Thank you."

Alys made one last kissing face at Lord Draven, then rushed off to the keep.

Embarrassed to the core of her soul, Emily opened her sewing basket.

"Tell me, milady, is your maid possessed of some strange demon that makes her dance about so?"

Smiling, Emily threaded a needle, then set it aside and retrieved her wet towel. "If the demon has a name, milord, I fear we must call it mischievousness."

She bathed Lord Draven's wound. His brow was warm to her touch, and unlike her father, Lord Draven didn't hiss as the cloth scraped his skin. He merely watched her with an intensity that seared her flesh.

"Most ladies would beat their maids for such insolence."

"Well, I am not hypocrite enough to punish her for a sin that is so dear to my own heart."

His gaze softened. "Aye, I have a feeling you could well tutor her on the subject."

"Comparatively speaking, she is but a novice and I a master craftsman."

As she brushed her hand through his ebony locks to hold them away from his wound, she was struck by their softness. His hair was like fine silk sifting between her fingers. Never before had she felt anything like it or the heat that his presence stirred within her. Her body felt vibrant and warm, and was possessed of a terrible throbbing.

"You smell like apples and cinnamon," he said gruffly.

Emily paused and held the cloth to his brow. " 'Tis a perfume my sister wears," she said softly. "I always told her she would attract more flies and bees with it than men."

He frowned. "Then why are you wearing it?"

"I miss her, and wearing it comforts me."

He looked away.

Licking her dry lips, she dipped the needle and thread in the cup of wine.

He sat with his legs wide apart and his hands on his knees. Emily tried not to notice the way he surrounded her as she stepped between his legs to stitch the wound. Nor how her breasts, which drew strangely taut and felt suddenly heavy, were level with his gaze.

And when he chanced to glance at them, she felt a peculiar, powerful ache between her legs.

Emily swallowed against the strangeness of her body as she prepared to stitch his brow. "I'm afraid this will sting a bit."

"I assure you, milady, I have been stitched enough times not to notice."

A point he proved well as she completed the first stitch. He remained as still as a statue. Her father would have cursed and jerked, as had any man she'd ever stitched. But Lord Draven just sat, his gaze on the ground behind her, as she made three tiny stitches to close the wound.

Stepping away, she retrieved her silver scissors from the basket.

"You have a gentle touch," he said, his voice deep and strange to her ears.

"Thank you, milord. 'Tis not in my nature to hurt people."

She cut the thread, then reached for the bag of herbs she kept in her basket. While she prepared a poultice to keep the swelling down and reduce the chance for infection, she felt him again watching her every move.

What was it about that icy gaze that made her both shivery and warm at the same time?

Again she wondered what it would be like to kiss him. Joanne had told her kissing was the best part of a man's embrace, and something inside told her that Draven's kiss would indeed be wondrous.

"What brought milady to the field this morning?" he asked.

Emily mixed her herbs with the wine. "I was wondering why no one was in the hall breaking the fast."

" 'Tis not my habit to do so until midmorning." He glanced away from her and she took a deep breath in relief to have some peace from that searing stare. "I shall have Druce inform the cooks to rise early and have your food prepared for you."

"Druce?" she asked as she spread the poultice over his brow. His skin was so different from her own. It was smooth, but not delicate. It was just masculine. And warm. Terribly warm, and very distracting for a maiden's virtuous welfare.

"My squire."

"Ah," she said as she finished her ministrations. When she bent down to reach for the towel, her hip inadvertently grazed his inner thigh.

He hissed sharply, then sprang to his feet so quickly she gave an involuntary shriek.

Before she could apologize, he was out of her hearing range.

Draven took long, deep breaths as he struggled with the lust coursing through the entire length of his body. His thigh ached as if someone had placed a hot iron to it. And his taut groin burned as if the fires of hell had descended into his lap.

Had he stayed one more instant with her, he would have dishonored them both.

With no thought save to put as much distance

between them as possible, he headed into the stable, which unfortunately was occupied by Simon.

"I thought you were in the donjon," Draven snapped at his brother, who was standing over the makeshift pallet Draven had made the night before.

"I heard from Druce that you had moved your things in here and sought to verify that fact."

Draven tried to ignore him as he removed his surcoat. "Where is my squire?"

"Eating last I saw. Here, let me assist you."

Draven gave Simon his back so that his brother could unbuckle and unlace his armor.

"Why did you give the lady your solar?"

Draven felt his jaw flex. " 'Tis none of your business."

"I know, but I've never seen you act so strangely."

Closing his eyes, Draven wished for once that Simon would just go away. But he knew him well enough to know Simon wouldn't leave until he had whatever answers he sought. 'Twas the most annoying habit of a man who had numerous annoying habits.

"I gave her my solar because 'twas the cleanest room in the donjon, and I moved my things out here because if I stay away from her I won't be able to harm her."

He felt Simon grip his mail hauberk in his fist. "How many times must I tell you, you are not your father?"

Draven shrugged his grip off, then jerked the heavy hauberk over his head. "You don't know me as well as you think, brother."

Simon gave him a feral glare of anger. "I have never once seen you strike out in anger. Why—"

"What of your arm?" Draven asked, interrupting him.

The anger fled from his features as his face paled considerably. "We were children, Draven, and it was an accident."

"It doesn't matter," he said, trying to banish the sight of his brother lying on the ground, wounded by his own hand. "I almost killed you that day."

"You've never raised a hand against me since."

"Because you've never made me angry."

Simon snorted. "Well, it certainly wasn't from lack of effort on my part."

"I don't find you amusing."

"See," Simon said triumphantly. "You're angry at me now and yet you do nothing to harm me."

" 'Tis not the same," he insisted. "I cannot—nay," Draven corrected, "I *will* not take such a chance with her welfare. Not when I've sworn to see no harm befall her."

Simon sighed. "More's the pity then. I was hoping her presence here would make you realize that you can be with a woman and not hurt her."

Draven wished he could believe that. But he knew better. He was possessed of the same rage as his father and as powerless to stop it.

How many times in battle had he killed without even feeling it? Once his rage took root in him, he became its pawn. He felt nothing, saw nothing, knew nothing until it passed.

And then 'twas too late for the poor soul who had crossed his path.

Having seen his own mother fall to that kind of rage, he would never knowingly jeopardize a woman's life for the sake of himself or of a need for heirs.

Nay, the curse of his blood would stop with him. He would make sure of it.

With a disgusted look on his face, Simon pushed himself away from the wooden post, then made his way from the stable.

Draven finished removing his armor and dressed in a black tunic and breeches.

As he left the stable, he caught sight of Emily heading back toward the donjon with Druce by her side. The two of them were laughing over something. The sound of her musical laughter rang in his ears.

What he would give to be free to make jests with her as well, and to see her eyes light up with humor.

With her head held high, and her pale blond hair and veil flowing behind her, she was a graceful, beguiling creature.

And for the first time in his life, he wanted Simon to be right.

What would it be like to have the life of a normal man? To sit before the fire while his lady went about her duties and tended his children?

To have her turn to him with a smile meant only for him?

He would sell what little soul he had left for it.

But it was a dream he'd left behind long ago out of necessity. Now with Emily's presence here it had resurfaced with such vengeance that he cursed Henry for his decree.

On my honor, I, Draven de Montague, earl of Ravenswood, will never lay hand to the Lady Emily in violence or in lust. She will leave my company in the same manner with which she was brought, or I shall surrender myself to the king's justice whatever it might be.

If it was the last thing he did, he would uphold that oath, his body and wants be damned.

Chapter 4

Emily had just sat down to break her fast with Alys when the door to the donjon swung wide. She frowned at Alys as people began rushing into the room in a flurry of activity.

A wiry man of about a score and ten years led the way, clutching a small black book to his right side. His black hair was thin and short, and a shock of his bangs continually fell into his eyes no matter how much he brushed it aside. He wore a bright orange tunic and whipped orders off his tongue with amazing speed.

"You, there," he said to one of the fifteen women. "You pick three others and immediately start cleaning the upper floor. I want four women in the kitchens scrubbing, and the rest of you can start in here. Master carpenter." He turned to the bearded older man at his right. "See that this hall is completely redone." He threw his left arm wide as he gestured toward the stark, faded gray walls. "They need to be reinforced, painted, and, well, whatever you think. I want it light and airy. Homey. Aye," he said with a satisfied smile, "let us strive for a homey feel."

"Milady?" Alys asked. "Who are these people?"

"I don't know," Emily said. "But I suspect the man in orange must be Lord Draven's steward." Or he was a lunatic to come unbidden into Lord Draven's hall and start making such changes.

Nay, he would have to be the steward.

As if sensing her thoughts, the man moved to her side. "Good day, milady," he said, his face bright and cheerful. "I am Denys, Lord Draven's steward."

He drew forth the book, opened it to the page that was marked by a small quill pen, and set it on the table next to her. He took a vial of ink from the satchel on his girdle and opened the top. Dipping the quill, he paused and looked up at her. "I was told to ask after your particular needs."

Before she could answer, there was another commotion at the door.

"Out of the way," someone shouted.

The crowd parted like the Red Sea as a group of four men hefted a large headboard through the door. The men paused just inside the hall and rested the intricately carved mahogany piece against the far wall. "Would someone tell us where to put this?" a young man asked as he panted.

"Well it certainly doesn't go in the hall," Denys muttered under his breath. He crossed the room and gestured to the stairs with his quill. "Up the stairs to the lady's room on the right."

Denys turned to one of Lord Draven's servants and instructed the man to show them the way.

Stupefied, Emily watched the men struggle up the stairs with her new headboard.

"What is going on?" she asked Denys when he returned to her side.

He smoothed his sleeve meticulously, then met her gaze. "Lord Draven woke me an hour before sunrise and bade me start preparations for your stay. He said the donjon was to look as if the king himself were staying with us."

Denys ran his finger down the list of items he'd written in his book. "I was told to find a house-keeper, a better cook, a baker, another brewer. There were shrubs and flowers to be ordered and a gardener. More cattle and hens," he said, frowning as he looked up from his list. "I was told to get a lot of hens."

"Hens?" she asked, confused as well.

"Aye, red ones, His Lordship said. Nothing but red hens for the lady."

Emily laughed at the very thought.

Denys looked back at his notes. "The house-keeper is named Beatrix and said that she could be here this afternoon. She's a widow woman who seemed very nice. If you have any problems with her, let me know and I shall deal with her forthwith. Now, what other items do you require?" Again he positioned his quill for her orders.

Emily sat perplexed. When she had spoken to Lord Draven the night before she had assumed she would be the one to put things in order. The best she had hoped for was a housekeeper and maybe a village girl or two to help with the cleaning. Never had she expected an army of helpers to descend on the keep, let alone all the other items Lord Draven had ordered.

"I can think of nothing," she said. She looked to her maid whose face mirrored her own amazement. "Alys?"

"Nay, milady. 'Twould seem His Lordship thought of everything."

Satisfied, Denys returned his vial of ink to his satchel and closed his book. "Very good, then. You and your maid may relax and know that I have everything in hand. Should you think of anything you need, please let me know."

"Thank you," she said, overwhelmed by Draven's generosity.

Denys had started away from her table when a thought struck her.

"Wait, Denys?"

He literally hopped back to her side.

Thinking what a peculiar man he was, Emily gestured toward where the lord's table should be set. "Did His Lordship perchance order a table and a dais?"

She could swear the steward's face lost some of its color. "Nay, milady, he did not."

"Then perhaps you should add that."

He hesitated. "I don't think that would be wise, milady."

"Whyever not?"

"Draven has little use for the pompousness of the aristocracy," she heard Simon say.

Emily looked over her shoulder to see him standing behind her with his hands behind his back.

How long had he been there?

" 'Tis not pompous, Simon," she said. " 'Tis expected."

"In other halls mayhap. Not here." Simon surveyed the activity. "As usual, Denys, I am impressed by your meticulousness."

"My pleasure is to please you, milord."

Simon laughed aloud. "And so you have. Draven on the other hand . . ."

" 'Tis what he ordered," Denys said defensively.

"Aye, but I can't wait to see his face when he enters this fray."

Denys nodded as if understanding whatever it was Simon meant.

Emily, on the other hand, was quite lost.

"Well then," Denys said, "if there is nothing else, I shall get back to work. Supervising and"—Denys looked to Simon—"and more supervising."

Simon excused him, then brought his arms from around his back to show Emily the fresh loaf of bread he held in his hands. "I swiped this from the baker's cart. He brought it with him from the village, and I thought you might like it more than what you have."

She thanked him as he set it on the wooden trencher and sliced her a bit of it. "It smells wonderful," she said, taking a small piece and placing it in her mouth.

And coated in honey butter, it tasted even better.

Swallowing the bread, she watched Simon as he looked around the hall.

"Why is it you think your brother won't be pleased?" she asked.

"He would rather have this place fall in upon his ears than see it—" He broke himself off as if catching his words. "Did I say that aloud?"

"Aye, you did."

Simon quirked his head. "Then Draven is right, I should better counsel my tongue."

"I say you should counsel it less," she teased. "For I would like to know."

"And I would like to keep my tongue in my head. Should Draven catch me spilling out his thoughts, like as not, I shall find it quickly removed."

She could well understand his wish not to make his brother angry. From what she had seen, Draven could indeed cause much damage to someone should anger possess him.

"Now, milady," Simon said with a curt bow. "If you'll excuse me, I should like to get this armor off for it chafes in places I cannot mention in mixed company."

Unsure of what she should say, she watched as Simon made his way through the bustling scrubbing maids and workmen.

"This is a strange place, lady," Alys said when they were again alone.

"It is indeed." Emily shared her bread with her maid. "Why do you think Lord Draven refuses to have a table?"

"I cannot imagine. Perhaps for the same reason you are breaking bread with your maid?"

Emily smiled gently. "You are more family than servant, you know that."

"Aye, but don't you think Lord Simon thought it strange that you sit here with me?"

She nodded. "No doubt he found my habit as strange as I find Lord Draven's. But I doubt Lord Draven thinks of servants as family. From what I have seen, he keeps his own company."

Nay, there was much more to His Lordship. Things she couldn't even begin to fathom.

"You know, milady," Alys said, drawing her attention. "Lord Draven has given you a perfect opportunity to seek him out."

"I was just thinking that," Emily said as she pushed her trencher aside. "After all, the least I could do is thank him for his efforts."

"A kiss should do as a nice thank-you."

"Alys," she scolded. "I could never be so . . . so . . . so forward."

Alys laughed so hard, she choked on her bread.

Emily patted her on the back. "You're not amusing."

"Nay, milady, but your comment certainly was," she said as she coughed to clear her throat. "I've seldom known you *not* to be forward."

Emily bit her lip impishly. "I know. 'Tis a terrible thing I am told."

"Terrible or not, if milady wishes to catch the raven, she must lay the trap, and no one ever laid a successful trap by being timid with the lure." Alys stood up and pulled at Emily's kirtle to lower the neckline.

"Alys!" Emily said insistently, trying to tug it back into place.

"Oh, 'tis just a little," she said, smoothing Emily's veil and pulling one curly tendril of hair free of the linen to drape on the right side of her face.

Alys tilted her head to study Emily's face, then squinted. "Nay." She shook her head. "Too nunnish for our intents."

Reaching up, Alys unpinned the veil from her head, placed the pins in her mouth, then fluffed and smoothed Emily's hair with her hands.

Again, Alys studied her for several seconds before she nodded and removed the pins from her mouth. "There now. Pretty as an angel. But remember, 'tis not angelic thoughts you should be having."

Emily rolled her eyes.

Alys pinched a bit of color into Emily's cheeks. "Moisten your lips and be off."

Emily did as told. "Wish me luck."

"Luck, milady, and good fortune."

With a deep breath for courage, Emily went to find Lord Draven to thank him properly for his deed.

Chapter 5

In the black of night, Draven made his way up the winding stairs that led to his bower. More weary than ever before, he felt the familiar burning in his knee of a wound he would just as soon forget.

All he wanted was peace, solitude, a place where no one would disturb him. A place where he could forget the world and the world could forget him.

He pushed open the door.

Draven took a single step into his room, then froze.

Emily sat in a large, gilded tub. She had piled her long golden hair atop her head, and several tendrils of it curled becomingly about her creamy shoulders.

The light from a dozen beeswax candles glistened against bare, milk-white skin. And his mouth watered for a taste of it.

Unaware of his presence, she lifted one supple arm up and lathered a cloth with soap. He could

hear her humming a soft, lilting tune as she drew
the cloth slowly over her arm, leaving a trail of
suds.

His body instantly attuned, he watched as she
tilted her head to the side and stroked the flesh of
her neck with her long, shapely fingers. He bit his
lip as he imagined what that skin would taste like
should he take it between his teeth and tease it with
his tongue.

His breathing ragged, he couldn't tear his gaze
from her as she started to lather her wet breasts
with gentle, massaging strokes. Her fingers splayed
over the tender mounds, teasing the taut nipples,
covering them with more suds and making his
groin hotter and harder than it had ever been
before.

Draven couldn't stand it. Unconsciously, he
moved toward her.

The tip of his sword scraped against the door-
frame, alerting her to his presence.

Looking up, Emily gasped as she jumped to
cover herself with her hands, sending water over
the edge of the tub and spilling it across the floor.

Their eyes met and locked, and a slow smile
spread across her face as she boldly unwrapped her
arms from around her bare breasts, gifting him with
the magnificent image of her wide-eyed and naked.

Then, to his utter amazement, she rose from the
water like a seductive nymph, completely
unabashed by her nudity.

He couldn't move as he feasted on the sight of
her creamy body glistening like wet silk in the can-
dlelight.

His mouth dry, he trailed his gaze from the top of her head to her sculpted breasts and then to the smallness of her waist. But what captured his gaze most were the damp, dark blond curls at the juncture of her thighs. Curls that beckoned him with the promise of wet, sleek heat welcoming him into the realms of paradise.

By all the saints, she was the loveliest creature on earth to him.

"I've been waiting for you, milord," she said as her face softened.

Draven couldn't speak.

She stepped over the edge of the tub and approached him with the slow seductive walk of a practiced courtesan.

Mesmerized, he still didn't move. Not even when she stopped before him and reached up to touch his face. Chills erupted through him, and he allowed her to tilt his head down as she rose on her tiptoes to meet his lips.

She pressed her breasts flat against his armor as she wrapped her arms around his neck.

Encircling her wet, bare body with his arms, he took possession of her mouth and ravished it fully. Draven moaned as he tasted the pure honey of her breath, her tongue. The scent of honeysuckle filled his head and he closed his eyes, reveling in the sound of her welcoming sigh as he ran his hands over her hips to cup her buttocks and press her closer to him.

Somehow, he found his armor in a puddle at his feet and he stood completely naked before her as she ran her hands over his chest.

Draven kissed a circle around her, from her lips to her neck to her shoulders. He came up behind her, running his hands over her taut breasts as she arched her back against his chest. He buried his lips against the nape of her neck as she hissed in pleasure.

"I want you, Draven," she whispered, her voice driving his throbbing body to new heights of need.

Brazenly, she took his hands and placed them again on her breasts. "Do with me as you will."

Leaning his head back, he gave his battle cry as he moved his hands from her breasts down her arms and to her hands. He laced his fingers with hers, then placed her hands against the wall in front of her.

Aye, he would have his way with her this night. Damn his oath and damn his past. For one moment, he would know what it was like to feel as if he belonged. As if he could have all he desired.

Her hair came tumbling down in a wealth of curls. He buried his face in her tresses and just inhaled the essence of her. Emily reached up over her head and buried her hand in his hair. "I love you, milord," she whispered, and for some reason he couldn't fathom, her words didn't terrify him.

She turned then, to face him, and took his lips with her own. Her hands explored his body boldly, hotly, as she rubbed herself against him, raising his desire to a ravenous need.

"You taste so sweet," she whispered, leaving his lips and nibbling a trail along his jaw to his neck.

Draven sucked his breath in sharply between his

teeth as she suckled the flesh of his neck. Then she moved lower. Down his chest, to his abdomen, his navel, and when she took him into her mouth, he thought he might very well die where he stood.

Only he didn't. Instead, he buried his hand in her hair and trembled as shivers of pleasure erupted through his entire body. Her lips and tongue teased him unmercifully with white-hot ecstasy. And just when he was sure he could take no more, she pulled away and rose slowly to her feet.

She took his hand into hers and led it to the sweet nectar between her thighs where she was hot and wet and ready for him. "Come inside, my sweet, where it is warm and inviting," she whispered.

Trembling from the invitation, Draven didn't hesitate. He braced her against the wall and drove himself inside her, up to the hilt. She moaned in his ear as she rose up onto her tiptoes, then lowered herself down upon his shaft.

It was heaven. Pure, blessed heaven. The likes of which he'd never thought to have.

He shook all over from it.

"Aye, Draven, aye," she moaned insistently as she gently milked his body with her own.

"Emily," he said at last, enjoying the feel of her name on his lips as he pulled himself back ever so slightly, then plunged himself deep inside her again.

"Milord," she said again even more insistently than before.

"Emily," he sighed.

"Milord!"

Draven came awake with a start as someone grabbed him by the shoulder. His first instinct to lay low his attacker, he barely caught himself before he yielded to that protective urge.

He blinked twice as he looked up into exotic, bright green eyes set in a puzzled face. The same catlike eyes he'd just been dreaming of.

Emily stood above him, fully clothed. And this was not his room where the dream had taken place. This was the old orchard behind the donjon.

"Are you all right?" she asked.

"Aye," he said hoarsely, shifting his body to keep her from seeing the hardness of him that jutted out like a ten-foot maypole.

He didn't know what annoyed him most, being interrupted from his dream or being caught in the midst of some adolescent fantasy, the likes of which he'd not had since he *was* an adolescent.

How could his dreams have betrayed him so?

And worse, in a castle full of people, why did it have to be Emily who awakened him?

Could he possibly be any more embarrassed?

Nay, not even if it were the pope himself who had awakened him.

"Are you certain all is well?" she asked again. "Your face is terribly flushed." She reached out to touch his forehead.

For an instant, Draven didn't move. He craved her touch so much that he was frozen.

Until his sense finally took hold of him. Jumping to his feet, he put a safe distance between them because if she were to touch him right then while the heat of the dream still tortured him, he might very well succumb to his body and take her where she stood.

"I am fine," he insisted, thanking all that was holy for his long supertunic that hid his embarrassing condition from her casual glance.

"Are you sure your wound isn't infected?"

Draven ground his teeth at the reminder of what had happened that morning. First he'd let her distract him to the point of being hit, and now . . .

What the devil was wrong with him? He'd always been in full charge of himself.

Emily stooped in front of him and retrieved the book he had been reading before he fell asleep. The low scoop of her dress was such that she unknowingly gifted him with the sight of the deep valley between her breasts, and the luscious mouthwatering mounds. His breath caught in his throat at the creaminess of her skin.

And his damned body grew even stiffer!

Cursing under his breath, he tried to distract himself by looking at a crooked piece of masonry falling off the wall behind her, and the sow trotting loose from its pen.

It didn't help. Not even a bit.

"Peter Abelard?" she asked, her soft voice entrancing him so much that he inadvertently met her curious gaze.

Those eyes . . .

What was it about them that enthralled him so? They were a deep, earthy green and shone with some inner light or spirit he couldn't name.

And suddenly those eyes grew puzzled.

Mentally kicking himself, he responded to her

question with the first stupid comment that came to his mind. "You find it strange I read a monk's writing?"

Because right then with the sun glinting in the highlights of her golden hair, monkish thoughts were the furthest thing from his mind.

"I find it strange you read at all."

"I would remark the same of you, milady," he said gruffly, taking the book from her hand. "I wasn't aware Hugh bothered to tutor his daughters."

"I could say the same of Harold." Emily bit her lip as soon as the words were out of her mouth and she saw the anger that lit his eyes.

She hadn't meant to offend him. "That is to say—"

"I understand what you said, milady," he said in a stiff, formal tone.

This was not how she meant for the encounter to go. But then she hadn't expected him to be so irritable. Especially given the tenderness in his voice when he spoke her name as she struggled to wake him.

Whatever was the matter with him?

Seeking to rectify whatever insult she had inadvertently given, she explained her unusual education to him. "My father thought it wise that we learn to read in order to make sure our steward never swindled his money. He always felt that a literate woman was a helpful one."

A bitterness darkened his eyes. "And my father believed that so long as the steward feared for his life, he wouldn't dare cheat his lord, literate or not."

That was in keeping with what she had always heard of the lords of Ravenswood. Their cold brutality had become legendary long ago.

And yet she couldn't imagine the vivacious Denys in fear of his life. In fact, he seemed most content in his official capacity.

"Is that more of your morbid humor?" she asked, remembering what Simon had told her about Draven.

His face didn't change at all. "You'll find I have no sense of humor. At least none of which I'm aware."

Emily paused. She had no idea where to go from that. So rather than taste any more of her foot, she deftly changed the subject. "I actually came to find you so that I could thank you for what you did."

"For what I did?"

"The castle," she said, taking a step toward him. "It was more than I—" Her voice broke off as she looked up into his eyes. Up close they weren't the frigid blue she had first noted, but were in fact a strange mixture of blues.

Never had she seen eyes quite like them. They reminded her of a stained glass window. Why, there was even a fleck of red in his left eye just below the pupil.

His gaze sharpened on her just the way Theodore's always did right before he attempted a kiss.

Emily stood completely still, both anxious and afraid that he might try it.

Lord Draven was so large compared to her, and no one had ever considered her slight of form.

Indeed, her father hardly had an inch on her height, but she barely reached Lord Draven's shoulders.

The soft wind caressed the dark locks of his hair. His gaze dropped to her lips, and she saw the raw hunger in his eyes. In that moment, she wanted to feel his lips on hers, to taste the essence of this man.

Breathless, she licked her lips in expectation of his kiss.

His head dipped ever so slightly and his lips parted.

Just when she was certain he would kiss her, he straightened abruptly. "I must be going," he said tartly, placing his book beneath his arm.

Annoyed by his dismissal, she watched him step around her and head toward the keep.

Emily put her hands on her hips and watched him walk away. "This is not going to be easy," she muttered beneath her breath.

How could she make him fall in love with her if he refused to stay near her?

Discouraged but not daunted, she headed back to the keep.

She had only come around it when Draven's squire almost ran her over.

"Beg pardon, milady," he said. "I must prepare His Lordship's horse."

Emily frowned as the lad dashed to the stable. Her consternation doubled as she entered the hall and overheard two knights speaking.

"I thought we weren't headed to Lincoln for another fortnight?"

"Seems Ravenswood changed his mind."

The other knight growled low in his throat. "I grow weary of this travel. We just returned from London."

"Were I you," the other knight said with a note of warning in his voice, "I'd not speak so loudly lest *he* hear you. Otherwise, you'll be pulling watch for the next two months."

They continued their conversation as they walked past her and out the main door.

Before she could recover, she heard Simon's voice on the stairs. "What do you mean you're bound for Lincoln?"

"You know the king ordered me—"

"But *now*?" Simon almost roared.

"Now is as good a time as any," Draven said in that low, almost lethal tone of his.

Simon snorted. "It's her, isn't it?"

Emily's heart leaped at the words. Hurrying to the wall just inside the hall, she pressed herself flat against it and listened carefully.

"Don't be absurd," Draven snarled. "I told you the lady is nothing to me."

"Then why have you moved your trip up?"

"Because it suits me to."

"And why is that?"

"Simon, lay the matter aside. I am bound for Lincoln. The lady is in your care until I return. I trust you can see to her safety?"

"Aye, I'll see to her safety. But know this, Draven. You can't run from her forever. Sooner or later you'll have to return."

She heard Draven pause just on the other side of

her wall. "Think so? I do believe there are plans for a Crusade brewing in Normandy. Perhaps—"

"Henry would never relieve you from his service long enough to crusade and well you know it."

"You'd be amazed what the king would do should I ask it of him."

There were several seconds of silence before Simon spoke again. "Very well, go to Lincoln. But know this. I never thought I'd see the day you retreated from anything, least of all a mere slip of a woman."

She turned her head to see Simon stalk angrily out of the door and then slam it shut. No sooner had the door closed behind him than she heard Draven's muffled words.

"And never did I think I would find a woman I wanted so badly." He sighed wistfully. "Beauty, you're a treacherous lure with a deadly hook, and this fish has no choice except to flee before it gets caught."

Emily flattened herself against the wall as he descended the steps, then followed after Simon.

For several minutes, she just stood there sifting through his words.

"And never did I think I would find a woman I wanted so badly."

Unlike remarks from Theodore, who constantly accosted her with such comments, Draven's words were special, for he had never intended another soul to hear them. A strange tenderness came to her. One she couldn't define and she wasn't really sure why she felt it.

They were just words. And yet . . .

They were special.

Emily smiled. If he truly felt that, then she stood a hope of her goal.

But not if she let him get away.

Chapter 6

"Milord?"

Draven turned from his horse at Emily's voice. Of all the wretched luck! One minute more and he would have been mounted and out of her reach.

"Milady?" he asked in a voice that bordered between confounded ire and pleasantry.

She came to rest in front of him and looked questioningly at his packed horse. "You're leaving?"

"I have royal duties in Lincoln."

"Lincoln?" Emily repeated, her eyes wide and beguiling. "Oh, I've always wanted to go to Lincoln. I've heard they have a most wondrous fair there this time of year."

"They do," Simon said as he came up behind her. Simon stared pointedly at Draven as he continued, "One of the largest in the region."

"Truly?" she asked.

"A fair is a fair," Draven groused, aggravated that Simon would dare attempt to manipulate him thusly. "You can't tell one from another."

She looked alluring, provocative, and so sweet he wanted nothing more than to take a gentle nip of her flesh to see if indeed she were coated in honey, or if the light golden glow was merely the true color of her skin.

"I wouldn't know, milord," she said softly, her face falling as sadness possessed her. "I have never been to a fair."

A twinge of something strange ran though him. It felt like a tugging at his heart for her having missed something she obviously wanted to do.

"Never?" Simon asked, his voice aghast.

Draven glared at his brother.

"Never," she said, drawing Draven's attention back to her. Her bottom lip poked out ever so slightly in an attractive pout. "My father wouldn't allow it. He said there was naught to be found at a fair save debauchery." She looked up at Draven. "I would so love to see a fair just once."

Draven barely heard her words, for his attention was captivated by the sparkle in her eyes. The moistness of her lips. Captivated by an image of him drawing her seductive bottom lip between his teeth and savoring the treasure of her mouth.

"Would it be possible for me to accompany you?" she asked.

Aye almost slipped out of his mouth before he caught himself.

Aye?! he railed at his treacherous mind. She was the whole reason he was headed to Lincoln! Taking her with him would defeat the entire purpose of the journey.

"Nay, milady," he said grabbing his horse's reins. " 'Tis impossible."

"But milord—"

"I have the king's duties to attend," he said far more gruffly than he meant to.

"Oh." Her face fell, and the sadness in her eyes tore at him. Draven didn't want to make her unhappy, any more than he wanted Henry to end his life.

And for some reason he couldn't name, her happiness became important to him.

"How about if I go with her?" Simon asked. "I can see to the lady's welfare while you attend your *business*."

Draven narrowed his eyes at his brother. Did the man want him to die? Rather Simon should take a dagger to his back than evoke Henry's wrath upon his head. The last thing on earth Draven desired was to be hanged, drawn and quartered over a woman.

Emily's face instantly beamed at the prospect of joining him. "Oh, please!"

His gut wrenched at her sweet voice and the look of anticipation on her face. How could he ever deny her so simple a request?

He made the mistake of looking at her again. She held her hands clasped between her breasts and bit her lip as if a denial from him would send her off into tears.

"I could be packed before you know," she said

excitedly. "And I promise I won't be a burden. Why, you'll not even know I'm along."

He doubted that. She had a terrible way of invading his thoughts.

"Please?" she begged.

This was a bad idea. He knew it with every breath he took and yet he couldn't find it within him to disappoint her again.

You have to die sometime.

Aye, but there are far more desirable ends.

Desirable perhaps, but then so was the look of happiness on her face. Besides, he could stay away from her in Lincoln and force Simon to look after her. And there would be Orrick's wife there to entertain her as well.

Aye, he could stay away from her. He *would* stay away from her.

"Very well, milady. If you hurry, I shall wait."

She bestowed a bright smile upon him that made him feel weak in the knees. Or mayhap in his head.

Aye, he was definitely weak in the head for allowing her to accompany him.

"Thank you!" she breathed, then did the most unexpected thing. She raised up on her toes and lightly kissed his cheek.

Draven's entire body erupted into flames, and it took every ounce of his control not to pull her to him and give her a much more satisfying kiss.

She took a step back, smiled again, then turned about and rushed up the stairs. His cheek burning from her lips, he watched the way her hips swayed as she ascended the steps and vanished inside.

He hated to admit it, but the lady had a most attractive bottom. And in that instant his dream came back to him with stunning clarity, and he actually swore he could feel himself well planted between her silken thighs.

Clenching his teeth, he winced. This was going to be a long, *long* journey.

Simon stepped forward and clapped him on the shoulder. "Nothing better than making a maid happy, is there?"

"Aye, there most assuredly is."

Simon cocked a puzzled brow.

"Skewering my meddlesome brother would definitely be better."

Simon laughed. "Then I'd best go pack so that I won't be directly in your sight for the next few minutes."

"You do that, Simon, and while you're at it, make sure to find your common sense and bring it along as well."

Two hours later Draven and his men hadn't so much as climbed into their saddles while they waited for the lady. Even Simon was beginning to look irritated.

"What the devil is taking so long?" Draven snarled as he paced before the steps.

"Druce," he called to his squire. "Go to the lady, *again*, and tell her we must be on our way lest we not clear the woods before nightfall. If she's not here forthwith, I shall leave her behind."

"Aye, milord."

Draven turned to glare at Simon.

Simon looked away sheepishly, and shuffled his feet.

The door of the keep opened.

"Here she is, milord," Druce called.

Draven glanced back over his shoulder and froze.

Emily descended the steps like a graceful angel draped in a dark green kirtle and veil. The sunlight caught on her gold girdle, which highlighted the gentle sway of her hips. She looked at him with a dazzling smile, and all his anger at her delay evaporated.

Until he saw the two trunks following behind her.

This was ridiculous! The last thing he needed was to have to bring along a supply wagon. He'd always been a man to travel lightly. Get where he was going and quickly return.

Take only what he needed.

By all that was holy, he had no intention of slowing them down just so she could bring her entire wardrobe. 'Twas bad enough to keep him waiting, but this . . . this was ludicrous, and he would be tested no more!

His anger mounted.

What did she think this was? A game?

Well, he would show her he wasn't one to toy with. He was a man of action. One in control of his destiny and of all those around him. He wouldn't be made a mockery by a woman.

"What did you pack now?" he asked in a deceptively calm voice, crossing the short distance between them.

"Only the essentials, milord," she said, looking up at him innocently.

Simon roared with laughter.

Draven narrowed his glare on the trunks. "We cannot carry all that. You'll have to leave it behind."

"But, milord—"

"Nay, lady, I will not yield on this."

"But—"

"One kirtle, one veil, and whatever personal items you require. That is all." He went to the horse Druce had saddled for her and pulled the saddlebags from it. "Whatever fits in here you may take. Everything else is to be left."

She looked incredulous. "My kirtle alone would fill *that* to overflowing."

"This is all you're allowed."

Anger sparked in her eyes. "This is beastly! Would you treat the king thusly?"

"Aye, I have, point of fact." And he had, too, to Henry's chagrin.

"Fine," she said, taking the saddlebags from his hand. " 'Twould serve you right if I stayed behind."

Draven was aghast. Only a woman would use *that* logic! "If you'll bloody well recall, I didn't want you to come with us to begin with."

"Don't you dare curse at me," she said defensively. She stood on her tiptoes and stared straight into his eyes.

Never before had anyone stood up to him and he found it. . . .

Entertaining, actually, he thought, as some of his ire dissipated. Far more entertaining than he would have thought.

Why, even Simon cowered beneath the weight of his anger. But not Emily. She stood her ground like a knight armed for battle.

"And," she said, stressing her words. "I'm coming, all right. I'll not let you deprive me of my adventure. I will enjoy it in spite of you."

She lifted her chin up in a final bout of daring and spun away as if her dignity had been greatly abused.

Her eyes narrowed, she lifted the top of the trunk closest to her and dug through it until she found a dark blue kirtle, matching veil, brush, and comb.

She made a grand showing of packing her garments. The last two items she picked up between her thumb and first finger, glared at him, then placed them in the saddlebags. She took her time tying the saddlebags closed, then returned them to his hand.

" 'Twould seem I am all packed now," she said. "I do have one question though."

This he couldn't wait to hear. "And that is?"

"Will my maid be allowed to join me or is she to be left behind as well?"

Though her actions and words amused him, he didn't dare let her know it. If she thought she had power over him, there was no telling what she might brave, and he didn't dare run the risk of her actually enraging him past his control.

"Milady, have you no sense to be testing me in this manner?"

"You will find I have plenty of sense, but I will not be bullied by you or any man for that matter."

"Bullied?" he repeated incredulously. "You think me a bully?"

"What else would you call it? You expect the entire world to dance when you snap your fingers. You know, milord, there are other people here besides yourself."

Draven felt his jaw slacken. "I could certainly say the same of you."

Instead of being offended, she gave him a sweet, beguiling smile. "I admit freely that I am spoiled. My father and sisters have harped upon it at great leisure. For that I would beg your indulgence. Now, is my maid to come along, or shall I send her back inside?"

That was well done, he thought as he watched her. He'd often heard people remark on someone being charming, but this was the first time he had ever witnessed it. No wonder her father spoiled her. How could one stay perturbed at such a sweet, inno-cent look as she admitted her flaws and begged indulgence?

"Bring her."

"Thank you."

Her head held high, she walked past him to the side of her horse.

Simon moved to assist her, but Draven pulled him back. "If I am the one she insults, then I shall be the one to set her on her arse," he said under his breath.

Knowing when not to laugh, Simon cleared his throat. "I'll see her maid settled."

As Draven approached Emily, he couldn't miss the look of challenge in her eyes, or the enjoyment she took from having bested him.

"Did you make me wait apurpose?" he asked.

She gave a tiny smile. "My maid said a lady should make a man wait for her. If a man stews long enough in anticipation, then he is more likely to savor a lady's presence."

"Well, if pleasures are greatest in anticipation, then the same can be said of trouble."

"Are you flirting with me?" she teased.

Draven went cold. Aye, he was indeed flirting with her! He, who had never attempted such before, was actually doing it now and with a woman who would be his death.

"I never flirt," he said, then placed his hands around her waist.

The smallness of her bones amazed him. She scarce weighed anything at all. His hands looked large in comparison to the size of her hips, and he could feel the heat of her skin through the cloth of her kirtle. What had he been thinking? He should have allowed Simon to do this.

But he hadn't.

Committed to the deed, he sought to end it as quickly as possible. He lifted her from the ground and set her on the back of her steed.

He diverted his gaze from her thankful smile and made the mistake of looking at her leg at the precise moment she adjusted her skirt around her. She flashed him the sight of one trim ankle encased by finely woven stocking that also hugged the contours of her calf.

Draven stifled a curse as his body reacted instantly. From what little he had seen, she had a beautiful leg, and nothing would give him greater pleasure than to lift her skirt and explore the length of it with his lips. His tongue.

Grinding his teeth, he forced the thought from his mind. He would think no more of her ankle, her toes, her . . . whatever.

She would be banished from his thoughts!

Leaving her side, he walked stiffly to his horse and mounted. Once Simon swung himself up on his horse, he gave the signal to start the journey.

Emily rode in silence. But her mind raced at all that had transpired.

You are mad for teasing him. You're lucky he didn't strangle you for your behavior, and in front of his men no less! What would Father say?

Well, he would be delighted since she tweaked the nose of his adversary, but were it any other man, her father would be appalled by her behavior. And in truth she was as well.

A little anyway.

But there had been no mistaking the fire of admiration that sparked in his eyes when she stood up to him.

And when he touched her . . .

Her body still tingled from the memory. His hands had been strong, sure, and he had hefted her up with no effort at all. Oh, but it had been wonderful to be in his arms if even for so brief a moment.

It had been then that she made up her mind for certain. He was her rose. And gruff though he appeared, she wanted him to be her husband, for no man had ever made her heart race the way he did.

It races from fear, her mind argued.

Nay, she argued back. It wasn't fear she felt at his presence; it was something else. Something she couldn't quite name or define.

But it was definitely something she wished to explore at great depth and leisure. And explore it she would.

He might be a warrior unparalleled in battle, but she intended to be a warrior unparalleled for his heart. She would scale the rose's thorny demeanor and brave the icy glares to see if the soul beneath it all could be reached. And if it could, she would claim him or else.

"En garde, mon seigneur," she whispered as she watched his stiff back. "For in the battle for your affections, I will surely emerge victorious."

Chapter 7

To Draven's amazement, they actually made it through the forest before nightfall. But not by much. Instead of finding a town or village where they could rest comfortably for the night, they were relegated to making camp in a small meadow.

He'd assumed Emily would complain about her accommodations, but instead she appeared delighted by the prospect of camping out in the open.

As his men prepared her tent, she walked around the area with a bright smile on her face while he tended their horses. She appeared interested in everyone and everything.

Indeed, he'd never before thought anything about how complicated raising a tent could be until she pointed it out to his knight Alexander.

"I'm impressed," she told the knight. "You're very skilled at it. Why, you make it look easy."

A stab of jealousy sliced through him. Draven looked askance to see her leave his knight, then stoop down to pluck a solitary dandelion from the ground. The soft material of her kirtle hugged her buttocks, giving him a nice view of her.

Grinding his teeth, he quickly looked away, but not before he noted the keen interest his men were also giving her.

His deadly glower sent them scrambling back to their work.

You'll not even know I'm along. He cringed at the reminder of her words. Ignoring her would be like ignoring an inferno.

Especially since the inferno was in his lap.

" 'Tis beautiful, isn't it?" Emily asked as she drew near him, holding the dandelion in her hands.

Draven frowned as he unsaddled Goliath. "The camp?"

She rolled her eyes. "The woods, silly."

Silly?

Him? His frown deepened.

She gave him a peculiar look, then laughed.

"What?" he asked.

She stroked Goliath's forehead and mane as he reached for a brush. When he straightened up, she said, "I bet you frighten small children with that glower."

Draven paused. Should he be offended?

He wasn't quite sure. She didn't seem to be deliberately insulting him, and yet how else should he take such a comment?

"I beg your pardon?" he asked.

Cupping her arm around his horse's neck, she

leaned toward him as if she were about to depart a grave secret to him. "You look so stern, milord. You should relax more."

In spite of the truth she spoke, he said, "I would say milady doesn't know me well enough to speculate on my nature."

She looked sideways at him as she toyed idly with Goliath's mane. "You'll find I'm quite intuitive about people."

"Is that so?"

"Aye, very, in fact."

Draven paused in his brushing and looked at her. "Then your intuition should tell you that I am not a man to trifle with."

"It does indeed," she said, stepping back ever so slightly and patting at Goliath as the horse nuzzled her shoulder.

"Then why do you trifle with me?"

"Because it gives me pleasure."

He blinked at the unexpected answer. She was a bold, honest woman, he'd give her that. But he didn't know what to do with such a person. Most people were reserved at best around him, deceptive at worst.

"You take pleasure in annoying me?" he asked.

Her smile became impish and warm. "Don't *you* take pleasure in my annoying you?"

"Nay, what makes you think that?" he asked, stunned to find that deep inside he actually *did* enjoy it.

She shrugged. "I know not, 'tis merely a feeling I have that tells me you enjoy my teasing in spite of your denials."

Perhaps she was as intuitive as she claimed. Still, it would serve no purpose to encourage her.

He brushed Goliath's side. "You are peculiar, milady."

"Among other things."

Draven paused again at the wistful note in her voice. He glanced over to her. "Such as?"

She took the dandelion in her hand and brushed it along his jawline. A thousand chills swept over him, but whether from the gentle caress or the warmth of her smile he was unsure. All he knew was the hot look in her eyes fair blistered him.

"You'll have to learn that for yourself, milord. In the coming year."

And with that, she withdrew from him.

Draven watched her walk away, his body so stiff it caused him pain as he strained against his suddenly tight chausses.

She was truly wondrous.

She stole a glance at him over her shoulder. Draven quickly looked away lest she catch him ogling her like some squire who had first glimpsed a pretty face.

He gave her his back and yet he couldn't quite dispel the image of her peeking at him. In spite of himself, he found his gaze drifting again to where she had stood.

To his disappointment, she was no longer there, but had taken herself over to her maid, where they talked over some matter.

"It's just as well," he breathed, stroking his horse's forehead. He didn't want her attention. Really he didn't.

* * *

Later that night, they all sat around the fire as they finished a modest supper of roasted hare, bread, and boiled dandelion greens.

Emily had just finished eating when Draven felt her gaze upon him. He looked up from his trencher to see her staring straight at him. Her warm, inviting smile set fire to his loins.

"Tell me, milord," she said in a voice that came dangerously close to a purr. "What duties are you to attend in Lincoln?"

"I am to review the tax rolls for Orrick, baron of Lincoln."

"Orrick?" she said happily. "He is one of my father's closest friends. Why, I've known him all my life." Her smile widened. "When I was a little girl, he used to ride me through my father's hall on his shoulders. My sister Joanne would ride on my father's shoulders and we would pretend to joust."

She bit her lip and her gaze dulled as if she were reliving those happy times. "I can't wait to see him again."

Draven's gut tightened at her words. If what the king suspected about the baron proved to be true, he would no longer have to fear his desire for Emily. For she would hate him passionately.

"Why must you review his accounts?" she asked.

Draven tensed. How did he tell her that a man she so loved might prove to be stealing funds meant for the royal treasury? Especially when the penalty for such was death.

"Because the king ordered it," he said simply, now dreading the journey and what it might herald.

She frowned as she thought over his words. "The king doesn't suspect him of—"

"I am simply to review his records," Draven said, cutting her off.

Emily nodded, but by the worry in her eyes, he could tell she knew he hadn't been honest with her. Draven sighed. He'd never before been deceptive with anyone, and it bothered him greatly that he had done so now. Especially with her.

Though for his life, he didn't know why. Anymore than he understood why her current subdued state made him ache for the words or actions it would take to make her happy again.

Forcing the thought from his mind, he concentrated on eating his food.

I have duties to attend. Duties that include staying away from the Lady Emily.

They arrived in Lincoln two days later.

As they entered the bailey of Laurynwick Castle, there was a great shuffling of servants scurrying to tend their mounts and unpack their belongings.

The Baron Orrick came rushing from around the side of the keep, belting on his sword. At two score and eight years, the baron was a slender, distinguished-looking man with a full beard. He wore his colors in a blue and gray surcoat, and met them at the foot of the steps with heightened color in his cheeks.

Orrick brushed his hands over his gray hair, trying to tame its unruliness before he joined them.

"My lord earl," Orrick said as he neared him. "I wasn't expecting you for another fortnight."

"My apologies," Draven said gruffly. "Something came up." Aye, and it had been up since the moment he met the little minx and her teasing ways.

Draven shifted his stance, trying to alleviate some of the discomfort *it* caused.

The baron appeared a bit nervous as he glanced around. "Then I make you most welcome."

It was then the baron saw Emily astride her small palfrey. "Lady Emily of Warwick?" he asked in disbelief.

Emily bestowed one of her more breathtaking smiles on Orrick, and though the baron was nearly a score of years his senior and married, Draven felt an unexpected slice at the look she gave. As well as a sudden urge to choke the man for making her smile a smile of pure affection.

"Lord Orrick!" she said with a laugh as the baron helped her down. "How fit you look."

"And you are as beautiful as ever, milady," he said, holding her arms out so that he could get a good look at her.

Draven narrowed his glare at them. How dare the man ogle her so blatantly! Indeed, Emily seemed to preen before the man.

He clenched his fists as the urge to choke the little man became even stronger than before.

Orrick kissed her hand. "But tell me, Emily, why are you here?"

"She is my ward," Draven said, his voice far sterner than he had intended.

Orrick's face paled as he glanced back to Draven,

then to her. His brows drew together in concern and fear. "Your father?"

"Is well," Emily inserted as the baron tucked her hand into the crook of his arm. She patted his arm affectionately. "I am more Lord Draven's political hostage than ward, I'm afraid."

Orrick cocked his brow. "The king allowed such?"

"The king *commanded* such," Draven corrected.

He didn't miss the flash of alarm that crossed the baron's face an instant before he caught himself and banished it. "Well, whatever brings your gracious form to my hall, milady, I thank it. Since my daughter married three years past, I find that I am sorely in need of some youthful company." Orrick covered her hands with his own and led her up the stairs.

As Draven followed, Simon joined him at his side. "Irritating, isn't it?"

"What?" Draven asked through clenched teeth.

"The way they look so happy together. You know, I hear tell Orrick's new wife is about the same age as Emily. Why, if something were to happen to the baroness, Emily could easily find herself Orrick's bride."

"Shut up, Simon."

As they entered the hall, Orrick called for his wife. "Christina, you must come and see who just arrived on our doorstep."

Draven turned at the sound of footsteps rushing down the curving stairs to his left. The steps slowed down as she neared the bottom.

Two seconds later, Draven saw a head peek around the wall. A white veil framed the face of what appeared a cherub, complete with a cupid's bow mouth and chubby cheeks and wide brown eyes. The lady appeared just under a score of years, though how much so he couldn't quite tell.

"Emily!" the lady squealed excitedly, stepping around the wall to show him the only round part of the lady was her face. Her short body was willow thin as she rushed to Emily and threw her arms about her. "Oh my gracious!"

Emily made some bizarre shrill sound herself as they embraced and twirled about in a dizzying fashion. He'd never heard such a sound from Emily before and in fact he found it hard to believe her capable of it.

"Oh, Christina, how have you been?" Emily asked as they pulled back and looked each other up and down.

"Just fine," Christina answered with a laugh. "Look at you! Aren't you as beautiful as always."

"Nay, not as beautiful as you."

"Aye, you are."

"Nay—"

"How long will they do that?" Draven asked Orrick in a low tone as the women continued to sing each other's praises.

"For a while, I'm sure. Christina was fostered at Lady Emily's home and all I ever hear from her is how much she loved Emily and her sisters."

Orrick motioned toward the great hall. "Come, gentlemen, let us give the women time to renew their friendship and seek our ale in a less ear-piercing environment."

Draven gratefully followed before he lost any more of his hearing to their happy, high-pitched chatter.

Orrick led them to a group of chairs set before an unlit hearth. Once they were seated a servant brought them tankards of ale. Still, he could hear the women in the foyer as they caught each other up on the details of their lives.

"You're the earl of Ravenswood's ward?" Christina fair shrieked. "I bet your father is near to bursting his gullet over it."

"Aye, he was far from happy about the king's decree."

"I'm surprised he didn't throw himself beneath the hooves of Lord Draven's horse rather than let you—"

"Can I offer you something to eat?" Orrick asked graciously, diverting Draven from their conversation.

Draven shook his head, and so they sat for several minutes saying nothing, their gazes darting about the room.

The women, however, continued their conversation out in the foyer. "And what of you, Christina? Are you happy here?"

"Aye, Orrick is a most wondrous husband . . . Oh, Em, I'm sorry, I didn't mean—"

"Nay, think nothing of it. I know well my status, but you . . . you look absolutely radiant. I am so grateful marriage agrees with you!"

"Aye, and I heard of Joanne. Is it true she is to marry?"

"She is."

Trying not to eavesdrop, Draven watched the baron carefully.

The baron's overt awkwardness didn't lend itself to friendly chitchat. Not that Draven was particularly adept at friendly chitchats, or even unfriendly chitchat for that matter.

Basically, Draven wasn't a chatty person in any shape, form, or fashion.

"Nice weather, you're having," Simon ventured. "Perfect for the fair."

"Aye," Orrick agreed, nodding his head. "Very pleasant. Mild, not too hot or cold."

And they sat some more in silence, nursing their ales.

"The fair is wonderful this year," Christina's voice covered their silence as the women continued to chat. "There is this one goldsmith you must visit. Remind me to show you the earbobs he made."

"Oh, I envy you that," Emily said. "My father would never allow us to pierce our ears. He was too afraid we'd develop an infection from the piercing and perish."

"How I wish your father would learn not to be so frightened of your welfare. Why, I'll never forget that time he whipped you for merely going out the postern gate with me to pick berries in the meadow behind the castle."

Draven frowned at their words. He had known Hugh was overprotective, but that went beyond the pale of acceptability. Not even to let his daughter pick berries?

He felt a strange wrenching in his chest. What else had Emily been deprived of?

And the thought of her father beating her . . .

'Twas a good thing Hugh was far from his reach.

"Aye, I remember it well," Emily said. "You can imagine how excited I was coming here. Why, I actually got to sleep outside in the forest!"

"Weren't you afraid?"

"With Lord Draven to protect me? Nay, I think he could well slay a bear with his bare hands."

In spite of himself, he felt a pang of pride at her words and admiration.

"In fact," Emily continued. "You should see him train. It takes my breath the way he moves. Never have I seen a man more handsome or strong. No wonder Queen Eleanor calls him the Rose of Chivalry. And did you know he reads for pleasure?"

Simon choked on his ale as he struggled not to laugh.

Glaring at his brother, Draven felt heat descend upon his face.

Blushing? he thought with a start. The maid had him blushing?

He'd never done such in his life.

"Do you think Lord Draven is . . ."

His entire body stiff and attuned to the women, Draven struggled to hear the rest of Emily's sentence, but for once they dropped their voices to a level that prevented it.

What the devil could they be saying now?

"I heard the king banned tournaments," Orrick said all of a sudden.

Draven had to bite his tongue to keep from shushing the baron as he strained to hear the women.

Why on earth would the man pick this instant to finally start talking?

"Aye," Simon answered in a loud voice, and by the glint in his brother's eye, Draven knew he did it purposefully to mask whatever words the women uttered. "Lost too many good men and soldiers to accidents. Henry says if we must partake of such foolishness, then let us go to the continent for it. Not to mention all the property that can be damaged, the peasants who get crushed when knights over-run the boundaries. You know all the things—"

"He knows, Simon," Draven snapped.

"Well," Emily said, "would you look at them."

Draven looked over his shoulder to see Emily and Christina standing side by side behind his chair. By St. Peter's hairy toes, what had they said about him?

Not knowing was near enough to drive him mad.

"Have you ever seen a more soured group?" Christina asked.

Emily laughed. "Not in a while."

The men instantly came to their feet and offered the ladies a chair. Emily took a seat in Draven's vacated chair and primly adjusted the skirt of her gown around her.

What had she said?

"Congratulations, Lord Orrick," Emily said.

"Congratulations?" Draven asked.

"Christina is expecting a babe," Emily explained.

Christina blushed. "I'm so excited, but scared as well. I have no idea what really to expect."

" 'Tis your first?" Simon asked.

"Aye."

"I keep telling her not to fear," Orrick said. "My first wife had six without any problems at all."

"But Emily's mother and two elder sisters died in their birthing beds," Christina contradicted.

Draven looked at Emily and saw the sadness in her eyes. He felt a strange urge to comfort her. To reach out and take her hand in his.

"Oh, I'm so sorry, Emily," Christina said quickly, placing her hand on the arm of Emily's chair. "I didn't mean to—"

" 'Tis fine," Emily said graciously as she placed a hand over Christina's. "I know you meant no harm. Just as I know God will take care of you. You shall be fine. You'll see."

Christina smiled, then turned to her husband. "Orrick, have you heard Emily's sister Lady Joanne is to marry Lord Niles of Montclef next month."

"Niles?" Orrick asked, his face shocked.

Draven searched his memory for what would cause the baron's reaction. He knew little about Niles or his family other than the name.

"You know Niles?" Emily asked.

"Aye," Orrick said with a note of reservation in his voice. "And I must say I'm surprised your father would approve the match."

"And why is that? We have heard nothing but good of him," Emily said.

Orrick shook his head. "It's been a good ten

years or more since I last saw him. We journeyed to Normandy together before the death of his father. There was just something about the man that sat ill-at-ease with me."

"Well," Emily said. "Joanne claims to love him, and she won't be swayed from the marriage."

"I'm still amazed your father would agree," Christina said. "Especially after what happened to Anna."

Emily's eyes grew dark and thoughtful. "Will you please excuse me," Emily said, interrupting Christina. "I'm suddenly very tired."

"Oh, forgive me for my discourtesy!" Christina said, rising instantly to her feet. "Come, let me fetch a maid to prepare your room and you can rest in my solar until it's ready."

Emily rose and followed after Christina. They waited until the women had left the hall before retaking their seats.

Draven sat in silence for several minutes as he thought over what he'd heard. And the sad, heart-broken look Emily had on her face at the mention of Anna.

"Who is Anna?" he asked Orrick.

"She was one of Emily's sisters who died about nine years back."

Draven nodded. That explained the sadness, but he suspected there was more to the story. However, now wasn't the time to dwell on the matter.

Draven looked back at Orrick. "Well, since we know this isn't a social visit, shall you have your steward fetch your accounts?"

"Now?" Orrick asked in a panicked voice.

Draven stared at him stoically. "Now is as good a time as any."

Orrick swallowed as he fidgeted with the hem of his sleeve. "Aye, then. I'll show you to my council room."

Orrick rose from his chair and looked about nervously. He set his tankard of ale on the mantel and patted at his purse before he removed a brass key and led them from the room.

"He's guilty," Simon whispered as they followed Orrick across the hall.

"I know," Draven answered, sickened by the thought. All in all, he had no quarrel with the baron, who had always appeared a decent enough fellow.

But if he had in fact swindled Henry out of his due, there was nothing Draven could do to save him.

Chapter 8

"Do you think me foolish?" Emily asked as she sat in the bower seat of Christina's room. She hugged a small red pillow to her breast as she poured out her scheme to her lifelong friend.

Christina sat across from her in a heavily carved chair that looked like a cross between a dragon and a winged frog. Christina glanced up from the needle-point in her lap.

Her face pensive, she met Emily's gaze. "Not for wanting to marry. I'm just not so sure *he* is the one you should choose. He's just so . . ."

Emily waited for several minutes. When it became apparent Christina wouldn't speak, she offered a word for her, "Forbidding?"

"Aye," Christina agreed.

"And moody?"

"Aye."

Emily waited, watching her friend struggle to

find another word to describe Draven. "And distant?"

"Aye."

Impishly, she added, "Strange?"

"Definitely."

Emily tossed the pillow at her. "No aye?"

Christina smiled and tucked the pillow behind her back. "I was growing bored."

Emily laughed. "He is not so strange."

"You think not? Orrick says in battle Lord Draven becomes crazed. That he plows through men like a plowshare over snow."

"I would think in battle that would be a virtue."

"In battle mayhap, but what if he does it at home as well?"

Emily arched her brow. "What, plow snow?"

"Emily! You're being obtuse."

"I know what you're saying," Emily said with a sigh. "But I have never seen him lose patience with anyone."

"You just met him," Christina reminded her.

"I know. It's just there's something about him that makes me feel all . . ." She bit her lip trying to think of the words. "Tingly inside."

Christina gave a knowing smile. "You've not been around many men, Em, and I doubt you've ever been around one such as he."

"You're right about that."

"You have an infatuation, I suspect."

"Infatuated? Me?" Emily asked with a laugh. "Now who's being ridiculous?"

"I'm not being ridiculous," Christina said, stabbing her needle through the linen. "It's that tingly, warm, giddy feeling you get when you look at a handsome man."

"I know the definition of it."

"Aye, but you've never felt it, I wager. How could you? Your father has never allowed a handsome man into his castle for fear of it."

That was true enough. Niles looked more like a woolly beast than a man. He was two inches shorter than Joanne and about as thick as an oak tree, with wiry brown hair and a thick beard. She'd never understood her sister's attraction to the man.

Emily frowned as she considered Christina's words. Could her own feelings be something as simple as a mere infatuation? "Perhaps. But what of you and Orrick?"

Christina shrugged.

"Nay, don't you dare get tight-lipped."

Christina laughed. "Forgive me." She returned to her sewing. "Orrick is good to me. Very good, in fact, and I have no reason to complain."

"But you're not entirely happy. I can see it in your eyes."

Christina gave a reluctant nod. "It's just hard going to bed every night with a man older than my father. In truth, my stepchildren are older than I am."

Emily sympathized. She'd known numerous women who had the same complaint. "At least you have a husband," she said wistfully. "And soon a babe."

Christina looked up at her. "I know how much you want a child. And maybe Lord Draven isn't so bad, as you say. And knowing your father as I do, you'll like as not have another chance to find a husband."

Emily's chest drew tight at the words. She didn't want to think about living her life alone, unwed.

What would she do if she returned to her father's?

"I have to make this work," Emily whispered. "I have to."

For the next two days Emily saw no sight of Draven as he scoured Orrick's accounts. Countless times she and Simon walked past the closed doors, listening for a sound from within.

Nothing. Not a snore, not a curse. Nothing.

It was downright eerie.

Orrick sent food inside, and back it came untouched.

On the third day, she and Simon were partaking of the midday meal with Christina and her husband.

"Does the man *never* sleep?" Orrick asked as he cracked his boiled egg with the side of his knife.

Simon snorted. "You'd be amazed how long a body can go without rest."

"Obviously," Orrick muttered. "I've never seen anyone apply himself so diligently."

Nor had she.

Well, then again, she herself could be pretty single-minded when the occasion warranted it. But going over accounts and taxes?

Quite honestly she'd rather be tied to a stake by her hair and drowned in pickle juice.

Seeking to dispel the moroseness of the diners, Emily turned to Simon. "Since Lord Draven seems content to live out his visit in the council room, is there any chance we might visit the fair today?"

Simon glared at the closed council room door across the foyer as if he despised it every bit as much as she did. "I don't see why—"

"Father!"

Emily jumped at the drunken shout that came from the doorway as the door was thrown back against the wall with a resounding thud.

All activity in the hall ceased as all heads turned to the foyer.

A man about four years her senior stumbled into the room with the help of two very frighteningly large men.

At first glance the two mountains appeared twins, until one looked closer. The man on the right had brown hair, brown eyes, and a scar that ran the length of his face. The other man's hair wasn't so much brown as it was an unwashed dark blond. Each one well muscled, they had stern, angry faces that promised a sound thrashing to anyone foolish enough to approach them.

The man in the middle she deduced as Orrick's son. With features similar to his father, he was as handsome as Christina had told her. He wore his dark brown hair clipped short and neat, but his clothes were wrinkled and stained.

The two hulking men brought him to stand before his father's dais. Orrick's son propped his left arm up on the table and gave a loud belch.

"Reinhold!" his father snapped. "What are you—"

"Not now, old man," Reinhold said disrespectfully as he rolled his head to look up at his father. "Let me introduce you to Fric." He clapped the man to his right on the shoulder. "And Frac," he slurred, pointing to the man on his opposite side.

"My name is Frank," the first one said in a thick Teutonic accent.

"And mine is Fritz," the other responded.

"Does it matter?" Reinhold asked, waving his hand dismissively. He scratched at his unshaven face and looked at Orrick. "I need twenty silver marks to pay them."

Orrick held his lips tight as he perused his son. Though Orrick sat tall, his spine stiff with pride, she could see the embarrassment on his face as he glared at Reinhold.

"Pay them for what?" Orrick asked.

Reinhold snorted. "Not killing me for one thing."

"He owes debts to our master," Frank said as he crossed his beefy arms over his chest and narrowed a vicious glare at Orrick. "Tam the Scot wants to be paid in full or else we're to make sure your son doesn't welsh on any more debts."

"Tam the Stewholder?" Orrick asked Reinhold in disbelief. "You swore to me that you'd never go there again."

"Well, here's a big surprise, old man, I lied. Now be a good boy and pay up."

Orrick's breaths came in short, sharp pants. One vein pounded at his temple.

Christina reached out and touched his hand, but he shook off her touch.

He looked first to Fritz, then Frank, and lastly his son. "I don't have it."

"You what?" Reinhold bellowed.

"You heard me, boy. I told you last time that I can't keep this up. You promised me—"

"Bullocks!" Reinhold shouted, slamming his hand down so hard on the table that it shook Emily's bowl. "You keep up your whore without complaints and yet you can't spare a copper for your own son?"

"Reinhold, please," Orrick begged. "I have company."

Reinhold looked at Emily and curled his lip. "You can afford to feed *them*, yet you have no money for me. Fine," he said, turning to the mountains. "What say the two of you take my stepwhore to work off my debt in the stew?"

Christina gasped as Orrick reached an arm out protectively.

The two men actually looked at each other as if considering the terms.

"All right," Frank said. "She should bring in enough in six months or so."

"Nay!" Orrick shouted, coming to his feet.

Fritz pulled a knife from his belt and angled it at Reinhold's throat. "Choose, my lord," he sneered. "Your wife or your son."

Suddenly, Fritz's eyes bulged.

"Since we're playing a choosing game, how about I give you a choice?"

Emily breathed in relief as Draven stepped around Fritz, and it was only then she saw the sword he had held to the giant's back. "Your life or the knife."

The giant dropped the weapon.

Draven kicked it across the floor, then sheathed his sword.

Fritz took one look at Draven's surcoat, then crossed himself.

Frank's face blanched. "My lord earl of Ravenswood," he said, cringing from Draven's presence. "We have no quarrel with you."

The look on Draven's face bore all the promise of hell, wrath, and brimstone.

"Don't you?" Draven asked in a voice so cold it actually sent a shiver down Emily's spine. "You come into the hall of my host, threaten him, his son, and his wife, and you think you have no quarrel with me?"

They gulped in unison.

"We just do as we are told," Frank said, his voice unsure and wavering.

Draven approached Fritz, who fair shrank before him. Like a wild wolf herding bulls, he backed them away from Orrick's table and Reinhold.

"Then I *tell* you this, as you value your putrid lives, you will leave here and make whatever lies you wish to your master. *Never*"—Draven paused effectively—"darken Lord Orrick's doorway again. For if you do, there is no corner of hell you can find to hide that I won't come seek you out. And I promise you, your master's wrath is nothing compared to mine. Do you understand?"

If they didn't they were too foolish to live, Emily thought. For Draven's deadly calm voice and heated glower sent chills of terror up and down her body.

"We understand," they said simultaneously.

Draven gestured to Orrick. "Then make your apologies to the lord and lady."

"We beg your pardons," they said, bowing before Orrick.

"Now, leave."

They bolted from the room.

Lord Draven raked Reinhold with that same menacing glare, then looked to Orrick. "This is the reason you've swindled the king?"

Emily saw the shame on Orrick's face. "Aye," he said simply. "For all his faults, he is my son and I would never see him harmed."

Draven took a deep breath. "And you are willing to give the king your life to save his?"

"Aye." Orrick pushed his chair back from the table and rose to his feet. "If you will give me but a moment in private to say good-bye to my wife, I shall go peacefully with you."

Draven stood there staring at Orrick. Emily couldn't read his emotions or his thoughts, and she couldn't imagine what terror Orrick must be feeling.

She opened her mouth to speak, but Simon touched her forearm and shook his head in warning.

"That won't be necessary," Draven said at last. "For your crime, I will extend your service to the king from two weeks this year to eighteen months."

Orrick sighed in relief and nodded. "Then I shall have my squire fetch—"

"I'm not finished," Draven said dispassionately.

"Forgive me." Orrick cast his gaze to his feet.

"Since your wife is with child, I think it best that your son serve the king in your place."

"What!" Reinhold shouted.

Draven turned to him and Reinhold shrank back from the heat of his glare. "I think eighteen months in London under the care of Master William will teach you the discipline you need to respect a man and woman who would risk their lives to shelter you. And were I you, *boy*, I would be grateful to them, for they are the only thing that prevents me from turning you over to Fric and Frac."

Emily bit her lip at Lord Draven's mercy. She exchanged a relieved look with Christina.

"Alexander?" Draven called.

One of his knights stood up from the lower tables. "Aye, milord?"

"Reinhold is in your custody. Come morning, I want you to escort him to London, and if he gives you any trouble, handle it as you see fit."

"Aye, milord." Alexander, whose size made mockery of the two mountains who were there before, came forward and took Reinhold by the arm. "If it pleases you, milord, I shall see him sobered forthwith."

"It would please me much."

Alexander nodded and led him away.

Orrick took a deep breath. "What of the money I owe the king?"

"What money?" Draven asked.

"The money I—"

"My Lord Orrick," Simon interrupted, his tone thick, "you misunderstood my brother's question. *What* money?"

Tears gathered in Orrick's eyes as he cleared his throat. "You would do that for me?"

Draven didn't answer; instead he turned on his heel and left the room.

Orrick sat down and wept.

Emily sat there in silence as Christina comforted her husband. Ill-at-ease, Emily excused herself and went to find Draven.

He had returned to the council room across the hall. She pushed open the door he'd left ajar and stepped tentatively into the room.

He stood with his back to her, closing up the ledgers he had been reviewing.

"Milord?"

He paused upon hearing her voice, then continued closing the books without turning to look at her. "Aye, milady?"

"Why did you do that?"

"He's a good man who loves his family. Why should I see him dead for it?"

In that instant, she realized that this was not a man who would raid a village and slaughter innocent people in their beds. Her father was sorely mistaken about Draven. "You didn't attack my father's village, did you?"

He turned around to face her, his expression aghast. "You think I would do such a thing?"

His look was too sincere to be feigned. "Nay, but my father thinks so."

"Don't take this the wrong way, milady, but your father is a fool."

"Tell me, milord," she asked with a smile. "Is there a right way to take that?"

He didn't smile back. Instead, he turned back to the books and finished putting them away.

Emily moved to help him. She saw the dark pain in his eyes. Something about all this troubled him.

"What is it?" she asked.

"What is what?"

She tilted her head and looked up at him with a frown. "There is a thought on your mind that you haven't voiced."

"There are many thoughts on my mind that I never voice," he said evasively.

"This one troubles you."

"They all trouble me in one way or another."

Oh, the man was frustrating! Why couldn't he simply talk to her?

"Well," she said, trying again. "My mother always said that you should share your troubles. If you let them out, then they are less likely to burden you, whereas if you keep them inside they fester your blood and taint your soul."

"Perhaps I like my tainted soul," he said simply.

"Perhaps. But you really should speak your mind. My father says it keeps one healthy."

His look droll, he spoke, "Then you are the healthiest person I know."

She laughed. "He says that too."

She handed him the book she held, and as he took it their fingers brushed. He froze and stared at her fingers. Something warm flickered in his eyes, brightening the multiple blue tones.

Kiss me, she begged silently, longing to feel his lips against hers.

But he didn't.

Instead, he took the book and placed it on the shelf with the others.

Emily sighed. "At least you're finished now."

"Aye. If we leave within the hour we should be at the inn by nightfall."

Emily's breath caught in her throat as disappointment filled her. He had completely forgotten her request to go to the fair?

"But . . ."

Draven turned at her squelched word. "But?" he asked.

He saw the disappointment in her eyes.

"Nothing," she said, hanging her head dejectedly. "I shall go pack my *saddlebag*."

Draven frowned at her as she left him. What the devil was wrong with her? Surely she wasn't still angry over the saddlebags?

She'd seemed so happy just a moment before and now . . .

He shook his head.

Women. What man would ever understand them?

Shrugging it off, he left the room and returned to the hall to find Simon still sitting at his place on the dais. Draven quickly averted his gaze from the lord's table to his brother. "Where is Orrick?"

Simon gestured toward the stairs with the grape he held in his hand. "Christina took him above until he could compose himself. 'Twould seem he is overwhelmed by your mercy." He popped the grape into his mouth.

Draven nodded. He'd pay the money to Henry from his own coffers, and as long as Henry had his full due, he'd leave the baron in peace.

"Have you any idea what is wrong with Emily?" Draven asked after Simon had swallowed his grape.

Picking through the bowl of grapes in front of him, Simon shrugged. "She was fine when she left here. What did you say to her?"

Draven stiffened at the implication. "I did nothing more than tell her to get ready to leave. We'll be departing as soon as everyone is packed and saddled."

Simon tossed the grape in his hand at Draven's head.

Easily, Draven dodged it and frowned at his brother, who leveled a droll look at him.

"You dolt!"

Draven lifted his brows at the unwarranted insult. "I beg your pardon?"

"I realize, *brother*, you're used to snapping your fingers and having your men follow you while they swallow any complaint lest you mangle them over it, but the lady isn't used to it. You don't just finish your work, hop on your horse, and make for home. Emily wanted to go to the fair."

Draven stared at him in disbelief. "We've been here three days. I assumed you had taken her already. That is why you came, is it not? Or are you here simply to gorge yourself on grapes and pester me?"

"Mostly the latter," Simon admitted with a smirk. "However, had you stuck your head out of the door in the last two days, you would have found that I twisted my ankle the evening of our arrival."

Suspicious, Draven crossed his arms over his chest. "Doing what?"

"Walking."

"Walking?" he asked tightly.

"Aye, walking," Simon repeated. "Unfortunately, I have been unable to escort the lady. The least you could do is take her for me."

"I don't have time for such frivolities."

"Oh, that's right, I forgot. You must get back home and walk about like some great brooding menace. How silly of me."

Draven stiffened at his audacity. "Careful, brother," he growled, "you overstep your bounds."

"Heaven forbid I should do that. But . . ." Simon paused and leaned forward on his elbow. "I would make a small request that you do take the lady. From what I have heard from Christina, Emily has never been allowed off her father's lands. She has never once seen a fair, and if you have any kindness in your heart toward her, you would let her go this one time. She'll probably never have another chance again in her life."

Simon was manipulating him. He knew it most certainly. However, from what he'd heard himself, he knew Emily had led a most sheltered existence. Having lived his childhood under his own father's strict dictates, he could well understand her wishing to do something entertaining. Even though he didn't care for such events himself, she would probably enjoy it.

No doubt she would even smile a bit.

His mood lightened instantly as he contemplated her winsome smile.

Pleasing her wouldn't be so bad, would it?

Draven looked blankly at his brother. "Twisted your ankle, did you?"

"Back to that, are we?" Simon lifted his right leg up to the side of the table so that Draven could see it. "As you can plainly see my ankle is quite swollen."

Not from what Draven could tell, but then Simon placed it back under his chair so quickly, he scarcely got more than a glimpse of it.

"We leave in the morning," Draven announced as he turned, about to leave. "Swollen ankle or not."

Chapter 9

With Alys trailing behind her, Emily came down the stairs, her heart heavy. She wished she could say a quick good-bye to Christina, but Christina was still in her solar with Orrick.

Though it would serve Draven right to wait for her again, Emily didn't have the heart even to torment him. Not when she felt *this* disappointed.

Crestfallen, she descended the stairs to find said ogre waiting by the door. Without a word, she handed Draven the saddlebags.

In turn he handed the saddlebags over to her maid. "Take those back upstairs," he told Alys.

Emily frowned as she raised her gaze from the floor to his face. "Now I'm not even allowed to take that with me?"

He shrugged nonchalantly. "You may bring it if you like, but you'll look rather odd carrying saddlebags at the fair."

Joy raced through her as her mood instantly brightened. "You'll let me go after all?" she asked excitedly.

Draven gave her a chiding stare. "You should have told me Simon had yet to take you. I never break my word, milady. The whole reason I allowed you to come here was to see the fair. I wouldn't consider returning you to Ravenswood until you've had the opportunity."

Impulsively, she threw her arms about him and squeezed him tightly. His body felt good in her arms. Too good, she realized as she felt his muscles flex against her.

He quickly stepped out of her hold.

Still, his actions didn't daunt her. She felt too wonderful at the moment to take any slight.

"Careful, milord," she said impishly, "else I might begin to suspect you're not the evil ogre you portray."

He didn't answer, but there was a subtle softening to his features.

"How long will it take us to get there?" she asked.

Draven felt the urge to smile at her, but he quickly caught himself. "Not long. The horses are saddled and awaiting you."

She rushed past him, then paused at the door and looked back to see he had yet to budge. "Well, come on, milord. Hurry!"

Draven did as she commanded, and this time when he helped her mount, he was most careful not to touch her any longer than what was absolutely necessary.

But the luscious honeysuckle scent of her hair

clung to him as he mounted his own horse and led her out of the bailey.

"Do you think they'll have jugglers?" she asked as soon as they passed through the barbican. "I so love to watch them. I bet they have a maypole. Christina used to tell tales of the annual fair in York. They always had a maypole even though the fair was in August.

"Have you ever seen an acrobat who could twist his feet over his head? One came to my father's years ago and I . . ."

On and on she went until his head rang from it. He'd never been around anyone who seemed to love to talk as much as the Lady Emily. Not even Simon.

In truth, he didn't see how she found so many words. Did the lady never run short of them or of ideas or questions?

She would pause only long enough for him to give a short, glib response and then she'd be off again.

After a time, he learned just to grunt when she paused for breath. Satisfied with his responses, she carried the conversation the entire way there, and in a while he started to take a strange comfort in the sound of her happy prattle.

When they finally reached the gathering, she fair jumped from the horse to the ground before he even had a chance to dismount. It amazed him that she hadn't hurt herself.

"Oh look," she breathed, her eyes shining as she twisted and turned about like a child at Christmastide. "Isn't it beautiful?"

Draven studied the field of crowded tents, tables, and milling people. He'd never cared for such events, but the Lady Emily didn't share his jaded view. The multicolored tents and pennants announcing wares and goods looked gaudy to him.

"Just make sure you don't stray from my side," he said in warning as he tied their horses to a pole and paid an attendant to watch over them.

"I won't," she promised.

Draven turned to her. "Then lead the way, milady. The rest of the day is yours."

Her face bright, she lifted her skirt up ever so slightly and made her way across the field. Draven had never seen anything like her as she moved through the crowd with the curiosity of an exuberant child.

The sunlight reflected off her golden tresses and the color pink rode high in her cheeks as she darted from booth to booth examining everything.

"Sweetened chestnuts for milady?" a merchant asked as she drew near his table.

Draven noted her hesitation before she shook her head in declination. "Thank you, but nay."

As she moved on to the next table, Draven nodded at the merchant and passed a halfpenny to him. Taking the shelled, roasted nuts that were wrapped in a thin sheepskin bag, he followed her to the next stand where she looked over an assortment of toiletries.

"Here," Draven said, passing the confections to her.

She looked from his hand to his face, then smiled. "How did you know I wanted them?"

"A simple guess."

Her smile widened as she took a single nut and placed it on her tongue. "Mmm," she breathed, closing her eyes and savoring the bite. " 'Tis wondrous."

But not half as wondrous as the lady before him. He'd sell whatever he had left of his soul to be the fare she sampled with such gusto. Licking her lips, she took the sheepskin from his hand.

"You must taste this," she said, selecting another nut and lifting it toward his lips.

Draven forced himself to part his lips. Her fingers burned his lips as she brushed them while placing the salty, sweet morsel into his mouth.

"Delectable," he said, more in response to the feel of her soft skin against his than to the taste of the food.

Something caught her eye then, and she turned her head away. Draven exhaled and stamped his soured leg against the ground in an effort to bring his lusting body under his control. The pain did very little to abate his desire.

"Oh, look! A juggler." She grabbed his hand and pulled him away.

Dumbstruck, he allowed her to pull him through the crowd. He knew her touch meant nothing to her, she was merely excited, and yet it burned him to the core of his very being.

He ground his teeth. Oh, but to have an instant to show her pleasures that would far exceed anything she saw here this day. As much as he ached for her, he could easily give them both an entire week of pleasure—if he dared.

But should he dare such, sooner or later the curse would surface and end their liaisons with a death knell.

Rubbing his hand over his eyes, he watched the juggler alternate from eggs to melons to knives.

When the juggler finished, she jumped up and down and applauded mightily while cradling the sheepskin of nuts to her bosom. He stared at the small bag nestled between her ample breasts with envy. At the moment he'd gladly trade places.

She turned to look up at him with a dazzling smile. "He was very good, wasn't he?"

Draven never had the chance to answer for she took his hand, spun him about, and headed in the opposite direction.

Her next stop was a table of ribbons and cloth. "A pretty ribbon for milady?" the old woman asked. "Or cloth for a kirtle or veil?"

Emily shook her head. "Nay. I am but browsing."

After a moment, Emily paused and looked back through the crowd for her next distraction and it was then he saw the sugar crystals on her bottom lip. Entranced, he stared, wanting desperately to kiss them away. To draw that lip between his teeth and lick the sugar away while he tasted the sweetness of her mouth.

She took a step and Draven pulled her to a stop. She looked up with a puzzled frown.

"You have . . . um . . . There's . . ." Draven paused.

It was just sugar, for the sake of St. Anne! What was the matter with him that he couldn't tell her to just lick her lips and be done with it?

He reached a hand out to touch the crystals, but

as soon as he saw the way it trembled, he dropped it back to his side.

"Is something amiss?" she asked.

"You have sugar on your lip."

There, he had said it.

Finally.

"Oh," she said, beaming. "Thank you."

The tip of her pink tongue darted out over the area, and if he'd thought the sugar bad, 'twas nothing compared to the lightning-quick heat that seared his loins at the sight of her tongue.

And then she ran her fingertip over her lip and he was damned near undone.

"Did I get it?" she asked innocently.

Not yet, he thought dryly, but he'd love to be the one who gave it to her.

Clearing his throat at the treacherous thought, he nodded. "Aye. 'Tis gone."

"Come one, come all," called a voice from the center of the crowd. "Alfred, King of Minstrels, is about to play."

A minstrel? Draven moaned silently. Surely Emily had better sense than to subscribe to their brand of ridiculousness about love and honor.

Personally, he would rather be flayed to death than listen to the crooning of some mewling musician.

"A minstrel!" she said enthusiastically.

He groaned aloud.

But she paid no heed to his pain. Grabbing his wrist, she practically ran through the crowd to the space that had been sectioned off for such torturous events.

Benches had been set up around a tree stump where a minstrel sat tuning his lute. Draven directed her to a bench to the left of the minstrel. After the area became crowded, the minstrel began singing a tale of a Norman lady and her idiot lover.

Draven didn't listen for long before he turned his full attention to the lady at his side.

The light breeze swept through her pale hair, moving wisps of it about her face. Absently, she lifted up one graceful hand and tucked the way-ward strands behind her ear. Her fingers caressed her ear and jaw, sending waves of molten lust through him.

Draven imagined reaching out for those tendrils and running his hands through them, pulling her against him and yielding to his desire to see her kissed well and fully.

Again his dream came to him and he saw the creaminess of her bare flesh shining in the candle-light as she walked naked toward him. And in that instant of desire, he swore he could feel her body pressed against his, feel her legs around his hips as he drove himself deep into her.

He clenched his teeth in desperation. How on earth could he live out a year with her and not touch her when all he could think of was claiming her?

What had Henry been thinking?

In that moment he could forget his past, his tem-per. Everything. Everything save her and the laugh-ter she brought into his empty life.

How did she do it? How could she find such thrill and wonder at things as simple as a chestnut or a ribbon?

Dear Lord in heaven give me the strength I need to hold my oath. Or send an archangel to kill me where I sit before I have a chance to corrupt my honor or hers.

He would not be his father. He would not forsake his oath! Never.

She turned and looked up at him, her expression tender.

Draven blinked and quickly averted his gaze to the minstrel. He had to focus on something. Anything other than her.

Determined, he listened to the song of a Saracen warrior and a Norman princess. The mewling love story of a man degrading himself for his lady was almost enough to turn his stomach sour.

At least he knew *he* would never be so foolish over a woman. Imagine a grown man actually walking naked through his enemy's army for the sake of love!

How ludicrous.

Revolting.

When the minstrel finished, Emily turned to him and sighed. "What a great tale. It has been my favorite since I was a little girl and a minstrel came and sang it in my father's hall."

He scoffed. "What a great fool for love," he said, thinking over the warrior the minstrel sang about. "No man would ever walk naked through his enemy's castle."

"But Accusain loved Laurette," Emily insisted. "That was his proof to her."

Draven curled his lip in distaste. "I leave such grand imaginings to milksops like yon minstrel. No man worthy of the title would do such a thing."

She leaned her shoulder against his arm and nudged him ever so slightly. "Perhaps not, but 'tis what every woman dreams of."

Draven refused to look at her lest he be taken in any more by her charm. "Then women and men have much in common, I think."

"How so?"

"Every man I know dreams of a naked woman walking through his castle gates in search of him."

Color rose high in her cheeks and he could tell he'd shocked her greatly. In truth, he knew not why he said such a thing to her. He'd never been so crude in the presence of a lady.

"You are wicked, milord." She laughed. "Truly, truly wicked."

Unfortunately, he hadn't been half as wicked as he longed to be. Point of fact, he would love to give her a whole new meaning to the word *wicked*.

And the word *pleasure*.

Especially since she was giving him a whole new meaning to the words *hard*, *desperate*, and *longing*.

The minstrel played two more equally repugnant tales before he took a break. Emily was on her feet before Draven could blink, pulling at him to rise.

He stood, then clenched his teeth at the stiffness in his knee. He hadn't realized his wince had been visible until he met Emily's gaze.

The concern on her face surprised him. "How did you injure your knee?"

His first instinct was to set her back on her heels with a smart retort. But before he could think of one, the truth came out. "I was run down by a horse in my youth."

Draven omitted the small fact that his father had been the rider and the event no accident, but a blatant attempt to murder Simon.

Her brows drew together into a deep V. "You are lucky it didn't make you lame."

Draven leaned heavily against the joint as the pain lessened ever so slightly. " 'Tis only by the effort of my will that it hasn't."

"It must have hurt terribly."

Draven didn't answer.

From the crowd they heard a small child crying. "Mama?" the girl wailed.

Emily looked past him. Before he knew what she was about, she headed off for the little girl a few feet away.

She knelt before the child and gently touched the girl's cheek.

By the ragged dress and unkempt hair, he surmised the girl was a peasant's child. But Emily didn't seem to notice. She took a corner of her mantle and dabbed at the girl's wet cheeks.

"Have you lost your mother, sweetling?" Emily asked.

"Aye," the girl wailed. "I want my mama."

"What's her name?"

"Mama."

Draven rolled his eyes as he moved to stand over them. That was certainly helpful.

Emily gave a gentle laugh. "Well, I daresay there are quite a few women here today who answer to that. What does she look like?"

"She's beautiful," the girl said with a sniff.

Emily glanced up to him over her shoulder. "A beautiful woman called Mama. Do you think we can find such, milord?"

"In this crowd, who knows."

Then Emily did the most unexpected thing: she reached out and chucked him on his good leg. "Milord, please. I am trying to comfort the girl. Not frighten her more."

Draven clamped down on his tongue. No man or woman had ever been so at ease in his presence that they would just reach out and touch him.

Not even Simon.

"What's your name, little one?" Emily asked the girl.

"Edyth."

"Come, Edyth. Let us find your mother. She must be looking for you too." Emily rose to her feet, and to his utter amazement picked the girl up and rested her on her hip.

"Milady," Draven warned, "she'll soil your gown."

"The tears will wash out, as will the dirt," Emily said dismissively.

The girl laid her head on Emily's shoulder and encircled her neck with her arms. He felt something strange in his gut as Emily cradled the girl to her side.

The feeling was something he didn't truly want to identify as he watched Emily give the girl her sweetened nuts and carry her through the crowd as she stopped and asked people if they knew the girl or her mother.

They hadn't gone far when he noted Emily growing weary of carrying the child, but she refused to put her down.

"Here," he said before he thought better of it. "Let me take her."

The little girl's eyes widened in fright as she shrank from his touch. "Will he hurt me, milady?" the girl whispered loudly.

"Nay, Edyth. His Lordship is a good ogre."

The girl looked doubtful. "Mama says noblemen hurt little peasant girls they find."

Emily stroked her hair back from her face. "Your mother is no doubt right and you should avoid them as a rule, but this one is different from the others. I promise you he'll not harm you one bit."

"But he's so big!"

Emily cast a glance at him over her shoulder, and her praise brought a strange warmth to his breast. "He is at that, but I bet you'll be better able to see through the crowd in his arms and find your mother."

The girl bit her lip, then nodded. She let go of Emily and held her arms out to him.

As gently as he could, Draven took the girl. He froze for a moment at the odd sensation of holding a child in his arms. He'd never done such in his life. But it felt good to have those spindly little arms of hers around him and to hear her young laughter in his ear.

"He's hard." The little girl laughed. "Not soft like you, milady."

Emily patted the girl's back, her hand brushing his as she did so.

Longing hit him so hard in his chest, he lost his breath for a moment. 'Twas the longing one felt from a remembered dream that had been banished and forgotten.

And for a moment he allowed himself to think of what life would be like if he dared take a wife. Of what it would be like to carry his own child in his arms.

But as soon as the thought entered his mind, he heard the echoed memory of screams in his head. Felt the pain of his knee and knew in his heart that he could never dare take such a chance.

"Edyth!"

He turned at the cry of alarm.

"Mama!" the girl shouted, kicking her legs against him.

Draven set the girl down and she ran to the peasant woman who opened her arms to scoop up her daughter.

"Oh Edyth, I feared I'd lost you forever! I told you not to wander off."

"I'm sorry, Mama. I won't do it anymore again. I promise."

Draven stood back as Emily approached them.

"Look, Mama," Edyth said, holding the sheepskin bag up to her mother. "The lady gave me sweet nuts."

The woman looked from the girl's hand up to Emily, then averted her gaze back to the ground. "My sincerest thanks, milady."

"It was our pleasure," Emily said. "You have a most wonderful daughter."

The woman thanked her again, took Edyth's

hand, and led her away. As Emily turned back to face him, he saw the sadness in her eyes.

"What is it, milady?" he asked.

"I doubt you'd understand." Her happiness dampened, she wended her way through the crowd at a much more subdued pace.

Draven said nothing more, but after a few minutes she spoke. "She was a sweet child, wasn't she?"

He shrugged. "Having never been around one before, I have no basis for comparison."

An unhappy smile curved her lips as she again brushed a strand of hair behind her ear. "I've been around many at my father's castle, our peasants' and the children sent to foster. But what I want more than anything is to be around my own."

"Then why haven't you married?"

Her eyes were bright from unshed tears. "My father refuses," she said wistfully as she walked onward. "No matter how I beg or plead, he won't have it."

"Why?"

"He's afraid."

"Of?"

"Losing us."

Draven frowned. "But for his own selfish ends, he would deprive you of what you want? That hardly seems fair."

"I know," she said, wrapping her arms about herself and walking onward again. "And on days such as this 'tis almost enough to make me curse him. But I know he means no pure malice. He acts out of love, and I could never find fault with him for that."

"I suppose I can understand."

She glanced up at him. "Do you? I think 'tis hard for others to understand his motives. I know you don't think much of my father, but he is a good man with a gentle heart."

Draven didn't respond.

"Even now," she continued. "I can see the look on his face the day my sister Anna died. When my eldest sister Mary died, it hit him hard. But Anna's death actually killed something inside him. I was but ten and one at the time, and he gathered me, Joanne, and Judith in his arms and swore that he would never allow a man to kill us."

Draven felt the blood drain from his face. "How did they die?" he asked, trying to banish the image of his own mother lying dead.

"Like my mother, they died in childbirth. To this day, my father blames himself for every one of their deaths. My mother's because he wanted another child, and my sisters because he agreed to see them married."

She took a deep breath. "At first I was grateful to him as I watched my friends marry men who were so much older than they. But as the years passed I started feeling this hole inside me."

Draven wondered why she was telling him this. He was hardly the type of person one saw as a confidant. But he remained silent as she spoke.

"Every time I see a mother with a child, I can feel it more profoundly. And now I wish . . ." She shook her head. "You think me foolish?"

"I think you are a woman who knows what she wants."

She met his gaze and smiled gratefully. "And what of you?"

"Me?" he asked in surprise.

"Do you not crave a family?"

The question set him aback. No one had ever asked him that before. "I have my sword, my shield and my horse. 'Tis all the family I require."

She frowned. "What of Simon?"

"Unlike your father, milady, I don't cling to people. For the most part, I enjoy my brother's company. But I know the time will come when he will leave. 'Tis expected."

"Are you not afraid of being alone?"

"I came into the world that way, and 'tis the way I shall surely leave it. Why should I expect the years in between to be anything else?"

Emily just stared at him as she digested his words. His calm acceptance amazed her. "Do you not wish it otherwise?"

"If you don't wish for something, then you can't be disappointed."

His words sent a shiver over her. How could he live with such a reality?

" 'Tis a cold place where you live, milord. And the fact that you seem to like it so well makes me pity you."

"You pity me?" he asked incredulously.

"Indeed I do."

Emily sighed. There was no need to further this discussion. He was a stubborn man and it would take some thinking to get past those prickly defenses of his. But she would succeed.

One way or another.

"Come, milord," she said, taking his hand again. "Let us not dwell on such serious matters while we are in the midst of merriment. I can see them getting ready for a wrestling match, and something tells me that you would much rather watch that than hear another minstrel's tale."

Draven nodded.

And so the rest of the afternoon went. Though Draven never really took part in any of it, he seemed content enough to watch her as she enjoyed herself fully.

Emily tried time and again to get him to loosen up a bit, but it was futile.

"Come, Lord Draven," she chided at the maypole. "Would you not like to kick up your heels and dance?"

"Should I do that, milady, the world would surely know just how uncoordinated I am, and being a knight of the crown and not a fool, I would shudder to make them laugh at me." He gently urged her toward the pole with a light nudge. "Go participate, if you must."

"Very well," she said as she left his side and went to take one of the red ribbons.

Draven crossed his arms over his chest as he watched Emily dance around the pole. She was truly breathtaking. Her hair and skirt flared around her as she turned in circles, twining her ribbon with those of the other dancers while she laughed and smiled.

How he wished he could live up to the words he had given her about his life. But in truth he did wish for something.

Her.

And there was nothing more than mere words standing between them.

And a curse.

Aye, the curse. Grinding his teeth, he tried to blot the image of his mother's pale face from his mind.

No matter his feelings, he would never forsake his word to Henry. Emily's safety would take precedence over his needs and wants.

He *would* control himself.

After the dance, she returned to his side, her eyes sparkling. "You should have joined us," she said breathlessly. " 'Twas most marvelously fun."

Impulsively, Draven brushed a stray strand of hair from her cheek. His fingertips lingered over the softness of her skin before he trailed them through the hair at her temples.

So subtle a gesture, and yet it sent heated waves of desire shooting through his entire body, rocking his equilibrium. He dropped his hand back to his side, but still the warmth of her skin clung to him, and he longed to cast his oath aside and take her once and for all.

I will not touch the lady in anger or in lust.

He would abide by his oath!

His will reaffirmed, he spoke. "I hate to take you away from the fun, milady. But 'twill be dark within the hour, and I fear we must be getting back."

"Very well." She reached out and tucked her arm into the crook of his elbow.

Draven stiffened, knowing he should withdraw, and yet he liked the feeling of her by his side.

Relaxing, he led her back through the merchants and their wares.

As they passed a goldsmith's booth, he noted the way Emily slowed down, her gaze drawn by the baubles. Draven stopped and reluctantly withdrew his arm from her.

"Here," he said, pulling a gold mark from his purse. "Go buy yourself a trinket to remember the day."

"I can't take this," she said, handing it back to him. " 'Tis too much to spend."

"Go ahead," he said gently as he pressed it into her hand. "I assure you there is nothing at this fair that would put a hardship on my finances."

She looked at him skeptically as she rubbed the coin between her thumb and forefinger. "Are you sure?"

"It would please me for you to spend it."

He watched as she crossed the way to look over the bracelets scattered about the top of the table.

"Here, milady," the merchant said, holding up an intricately set emerald necklace. "This necklace would be a perfect match for your eyes." The merchant's female assistant draped the piece around Emily's throat.

Her long graceful fingers stroked the gold braid as she lifted up the large tear-shaped emerald to study it. " 'Tis very beautiful," she breathed.

"Aye, milady does it justice," the girl said.

Draven agreed.

Taking a deep breath, he looked away. He knew it did no good to lust after that which he couldn't have. He'd learned long ago not to stare at the sun lest it blind him.

And so he forced himself to watch the people around him as they moved through the crowd.

Several minutes later, Emily was back at his side.

"Did you get the necklace?" he asked.

She shook her head, and before he could move, she seized his cloak. Draven frowned as he watched her hands gather the black fabric under his plain brooch, then unpin it. She placed his brooch between her teeth, and in its place she pinned an elaborate gold piece inlaid with a black enameled raven that was surrounded by dark red rubies.

She pulled his old brooch out of her mouth and smiled. "It reminded me of your emblem," she said, smoothing his cloak. "And I thought you might have more need of a happy memory than I." Her hands lingered on his chest as she tilted her head to look up at him.

Overwhelmed, he didn't know what pleased him most. Her smile, the feel of her hands against his chest, or the fact that she had thought of him. Those three things touched him to the very core of his soul.

"Thank you, Emily," he said, his voice thick. "I will treasure it always."

Her smile widened. "Do you realize that is the first time you have used my name while addressing me? I had begun to wonder if you even remembered it."

She took his arm again and started back to where they'd left the horses.

"Thank you for the day," she said warmly. "It was one of the best ones I've ever had."

He swallowed. It was without a doubt the best day of his life, and he would give anything for it not to end.

He covered her hand with his and reveled in the feel of her fingers beneath his own. Her skin felt like warm velvet, and he longed to sample the taste of it with his tongue.

Draven gave a gentle squeeze and led her to their mounts.

She wasn't nearly as talkative on the way back, and about halfway there, Draven turned to see why. She had her eyes closed and looked as if she were trying to sleep. She jumped as if startled and then blinked her eyes as if to clear them. And then she covered her mouth with her hand and gave a wide yawn.

Draven reined his horse to a stop and caught her reins. She looked at him with a frown.

"You'd best ride with me before you fall from your horse."

Before she could protest, he lifted her from her saddle and set her down across his lap. Her hips pressed against his loins, searing him with molten heat.

She said nothing as she wrapped her arms about his waist and settled herself against his chest like a babe. The top of her head brushed his chin, and he could feel her heat the length of his entire body. Her breath fell softly against his throat, raising chills all over him.

For a moment he couldn't move as he fought against the urge to kick his horse into the woods and lay her down upon the grass and take her. Over and over, he could imagine her sighs of pleasure in his ear as he rocked himself between her milky thighs and took possession of her both body and soul.

Could there be any greater pleasure?

Draven tightened his grip on the reins. He would not touch her. By all that was holy, he would not!

Forcing himself, he tied the reins of her horse to his saddle and continued on toward Orrick's home. His horse had barely gone three yards before she drifted off to sleep. It was only then he allowed himself to relax.

Impulsively, he tilted his head down to rest his cheek against the top of her head where he could inhale the sweet honeysuckle scent of her and feel the soft strands on his skin, his lips.

"Ogres can be fun," she murmured under her breath, never waking from her sleep.

"Even in slumber you speak," he said, amused by the knowledge, and even more by the fact that no other man knew that about her.

Only him.

Draven tilted her head and stared into her face. He rested her cheek against his shoulder and gently cupped her chin in his hand. Her lips were parted ever so lightly, and it would be so easy to lean forward and take possession of them.

If only he hadn't given his word.

All his life, his word had been his bond. He'd never once broken it. But never before had keeping it been so torturous.

"Lilacs," she whispered. "There are lilacs afoot."

Whatever was she dreaming of? He couldn't imagine.

Tenderly, he ran the pad of his thumb over her bottom lip, remembering the sugar that had been there earlier. She poked her tongue back out, touching it lightly to his thumb.

Draven drew his hand back as if she had scalded him, and indeed it felt as if she had.

Still, she called out to him, and once more he found himself stroking the softness of her face. Before he could stop himself, he leaned forward and pressed his lips to her cheeks. Draven sighed as his entire body erupted into flames.

Her skin was soft and alluring and tasted like the very sunshine above. He pulled her tight against him and buried his face in the hollow of her throat where he could feel her heart beating beneath his lips. She sighed in his ears.

Heaven help him, but he wanted her, and in that instant he felt his control slipping.

Upbraiding himself for his foolishness, he straightened in his saddle and spurred the horse to get them back before he yielded to his lust.

Once he was within sight of Orrick's walls, he gently shook her awake. Emily stretched languidly against him like a soft kitten. The material of her kirtle stretched taut over her breasts, and again he felt himself stiffen in response to the sight.

When she opened her eyes and saw his face, she jumped ever so slightly.

"My goodness," she breathed, "I forgot you were holding me."

If only he could have forgotten. "I thought it best

you be back on your own horse before we enter the outer bailey."

Stifling a yawn, she nodded.

Draven dismounted with her, then placed her on her own horse. Her warmth clung to him for a full minute before it evaporated and left him longing for it again.

Mounting his horse, he led her into the castle.

When they entered the hall, there was a banquet fare spread out that would rival one of the king's feasts. Servants bustled about in haste as they brought food from the kitchens and decorated the tables.

"At last you return," Orrick said in greeting as he approached them.

"What is all this?" Draven asked.

"Simon said you would leave in the morning, so I thought we'd have a farewell for your journey."

"It smells wonderful," Emily said, crossing the few feet that separated her from Christina.

Draven eyed the dais draped with red cloth, a sense of dread spreading through him. In truth, he preferred his meals in private. But there was no way to decline the offer lest he offend his host.

"I tried to tell him not to," Simon said in a low voice as he came up behind him. "He wouldn't listen."

Draven noted Simon's obvious limp as he paused next to him. "How's your ankle this evening?"

"Better."

"So I see."

"What do you mean?"

"This afternoon when I left, 'twas the other foot you favored. Perhaps it wasn't your feet you injured, but rather your head."

A wide smile split Simon's face. "You caught me. Well, at least I no longer have to worry about hobbling about." His gaze dropped to Draven's chest. "Nice brooch. Did some demon possess you that you would buy it?"

Draven glanced to where Emily talked with Christina. Pain stabbed his heart and he sighed. " 'Twas but a bit of foolishness. If you'll excuse me, I need to speak with my squire."

Emily frowned as she saw Draven leave the hall.

"I wonder where he goes?" Christina said from her side.

"I can't imagine."

"Well, 'tis just as well, now I don't have to worry about him overhearing us."

"Overhearing what?"

Christina turned to face her with a determined set to her jaw. "Emily, as there is a God in heaven above, we have got to find some way for you to get Lord Draven to the marriage altar."

Chapter 10

Emily stared in disbelief at Christina's declaration. "What brought about this change in you?"

"Oh, Em, he's wonderful!" she gushed. "What he did for Orrick . . . I can't tell you how afraid Orrick has been all this time over what would happen to him when Lord Draven came. And then taking you to the fair . . ." She paused as if another thought occurred to her. "Did you have a good time with him?"

"Aye, but—"

"But nothing," Christina said, interrupting her. "I have hired several of the musicians from the fair to play tonight. There shall be dancing and you will have to entice him."

"How? He barely seems to notice me. Although . . ." Emily paused as she remembered what she'd overheard.

"Although?"

She shrugged. "I overheard him talking to himself before we left."

"About what?"

"Me," she confessed. "He said he desired me and yet I see no proof of it. I'm afraid I'm at a loss as to how to deal with him. He is unlike any man I've ever known." Emily looked at her. "What of you? How did you catch Lord Orrick's notice?"

"I breathed," she said wistfully. "He knew my mother and elder sisters had all survived multiple births and that I had a nice dowry. 'Twas all I needed."

That wouldn't help her cause any.

"Lord Draven doesn't seem to care about either of those."

"Nay," Christina agreed. " 'Twill take some thinking." Christina bit her lip and scanned the hall. Her eyes widened, then she smiled. "And I think I know who can help us with the thinking!"

She grabbed Emily's arm and literally dragged her to Simon's side.

"Milord," Christina said. "Might we borrow you for a moment?"

"Nay, Christina," Emily breathed. "You can't be serious! He'll tell Lord Draven."

"Not if we swear him to secrecy. You are a man of your word, are you not, Lord Simon?"

"Depends on the word," Simon said evasively, looking back and forth between them. "I sense mischief afoot, and there is nothing I treasure more than good mischief." He rubbed his hands together. "What is it you ladies are up to?"

"First, you must swear yourself to eternal secrecy," Christina said.

"Very well, my lips are eternally sealed." Simon pinched his lips closed with his thumb and forefinger.

Christina nodded her approval. "Emily wants to marry your brother."

"Christina!" Emily gasped, horrified that she would just blurt it out so indelicately. "How could—"

"Oh, shush," Christina said. "No need in beating around it. Time is of the essence. You need a husband and Lord Draven needs an heir. Is that not right, milord?"

Simon looked askance as he appeared to ponder the question. He stroked his bearded chin. "How should I answer this?" he asked, covering his lips with two fingers. "The greedy part of me that is in line for Draven's lands says nay. He needs no heir. I would like greatly to have such wealth, however the dutiful brother in me would agree with you."

His teasing air sobered as he met Emily's gaze. "What of you, milady? I would know your feelings for my brother before I commit myself."

Her feelings. That was a hard question to answer. "He seems suitable enough for a husband."

Simon snorted. "Is that all you require?"

"He needs someone to take care of him," Emily tried again.

Simon laughed. "That is the last thing he needs. I assure you, he can handle himself well enough. Try again."

Christina nudged her. "Tell him what you told me, Em."

She shook her head.

"He makes her breathless, and she is quite infatuated by him."

Emily opened her mouth to reprimand her friend, but Christina would have none of it. "She senses a goodness in him. Is she right, milord?"

Simon nodded. "Very well, I will help you." He glanced away and paled. "Now, here he comes. Pretend there's nothing amiss."

Draven frowned as he crossed the hall to see Simon, Christina and Emily together in a tight circle as if plotting some mayhem.

At his approach, Simon began whistling, his gaze darting about while the women seemed engrossed in a conversation about veils.

Emily twined her fingers together as she talked to Christina. "The green is the best color for . . . for . . . for . . . things."

"Oh, aye. 'Tis good for lots of things, like . . . things."

"What is going on here?" Draven asked suspiciously.

Three faces turned to him with such a look of innocence it would have made any other man laugh.

Draven cocked his head and suddenly felt like a cat cornered by three mice. "What sort of conspiracy is this?"

"Conspiracy?" they asked almost in unison.

Simon clapped him on the back. "You've served the king so long, you're now imaging evil where it doesn't exist."

Did they think him a fool that he couldn't see through them?

Obviously so.

"Come," Christina said, taking Simon's arm. "Let us adjourn to the table and partake of the culinary mastery of our cooks. You should like the roasted pheasant," she said to Draven. "The elderberry sauce is the tastiest in all of Christendom."

Reluctantly, Draven followed, still unable to shake the uneasy feeling that his own goose was the only thing thoroughly cooked in the hall this night.

Christina sat him at the table between Emily and Simon. He felt trapped, unable to escape. His throat tight, he remained silent as the servants served the meal.

Simon leaned over. "Are you all right?"

Draven took a deep breath and nodded, though he could feel himself beginning to perspire.

"Milord?" Emily asked, drawing his attention to her.

When he met her gaze, he saw a gentleness in her features that eased the knot in his gut.

"Forgive me for my forwardness," she said, "but Christina tells me there will be dancing after the meal. Would you care to join me?"

An image of her dancing around the maypole flashed in his mind. There was nothing he could think of that would give him greater pleasure than to dance with her.

"Nay, milady, I cannot."

Disappointment darkened her brow.

"I would love to dance with you," Simon said, leaning across Draven to talk to her.

A stab of jealousy sliced his heart, but he said nothing. Instead, he focused his thoughts on serving food to Emily. He watched the grace of her movements as she ate. And when she reached for the goblet and placed her lips to the very spot he had drunk from, chills went through him. There was something so very intimate about the gesture. Almost as if they had shared a kiss.

"Is the food not to your liking?" she asked in a hushed voice when she noticed he hadn't eaten anything.

Draven shook his head. "The fare is fine."

"Then why do you not eat it?"

"I am not hungry."

"You know, milord, I haven't seen you eat enough to sustain a bee. How is it you've grown to such a size with only air to sustain you?"

"I leave it to Simon," Draven said dryly. "He eats enough for both of us."

Emily laughed as she looked to Simon's trencher, which he'd heaped with a king's portion of chicken, pheasant, roasted apples, and leeks.

"What?" Simon asked as he noted her attention.

"She merely admires your gluttony."

Simon swallowed his mouthful of food, then reached for his goblet. "Good food, good music, and good women are all I require in life to be happy. One day, brother, I hope you will try the combination."

Draven leaned back in his chair, refusing for once to rise to the bait. In truth, he didn't feel up to it. All he wanted was to leave this place.

Emily's presence at his side was the only comfort he had.

He watched as she delicately bit into a tender piece of chicken, licking the juices from her ruby-red lips. His comfort turned into a needle-laced bed that stabbed him all over.

It would be rude to leave. He knew it.

And yet . . .

You've suffered worse.

Had he? He couldn't remember even his more serious battle wounds stinging as much as his loins did just now.

It seemed as if an eternity had passed before the musicians were summoned and people began to rise from the tables. Simon made haste in taking Emily by the hand and leading her off to dance.

Draven watched in envy. There was no limp to Simon's gait, no pain in his stride. And for a moment he wished he hadn't run in front of his father's horse.

Shame filled him at the thought. Simon's life had been well worth it. Better he should lose his leg than Simon his life.

He just wished that for once in his life, *he* could be the one to dance.

Sighing, he rose from the table and went to seek whatever solace he could find out on the battlements.

* * *

Emily broke off her dance as soon as she saw Draven leave. A darkness seemed to cling to him as if the merriment of the night depressed him.

"Where does he go?" she asked, wondering if there was any truth to her suspicions.

Simon turned to look. "The battlements, no doubt."

"The battlements?" She frowned. "Why?"

Simon shrugged. "He's done that as far back as I can remember. He spends most of the night walking them."

"Why?" she repeated.

Simon motioned for her to follow him to a secluded corner of the hall.

Once they were away from others, Simon spoke. "What I am about to tell you, you must swear to never repeat."

"I swear."

Simon paused a minute as if gathering his thoughts. A deep sadness darkened his brow. "You cannot imagine the childhood Draven survived, milady. His father never wanted a son. He wanted a legacy. He wanted Draven trained to be a warrior, not a man, and he did everything he could think of to kill the human side of him."

Emily stared at him as she tried to fathom what he was telling her. "I don't understand."

The sadness in his eyes intensified. "Draven doesn't sleep much because his father viewed sleep as a weakness. To sleep is to be vulnerable. Whenever he caught Draven slumbering, he would beat him awake."

She remembered the rage she'd seen in Draven's eyes when she awoke him in the orchard. For a moment, she had actually feared Draven would strike her.

"How could Harold do such a thing?" she asked.

"His father had no heart," Simon whispered. "The earls of Ravenswood are such great warriors because they are all taught to feel nothing save anger and hatred. It's easy to stand strong in battle when you have nothing in life to hold onto. Indeed, they have always welcomed death and the relief it gave them from their miserable, lonely lives."

Her heart stopped. "And Draven?"

"In most ways, he is different. There is much of our mother in him, though he denies it. She lived long enough to show him what kindness was, what it felt like to be held and protected. He knows how to protect and love, but for some reason, he refuses to see that side of himself. Instead he sees only the part of him that is like his father. If you can just make him see that he is nothing like Harold, then you will have a husband who will never stray from your side."

A quiver of doubt went through her. Could she show love to a man so hurt?

"I promise you, he is worth it."

"But how, Simon? I don't know how."

He sighed. "Nor do I. Draven closed himself off so long ago that even I cannot reach him. I never knew a man could be too strong, but in my brother's case I would say he is."

Emily's mind sifted through thoughts until a verse from her favorite chanson leaped forward.

"Of course!" she said excitedly to Simon. "Accusain and Laurette."

Simon frowned. "I don't understand."

" 'Tis a tale we heard today at the fair. It is of a Saracen warrior and a Norman princess. They were from two entirely different worlds, and yet love allowed them to reach out to each other. It healed his wounded heart and allowed him to love her."

"But that is just a story and this is reality."

"Perhaps, but I am nothing if not a dreamer, and as a dreamer I would be remiss if I didn't do what Laurette would do in my place."

Simon cocked a brow. "And that is?"

"Seek out my prince where he lives." She patted Simon on the arm. "Wish me luck."

Simon waited until she was gone before he whispered. "I wish you much more than that, Emily. I wish you success."

Draven stared out into the dark night around him. Rushlights had been lit to illuminate the gate and portcullis, but beyond that he could see nothing. Just an empty blankness.

He'd always found comfort in the dark. Like a mother's arms, it gave him solace to be the only one about. It reminded him of death and if he closed his eyes, he could pretend that the world had ended. That there was nothing. No pain, no loneliness, no past. No future.

Nothing.

But when he opened his eyes, the reality of it all came rushing back.

When would it all just end?

"Milord?"

He turned at the soft voice coming from behind him. "Milady," he said gruffly. "What is it you do here?"

She pulled her cloak tighter about her shoulders. "I came to find you."

"Why?"

"Why not?"

"Are you being flippant?" he asked.

"Aye."

What was it about her that she would dare what no other had ever dared before with him? "I'm in no mood for games, milady. You should return inside before you become chilled."

"Are you coming inside with me?"

He shook his head.

Laughter filtered out from the hall.

"The jester," Emily said softly. "You should have stayed to hear him."

"Why?" Then he added before she could. "Why not?"

She smiled. "Actually I was going to say that it wouldn't hurt you to learn to smile once in a while. Laughter is the nectar of God."

She took a step toward him, and to his astonishment she reached up and placed her hands against his cheeks. They were amazingly warm given the chill in the air.

With her thumbs, she pulled his cheeks back into a semblance of a smile. "See," she said. "It doesn't crack your face."

Draven stepped back from her touch and returned to leaning against the battlements to look out into the dark forest. Emily moved to stand beside him, mimicking his pose.

Minutes passed while they just stood there. Even though they didn't touch, he could feel the length of her body every bit as profoundly as if they were shoulder to shoulder, toe to toe, hip to hip. Indeed, he could feel her with every fiber of his body.

Draven tried to ignore her, but the wind caught her gentle, feminine scent and carried it to him.

The laughter in the hall settled down as music again played.

"Enough of this," Emily said, her voice startling against the quiet. She took his hand and turned him to face her. "I *will* dance with you."

"I don't know how," he confessed.

"Aye, but you do. You forget that I've seen you train, and any man who can twist and maneuver the way you do in the list can most assuredly dance."

"I'll crush your toes."

"They will heal."

He didn't know what to say to that and so he let her take his hands and show him a few steps. To his amazement, he didn't step on her toes, and even more amazing was the enjoyment he felt from something so innocuous.

He was attuned to everything about her as she swept around him. To the moonlight playing in her pale tresses. The laughter in her eyes. The feel of her body so very close to his.

She stoked the hunger in him to a ravenous

frenzy that roared and hissed, demanding he take her. The waves of it crashed over him, and it was all he could do to stand strong against the gale force.

She twirled about and then stumbled. Draven barely caught her before she fell.

He held her tilted back in his arms. Her lips were so close that barely a handsbreadth separated them as her breasts pressed against his chest.

He stared at the rosy hue of her lips, wanting so much to dare the king's wrath by sampling them.

So very easy . . .

Emily clung to him, her green eyes wide in gratitude. "My hero," she whispered.

Draven stared at her. The title *hero* had been given to him years ago by fools who knew naught of him, and for deeds he didn't even want to remember committing. But for the first time in his life, he truly felt heroic as he saw himself reflected in the dark pupils of her eyes. And even more surprising was the joy her words brought to him.

It suddenly became important to him that she see him as such. That he never disappoint her.

A need of her own darkened her eyes as she watched him in the rushlights.

"What is it you want of me?" he asked as he straightened her to stand before him.

She bit her lip. "I suppose I should be coy about this, but then I've never been such. I've found that frankness is often the best way to deal with matters, and so I shall be true to my nature and tell you exactly what I want."

She tilted her chin up to look at him, her expression one of supreme sincerity. "I want *you*, milord."

He stared at her blankly, not quite comprehending her meaning. "You want me for what?"

"For husband."

His jaw went slack. What on earth was the woman thinking? Had she any sense?

"Have you any idea what you are saying?" he asked.

"Well, aye, of course," she said indignantly.

Draven took a step away from her. He didn't know what had possessed her, but this was indeed foolishness of the first order.

"You have no idea what it is you ask, milady. What it is you would condemn yourself to."

"I disagree." Taking a step toward him, she reached out for his arm.

Once again he pulled away. "You know me not at all."

"And my mother knew nothing of my father. Indeed, she never saw him until the wedding, yet they grew to love each other. Greatly."

"You say that as if 'tis a simple matter."

"Marriage often is."

"You are being foolish, lady. Now off with you." He turned his back to her and started for the donjon.

She rushed around him and blocked his path. "You cannot escape me. I won't let you."

Anger coiled through him that she would dare block his way. Especially when all he wanted to do was flee her and all the confusing thoughts and feelings she evoked.

"Is this your way to get me to send you home to your father?"

She looked at him as if the mere thought

offended her. "The last thing I want is to be sent back home. I want a husband."

"Then take yourself to the hall and seek another."

And before he knew what she was about, she seized his face in her hands, rose upon her tiptoes, and laid her lips against his.

Molten desire flooded every fiber of his body.

Reacting on pure primal instinct, Draven pulled her into his arms and molded her body against his own. She surrendered herself to him fully as he opened her mouth and sampled the sweetness of it. She wrapped her arms about his neck and sighed contentedly.

Draven's head buzzed as if he'd drunk too much ale, and all rational thought fled his mind.

There was nothing except the feel of her hot, supple body against his, the taste of her mouth, the smell of honeysuckle from her hair, and the sound of her rapid breathing in his ears.

Her kiss was one of innocence and timidity, yet curious and bold. Never had he felt the like, nor had he ever wanted anything more than he did a private bed for the two of them.

In her excitement, she pressed her breasts against his chest, inflaming him even more as she rubbed up against him, her hip brushing his hard, swollen shaft.

He left her lips with a groan and dared what he'd been longing to do. He buried his lips in the hollow of her throat and nipped her tender flesh with his teeth. She hissed in pleasure as she buried her hands in his hair and held him tightly against her.

The salty sweet taste of her skin branded his lips

and his tongue as she shivered in his arms. He wanted her. Here and now.

His body burned for her, and he could think no thought save having her.

Emily moaned ever so softly at the feel of raw power emanating from him as his tongue and lips worked magic on her body. A thousand ribbons of pleasure tore through her simultaneously until her entire body throbbed with a foreign, aching need.

Brazenly, she pressed her lips against his stubbled cheek, delighting in the taste and feel of his masculine skin. She felt him tremble as he ran one hand over her right breast and gave a tender squeeze. She jerked at the strange sensation that ripped through her, and her bittersweet torture only increased as he cupped her breast and dipped his head down to the low scooped neckline of her kirtle and kissed her flesh just above her taut peak.

Oh, 'twas wondrous. The feel of him strong and demanding in her arms as he gave her pleasure. Never had she felt the like, and at that moment she knew she would never rest until she possessed him for her own.

And when he dipped his hand inside her neckline and touched her bare breast with his fingers, she thought she might very well faint from pleasure.

Draven groaned at the feel of her heavy breast in his hand, her taut nipple in his palm as he moved his lips to sample her ear. He teased the chills on her skin with his tongue while he damned the fabric that kept him from touching her all over.

His senses whirling, he returned to her lips and pushed her back against the wall.

Emily cupped his face in her hands as she delighted in the feel of his body pressing her against the cool stone. She kissed him fiercely as he plundered her mouth. Never had she tasted anything like him. Felt anything so incredible. So wonderful.

She only vaguely realized he was lifting up the hem of her dress. He ran his hands over her bare buttocks, branding her skin with heat and pleasure. And before she knew what he was about, he reached down between the two of them and gently separated the nether folds of her body to touch her as no one had ever touched her before.

"Oh, Draven," she moaned as his fingers brought relief to the throbbing ache at the core of her body and she instinctively rubbed herself against his hand.

Draven froze at the sound of his name on her lips, reality crashing down around him.

One more minute and he'd . . .

With a curse, he forced himself to pull away from her before it was too late.

She took a step toward him, and he grabbed her arms to keep her at bay. Her lips were swollen from his kisses. And by the look in her passion-dulled eyes, he could see she wanted him as much as he wanted her.

But to take her would be his death.

"Is your hatred of me so great that you'd sacrifice your virginity to see me dead?" he asked fiercely.

She blinked in confusion. "I do not hate you, Draven. How could I?"

Whatever spell she had woven evaporated with those words, and once again clarity reigned in his head. "It seems to me, the question would be how could you not?"

Chapter 11

Stunned by his question, her body still inflamed by his touch, Emily could do naught save watch as Draven abruptly left. She stood on the battlements, baffled. How could he not see what she herself saw?

You know me not at all.

There was truth to those words and yet . . .

She had seen enough of his kindness to know he was a good man. And though he might not know what he needed, she did.

His words to the odious pair with Reinhold earlier that day came to her mind.

Stiffening her spine in determination, she narrowed her gaze on where he had vanished. "There is no corner you may find, milord, where I will not seek you out. You are going to learn that I am as stubborn as the day is long, and when I set my mind to something . . . Well, iron will you may have, but 'tis no match for my own. I will win you. See if I don't."

She touched her lips with the backs of her fingers. He had responded to her with passion and longing. Even a virginal maid could tell that. And if he desired her, then he held some feeling for her.

Lust wasn't the only feeling she wished to stir within him, but it was a beginning. A beginning she needed, and one she could most definitely use.

Draven ground his teeth as pent-up emotions swept through him. Anger, torment, lust. He had broken his word to Henry, but worse than that was the stinging desire flooding his body. All too easily he remembered the way she had felt in his arms. The way she had writhed to his touch.

Dear God, she would have let him take her!

"For husband."

The words echoed in his head as his lips burned, branded by her innocent kiss.

What could she possibly be thinking?

Her father would perish in shock if he knew her plans. Indeed, 'twas almost worth telling Hugh just to have the earl out of his way.

Well, she could think those foolish thoughts all she wanted. Wishing didn't make something reality. Of all men, he knew that for truth. And now that he knew her game, he would guard himself even more closely.

By all that was holy, he would not touch her again! Not her hand, not even the hem of her sleeve. Aye, from this moment on, he would avoid every part of her.

* * *

The next morning as Draven made his way down the stairs, Emily stumbled from the step above him. She fell full against him, touching every part of his body from cheek to toe.

The weight of her body pressing him against the wall was more than enough to make a mockery of his will as the memory of the night before came crashing back.

All too easily, he remembered the feel of her body in his hands, the taste of her lips, the sound of her murmured sighs in his ears.

"Are you all right, milord?" she asked, her sweet, warm breath tickling his throat. "I didn't see you there."

Yet there was a light in her eyes that made him question her sincerity. Especially combined with the fact that she had yet to withdraw from him and her lips remained dangerously close to his own.

"I'm so glad you were here," she gushed, "else I would have stumbled the whole way down the stairs, and like as not broken my neck."

Draven still couldn't speak. Not while his arm was trapped between her ample breasts and her legs were entwined with his own. He could feel her heart pounding beneath his forearm and when she moved back, her hip brushed against the part of him that ached the most to possess her body.

A tremor shook him.

And by the hot look on her face, he could tell she'd felt his erection plainly enough.

An attractive blush darkened her cheeks, making her catlike eyes glow. "Thank you for your chivalry, milord. I think henceforth I shall call you the hero of my heart."

At last he found his voice. "You credit me too much," he said quickly. After all, the last thing he needed was for her to misinterpret his actions. "I didn't even know you were there until you fell into me."

"Oh," she said, adjusting her kirtle around her.

Draven watched suspiciously as she drew the material tight against her body, highlighting the curves of her hips. And if that wasn't bad enough, she bent over, exposing the tops of her breasts to his starving gaze.

His groin tightened even more as he remembered the feel of those ripe peaks in his hand. By St. Peter, he was actually starting to salivate!

"I hope you'll forgive my clumsiness," she said as she straightened. "I was trying to hurry so as not to keep you waiting this time."

"How courteous," he said stiffly.

Better she should make him wait the next fortnight than reignite his blood with this inferno.

He moved away from her.

"Milord," she said, her tone chiding. "You act as though you are afraid of me."

Draven stopped dead in his tracks and looked back at her. "I fear no man."

"But I am not man."

"Do you think me daft that I don't know that?" he asked, glowering at her.

She raised a sharp brow at the anger in his voice. "Well, the way you treat me would leave me to think otherwise."

Sensing his imminent defeat, Draven sought to retreat to safety. "If you'll excuse me—"

"See," she said triumphantly. "There you go."

He paused in confusion. "There I go what?"

"Treating me as if I'm something other than a woman."

His head ached from her logic. "If I'm not treating you as a woman, then what, pray tell, am I treating you like?"

There was an odd look in her eyes. "I don't know."

"You don't know?" he asked incredulously.

She blinked innocently. "I don't know."

"Then why are we having this discussion?"

"Why not?" she quipped.

Draven looked sideways at her. There was a playful air about her, and a note of mischief. "You are toying with me, aren't you?"

The devilish light in her eyes deepened. "And if I were?"

"Then I'd say stop it."

"Why?"

"Because it annoys me." He started back down the stairs.

"I'd rather be annoying than ignored," she said, raising her voice as she followed down the stairs after him. "That is what you've been doing all morning, is it not? Ignoring me?"

"And if I were?" he asked without stopping.

She lifted her chin. "Then I'd say stop it."

Draven pressed his hand to his temple in frustration at her using his words against him.

He stopped on the bottom step and looked at her. "How is it you do this to me?"

"Do what?" she asked with such a look of innocence on her face that it almost made him laugh.

"Talk circles around me. I swear I'm becoming quite dizzy from it."

Her gaze dipped to his lips and he saw her hunger. "Perhaps you are dizzy from something else?" she asked, her voice low and seductive.

"And that would be?"

She shrugged, smiled, and descended the stairs. "How should I know?" she tossed over her shoulder. "I'm not the brooding ogre. I'm just a woman, plain and simple."

Draven growled low in his throat. *Plain and simple* described her like *pebble* described Gibraltar.

"I'm not a brooding ogre," he called after her.

She paused at the door and looked back at him impishly. "Nay, you are right. But do you know what you are?"

Did he dare ask it?

He did. "What?"

She licked her lips as her gaze branded him with heat. "You're a very handsome man, with beautiful eyes."

Stunned, he didn't move as she continued her way out the door.

Never in his life had anyone said such a thing to him. Ogre, demon, son of the devil, horse's arse. He'd been called any number of insults. But no one in his life had ever given him a compliment on anything save his battle prowess.

"Beautiful eyes," he repeated, both repulsed and yet strangely flattered.

Did he in fact have—

"Oh bugger that," he snapped under his breath. Who cared what his eyes looked like as long as he could see with them. He wasn't some winsome maid to have his head turned by flattery. He was a knight sworn to keep his hands off the Lady Emily.

And keep his hands off her he most surely would.

"Could you give me a hand, milord?"

Draven cringed at Emily's question as she waited by her horse for his assistance to mount.

What had he said inside the castle but an hour ago about keeping his hands off her?

He looked about for Simon, but the man seemed to have vanished. His other men were already mounted.

Resigned to it, he nodded.

Just pretend she's a fat, hideous nun.

Aye, one who smelled of honeysuckle and sunshine. His body leaped at the scent of her, and he could feel the muscles of his arms constrict.

As quickly as he could, he lifted her up. But she didn't take her saddle.

"Is there a problem?" he snapped.

She batted her lashes at him quite innocently. "I can't seem to get seated."

He stifled the urge to toss her over the horse like a sack of grain. "You're doing this apurpose," he said in a low whisper.

Her playful look confirmed his suspicion. "I told

you what I wanted, milord, and I am not above using any means to win."

He dumped her in the saddle. "Perhaps I should warn you, milady. No one has *ever* bested me."

"Then I would say you are due for a good besting."

He opened his mouth to respond when he caught sight of Simon joining them.

"Ah," Simon said as he passed by. "I see you've taken care of the lady. A good thing too."

"Why? Did you perchance twist your arm?" Draven asked sarcastically as Simon took his reins.

"In fact, I did. I think I shall be quite put out for some time. Won't be able to do anything chivalrous."

A conspiracy.

He should have known. Well, he was no pawn to be pushed about. To the devil with them both!

Swinging himself up on his horse, Draven waited while Emily said good-bye to Christina, who held a large, leatherbound book in her hands.

"You will write as soon as the babe is born?" Emily asked.

"I will, and you'll have to come see me again."

Emily cast a glance to Draven. "I will see what I can do."

Nodding, Christina handed the book to Emily. "This is for you."

"For me?" Emily started to open it, but Christina slammed the book shut and shook her head. " 'Tis for you alone in the privacy of your room."

"But—"

"Emily," Christina interrupted with a stressed

tone. " 'Tis for you *alone*. It concerns the matter we spoke of earlier this morn."

Emily's mouth formed a perfect O as Christina's meaning dawned on her.

Draven exchanged glances with Simon, who shrugged as if he had no idea what the women discussed.

But Draven knew. There was more conspiracy afoot. And he couldn't wait to lay hands to said book to see exactly what mischief they plotted, for there was little doubt in his mind whom they plotted against.

Christina helped Emily secure the book in her saddlebags. "Godspeed you all."

Emily touched hands with Christina, then said good-bye to Orrick.

"I am ready, milord," she said to Draven. "And I thank you for your patience."

Draven gave a curt nod to Orrick before he kicked his horse forward and led his party through the bailey. At least for the next few days he wouldn't have to fear being near the lady. The journey would see her on her horse and him on his.

At last he would have peace.

"What do you mean her horse has gone lame?" Draven snarled, looking at his knight Arnold.

"You may see for yourself, milord," he said, standing back.

Draven lifted up the back left hoof and saw it. An injured horse?

Was fate itself conspiring against him now?

If he didn't know better, he'd swear Emily or

Simon had something to do with it. But he'd kept his eyes on the lady the whole time and knew for a fact she'd done nothing to harm the horse.

It was merely one of those wretched, awful, gut-wrenching things.

"Very well," Draven said, lowering the horse's hoof. "Remove the saddle and I'll trust you to bring the horse to Ravenswood at a slow pace to keep from injuring her more."

"Aye, milord."

"Simon," Draven said, looking to his brother, who sat on his horse observing them. "The lady rides with you."

Emily crossed the short distance that separated them and said in a low voice, "I'll not ride with him, milord."

"You'll do as you are told."

She lifted her brows in censure. "You'll not take that tone with me."

"Woman," he growled in a voice that had sent grown men to their knees quaking in fear. "This is not a game."

Her face sobered, but there was none of the accompanying fear he was used to seeing. If anything his growl seemed to challenge her.

"You are quite right, milord. It isn't. I will either ride with you or I shall walk."

Draven glared at her. "Have you no sense to press me so?"

"I have plenty of sense."

"Then ride with Simon."

"Nay."

By the stubborn set of her jaw he could tell she

had no intention of ceding the matter. "If you are the meekest of Hugh's daughters, then I am thankful I have never had the privilege of meeting your sisters."

Realizing arguing with her would do nothing save waste more time, Draven relented. "Mount the damn horse."

Emily sensed she might be pushing him too far. Perhaps she shouldn't be so bold after all. But then her father had called her boldness one of her more endearing qualities.

As she took the saddle, she didn't think Lord Draven agreed with him. In fact, judging by the stiffness of his body as he mounted behind her, she didn't think he thought much of her at all at present.

She opened her mouth to apologize.

"Don't speak," he snapped. "Not one single word."

Emily clamped her lips together and vowed not to open them again until he apologized for his sharp tone.

Draven felt her go tense in his lap and knew he had offended her. So be it. He didn't think he could stand feeling her pressed against him while that silken voice of hers addressed him. Indeed, his entire body ached with longing to the point he didn't know if he could stand it.

If they passed a single village, town, or manor on this trip, he would stop and buy her a horse no matter the price. In fact, he'd gladly trade everything he owned for one wayward nag.

* * *

The day wore on in silence while Draven tried his best to distance his mind from his body. But it was impossible. Every stinking hoofbeat drove her against him in a sensuous rhythm that rocked his equilibrium and tolerance all the more. And with every hour that passed, his anger mounted and his shaft stiffened far beyond pain.

The wind blew tendrils of her hair against his face, caressing his cheeks and sending her honeysuckle scent through him.

Oh, but it would be so easy to spur his horse forward, find a secluded place in the woods, and lay her beneath him. To drive himself into her over and over again until he finally found the peace his body screamed for.

The memory of her kiss and feel of her flesh tortured him even more.

"Milord?"

He winced at her voice. "I told you not to speak."

"I didn't want to," she said petulantly, "but I have no choice."

"Aye, you do."

"I do not," she said firmly.

He looked down at her and saw the blush on her cheeks. "What is of such—"

"We needs take a rest."

"I wish to cover—"

"Milord," she said, cutting him off. "You misunderstand me. We *needs*," she stressed the word, "take a rest." She shifted her gaze meaningfully from his face to the trees they passed.

Dawning fell upon him.

"Oh," he said, holding his hand up to signal the others that they were slowing down.

Draven directed his horse to a small copse of trees. Reining to a stop, he helped her slide down the left side of his mount.

"Thank you," she said coldly, then turned to make her way into the woods.

Draven took the time to check on his horse to make sure their combined weight wasn't overly tiring to the animal.

Simon drew near. "Are you all right?" he asked.

Draven glared at him.

For once Simon had the sense not to press him. He held his hands up and took a step back. "I can see the answer to that is definitely nay."

Draven straightened from looking at his horse and pressed the palm of his hand to his thigh in an effort to pull his breeches further away from his swollen shaft. He didn't know how much longer he could stand this without being driven mad by it.

How much unsated lust could one man be subjected to before he expired from it?

And why in the name of Lucifer did he have to be the experiment to see just how much one man could take?

All Draven had wanted was peace. He'd have never gone to London at Henry's bequest if he'd had any idea of the outcome, and right then the thought of handing himself back over to the king for execution seemed appealing.

He glanced to Simon, who was looking into the trees where Emily and her maid had vanished.

"She wants to marry me," Draven muttered to his brother.

Simon locked gazes with him. "She said as much to me."

"Did she say *why*?"

He shrugged. "For some unfathomable reason, she likes you."

"Don't be ridiculous." Draven smirked. "No one *likes* me. She wants me dead is what she wants."

"If I believed that for one minute, I'd never . . ." Simon's voice trailed off.

"You'd never what?" he asked suspiciously.

Simon paused as if considering his words, then finished hastily, "I'd never tolerate it."

Draven pulled his dagger from his belt and handed it hilt first to Simon. "Here, take this."

Simon frowned. "Why?"

"Take it and drive it straight through my heart before I perish in flames."

Simon laughed and sheathed it back in Draven's belt. "You know what they say. Lust cannot keep. Something must be done about it."

"Are you so desperate for my lands that you would have Henry kill me for it?"

"Hardly," he said, offended. "Marry the girl and take her at will."

Draven sighed. "Think you for one moment her father would tolerate me as his son-in-law?"

"He'd have no choice if you went to Henry."

For the first time in his life, Draven allowed the thought of matrimony to tempt him. "You would condemn her to life with me?"

" 'Twould certainly be better than life spent with her father. You at least would allow her a moment or two of fun, I'd wager."

"Perhaps, but at least with her father she would live out her life. With me there would be nothing save an early grave."

"Draven, you are not—"

"Don't say it, Simon, for I know the truth. You see in me what you wish to, but I know what lies within me. I feel it as a constant companion."

Simon clapped him on the back. "You worry too much, brother. You need to learn to relax and just enjoy life. Take one moment and live." Simon nodded toward the trees.

Draven turned his head to see Emily rejoining them.

"You could learn much from the lady," Simon said in a low tone. "She knows how to make the most of what God has given us."

Draven considered his words.

Simon made it all sound so simple, but the consequences were too high. If he listened to his brother and married, there was much more than just a slim chance he would one day kill her.

So far he had maintained his temper around her, but she held no fear of him, and he cringed at the thought of her one day pushing him past his limit.

It would take only one occurrence . . .

Nay, 'twas a chance he'd never take. One he *refused* to take.

Emily didn't say a word as she neared the men. Draven looked away.

She exchanged a frustrated look with Simon before speaking to Draven. "Can we enjoy food now, or do you plan to ride for the rest of the day?"

Draven ran his hand through his hair, but still refused to meet her gaze. "My horse needs more rest. Take your time."

She threw her hands up at Simon, then impulsively made a gesture as if she were going to choke Draven.

Just as she reached for his neck, Draven turned to see her gesture.

Emily drew her arms back to her shoulders and smiled.

"What were you doing?" Draven asked suspiciously.

She smiled sweetly. "Nothing."

He looked to Simon. "What was she doing?"

"Nothing," he said, giving her a wink.

Draven gave a weary sigh. "I don't have time for this," he muttered, then made his way toward his men.

"He is a stubborn man," Emily said to Simon once they were alone.

"To the very core of his soul."

"What am I to do?"

"Keep at it. Sooner or later he's bound to give in and admit his feelings."

Emily watched as Draven spoke to his knights. He seemed completely oblivious to her presence. "What if he has no feelings for me?"

Simon laughed. "I assure you, if that were true, he wouldn't avoid you so."

"Are you certain?"

"Quite."

Emily considered his words for a moment as well as what she should do next. "Do you think I'm being too bold in seeking him out so often?"

"Is boldness part of your nature?"

"Unfortunately, aye."

"Then I would say follow your inclinations. So long as milady is being true to herself, there is nothing to fear."

She found that hard to believe. "Nothing to fear from a man who is feared by more than half of Christendom. Simon, are you certain?"

He nodded. "Trust me, milady, you'll know when you've pushed him too far."

"Very well, then," she said with an almost reluctant sigh. "Please, excuse me while I go make more nuisance of myself."

Chapter 12

Draven actually groaned as she came near him, and for an instant Emily felt contrite.

But only for an instant.

"Can you not give me a moment to myself?" he asked as he placed a pail of water on the ground for his horse.

She paused by his side. "Offhand, I would say you've had too much time to yourself."

He straightened to look her in the eye. "Did it never occur to you that I might prefer it that way?"

"It occurs to me that you might not know what you prefer since I doubt you've ever spent much time around anyone save yourself. If you have nothing to compare solitude to, how do you know you prefer it?"

"I've never had my arm cut off either, milady," he said as he stroked his horse's neck. "But I'm relatively certain I would prefer not to lose it. Some things one just knows."

Emily nodded in agreement. "Point well taken, but I must confess to being greatly offended by your words since you liken my presence to mutilation. I never realized before I was so distressing. And all this time, I mistakenly thought I was a rather likable person."

And then she saw it. It was subtle really, just a touch of softening around his lips and eyes. A new sparkle in the icy depths of his gaze.

"Aha!" she said. "So, 'tis possible to amuse you."

His features hardened once more. "I am far from amused."

She ignored him. "You know, I think it wise that you not smile."

"And why is that?"

"As handsome as you are, you'd probably make a woman faint dead away if you ever smiled at her."

He rolled his eyes at her. "You're being ridiculous."

"Nay, I'm quite serious," she said, taking a step nearer to him until they stood so close she could actually feel his breath fall against her cheek. If she leaned forward even a fraction of an inch they would touch.

Her entire body trembled at his closeness as she remembered all too easily the feel of his hands on her body. The taste of his powerful lips.

She half expected him to pull away, but instead he stood perfectly still as if waiting for something.

Emily smiled at him as her heart raced. "I

remember my mother telling me a story of when she was a young girl at court. There was a count who came from the continent, and she said that six courtiers fainted as soon as they laid eyes upon him. I should think you would be every bit as devastating to a woman's senses. Indeed, you have very white teeth, not blackened as so many lords I've met. Your shoulders are broad, your arms strong, and your features far more than just pleasing. Why, one could actually call you pretty. If one dared."

His face stoic, he just stared at her. "You do nothing more than flatter me."

"I speak honestly."

"Then tell me *honestly* what it is you hope to accomplish with your flattery?"

"*That* I've already answered, and you know it well enough." Emily dipped her gaze to his lips, remembering well the way they had felt against her own. And how much better they felt against other parts of her.

"Milady—"

She placed a finger against his lips to silence his words. "There is something I would ask of you," she said, her heart pounding. "I know I have made a nuisance of myself to you, and for that I do apologize. When I set my mind to something, I am never easily swayed."

She paused and took a deep breath for courage as she dropped her hand from his mouth to his chest. "I want an honest answer from you. Do you find me attractive or likable at all?"

Draven knew this was the one moment where he

could send her packing with one word. 'Twas the chance he'd wanted, and yet as he stared into those vibrant green eyes and saw her fear of his rejection, he couldn't bring the lie to his lips.

His words failing him, he answered her the only way he knew how—with his body.

Encircling her with his arms, he pulled her against him and claimed her lips with his own. Her arms came around his shoulders, clutching him closer as he explored the nectar of her mouth. God help him, but she was his ambrosia and his Achilles' heel.

Emily sighed in contentment at his answer as she ran her hands through the sable thickness of his hair.

He wanted her. He could have walked away or hurt her feelings, but he hadn't. Whether he admitted it or not, he was a good man.

And she wanted him.

With a curse, he pulled away. "I refuse to do this," he snarled, taking a step back from her.

"Draven—"

"Leave me," he shouted at her. "I don't want you near me. Can you not understand that I have given my oath and I will abide by it?"

"Then marry me." The words shocked her as much as they did him.

He stared at her. "I cannot."

"Why?" she asked, her tone demanding. "People do it every day."

"There are many things people do every day that I have no wish to do. Now leave me in peace and tempt me no more."

Emily started to press him, but something inside

told her not to. "Very well, milord. I will trouble you no longer. At least not for the moment. But I do wish for you to think the matter over carefully."

She started away from him, then stopped and turned back. "By the way . . ." Emily waited until he looked at her. "I will get a laugh from you yet."

Something strange fell over his face, as if he saw some nightmare playing before his eyes. "There is no laughter inside me," he whispered. "It died long ago."

Emily frowned. "Don't be silly. Everyone has laughter inside him."

"I don't," he said, then made his way to his horse.

Emily watched after him, her thoughts swirling. Unwittingly, he had just dropped another gauntlet for her to pick up. And pick it up she would.

"I will make you laugh, milord," she said to herself. "And when I do, I will know you belong to me."

Hours later, they stopped for the night next to a pleasant stream. While the men set up camp, she and Alys took a few minutes in private to freshen themselves by the pond.

When they returned to camp, their tents had been raised. Emily paused to watch Draven as he swung a heavy mallet to drive the tent stakes deep into the ground. His white linen tunic stretched taut over his muscles as he lifted the mallet above his head and brought it down.

Her blood raced at the sight. Never had she seen a man so well formed, so strong. Indeed, it stole her breath to watch him.

And when he was finished, a fine sheen of sweat covered him. He said something to one of his knights, before draping his saddlebags over his shoulder and heading for the pond.

He was going to bathe, she thought with a start.

And all she had to do . . .

Oh, nay, her mind snapped, you cannot do that!

Emily bit her lip. Aye, she could. Who would know if she spied upon him?

"Go on."

She jumped at Alys's voice in her ear. "Excuse me?" she asked.

Alys gave her an impish smile. "I know what you're thinking, milady. I saw your gaze follow His Lordship to the woods, and I say go on and see him for yourself."

"But Alys—"

"But Alys nothing. A lady ought to have a chance to inspect the goods before she commits herself to the deed."

Heat flooded Emily's cheeks. Her maid could be so very crude at times, and yet . . .

It was rather tempting.

Alys nudged her. "Go on. I shall whistle if anyone enters the woods behind you."

"And if he catches me?"

"Say you lost your way. That is *if* he is of a mind to question you. Who knows, he might welcome your presence."

Emily glanced about the camp in indecision. Everyone was there, including Simon, who sat with two of the knights drinking ale from a skin.

Did she dare?

"If you'd like, I'll go with you."

Emily blinked at her maid. "You'll what?"

Alys gave her an evil grin. "Be most happy to go along with you, if the truth were known."

Emily didn't know what to say to that, until Alys spoke again, "Surely milady isn't *afraid* to?"

"Don't be ridiculous. I'm not a child, Alys, and you can't goad me into this by calling me craven."

"I would never do such," Alys said innocently, but the look on her face belied her words.

Alys trailed her gaze down to the bucket next to Emily's feet.

"Oh look," Alys exclaimed dramatically. "I'm all out of water. How absolutely horrible. Why, I believe I needs go fetch more." Alys scooped up the bucket and sauntered toward the trees. "Would milady care to join me?"

"You are incorrigible!"

Emily had a bad feeling about this, but by the look of her maid she knew Alys was not to be swayed.

"Hand me the bucket and I—"

"Oh nay, milady," Alys said, blinking her eyes in an exaggerated manner. "I could never allow *you* to fetch water. What would His Lordship say?"

"Alys!"

Her manner instantly changed to her normal demeanor. "Now you've got my curiosity up, milady. I have to go with you, but I'll only stay a minute." Her face turned to pleading. "Just a quick glance?"

"We'll both take one quick glance, then come straight back."

"Both of us?"

"Both," Emily repeated, then taking a breath for courage, she joined Alys, and the two of them made their way carefully through the trees.

It didn't take long to find Draven. He'd already shed his clothes and was waist-deep in the water. Emily's face flamed as she and Alys squatted behind a large bush to watch him unobserved.

"Lord's toes, lady," Alys breathed. "But I've never seen the like."

Neither had she. Emily's throat was parched as she saw the deep, rippling muscles of his back. Tawny skin glistened with water, and every part of him was well muscled and strong. His broad shoulders tapered to a narrow waist.

And around his neck, he wore a small charm on a leather cord.

Water trailed over his flesh, pooling in the small hairs of his chest. Even from this distance, she could tell how solid his chest was, and too easily she remembered the feel of being held close to that rock-hard body. The feel of his lips and hands on her flesh.

She bit her lip at the memory and wished she had the audacity to walk the short distance that separated them.

Draven bent down to wet his hair, giving her a peek of perfect tawny buttocks and a rear so well formed that it jolted her with forceful lust.

Emily's entire body throbbed as she watched him reach up and lather his hair. His strong fingers stroked the sable locks, and the sight of his rippling, wet arms did the strangest things to her.

"I could do me laundry on that stomach," Alys breathed. Then she nudged Emily with her elbow. "But you know what's even better than laundry to rub on a man's stomach?"

Before Emily could answer, she heard something rustling in the trees behind Alys.

Her eyes widened. "I think we've been caught," Emily whispered, indicating the direction of the sound with a tilt of her head.

Alys turned around to look at the same moment a wild boar broke through the hedge.

For an instant Emily couldn't move.

Then Alys gave an ear-shattering scream.

Draven turned at the loud shrieks, only to see two women bolting into the stream and toward him. He barely had time to brace himself before they ran him over and knocked him down.

He came up from the water, sputtering, to find Emily and her maid jumping up and down, screaming at him, and gesturing wildly toward the bank.

"A boar, a boar, a boar!" the maid repeated.

"Quiet!" he demanded in a fierce, low tone. "And for the sake of your lives, stop moving."

To his amazement, they instantly obeyed. Draven took a cautious step forward to place himself between the women and the wild pig.

He looked to where his sword lay useless a few feet from the panting beast. It pawed at the ground and eyed them fiercely.

"It's going to charge us," Emily said, her voice high-pitched.

"If you remain perfectly still it won't charge," he told her.

"I'm not moving," Emily whispered. "I will stay here until Gabriel sounds his golden horn."

"What are we to do, milord?" the maid asked.

Personally, Draven wanted his clothes. Especially since Emily had him by his left arm in a grip so tight his hand was starting to tingle from lack of blood flow. He started to shrug her hold away, but didn't dare lest the movement entice the boar or, worse, make Emily panic and run.

"Can we outrun it?" Emily asked.

Draven didn't take his eyes from the boar. " 'Tis not so much outrunning the boar, milady, as it is outrunning your maid and myself."

"*Now* you find humor?" Her voice was aghast.

Moving his arm as slowly as possible, he shrugged off her grip. " 'Tis not humor. Just a practical fact."

Slowly, carefully, he waded a little closer to his sword.

The boar snorted and shook its head.

Draven froze.

Emily swallowed in fear as she watched him near the beast. How could he remain so calm while her heart pounded so fiercely she half expected it to leap from her chest?

"Emily?" Simon called through the trees.

She held her breath at Simon's shout.

The boar turned at the sound.

"Simon, fetch a crossbow," Draven shouted.

The boar looked back at Draven and moved two

steps nearer. Draven didn't budge as he stared the animal dead in the eye.

Emily swallowed the lump in her throat.

"A crossbow? Why?" Simon asked as he came through the trees.

The boar snorted once, stamped its foot, then charged at Simon.

With a foul curse, Simon literally jumped up a tree. Draven ran for his sword and seized it while Simon pulled himself up and out of the reach of the boar's pitching tusks.

"Keep it distracted," Draven ordered.

"Oh, aye," Simon growled as he tucked his legs up beneath him. "Keep it distracted, he says. Kill the damned beast, would you?"

As Draven inched near it, the boar turned to face him. Draven stopped moving.

Time seemed suspended as Emily waited for the boar to charge Draven's naked form. Even though he held his sword, she knew not even he was a match for the beast. Worse, once a wild boar charged, it wouldn't stop until it was fully dead.

And the more it was wounded, the more damage it would do to the person who had wounded it.

Terrified, she knew she had to do something to help him.

"Here, piggy-piggy," Emily called before she could stop herself.

"Milady!" Alys screamed.

Ignoring her, Emily splashed at the water. "Here, piggy-piggy."

The boar looked at her.

Her chest tight, Emily trusted that somehow, some way Draven would keep her safe as she continued to entice the boar away from him.

The boar came at her and Draven charged at it. The boar spun about in confusion as Draven raised his sword. As if realizing death was imminent, the boar squealed in terror, then bolted back into the forest.

Relief swept through her so quickly, her legs buckled. Emily knelt in the water, trembling and laughing hysterically.

The next thing she knew, Draven was by her side, helping her to her feet.

"Are you all right?" he asked.

She nodded, leaning on him for support. "I am merely thankful, milord, that even wild beasts are afraid of you."

She heard Simon's laughter as he descended his tree, and it was only then she realized Draven had taken a moment to pull on his breeches.

"What were you doing here?" Draven asked her, his tone sharp.

Heat crept over her face. She didn't dare tell him the truth.

"Water," Alys said before Emily could speak. "We came to fetch water for the camp, milord. Our bucket is beyond that bush where we dropped it."

Draven let out a loud breath as he released her. "The two of you should be more careful."

Then he looked at his brother. "And you . . . You were supposed to be watching them."

"Why do you think I came when I did? I heard them scream."

Draven glared at him. "Did you not think to fetch a weapon before you came in search of them?" He shook his head. "By my troth, Simon, some things a man should do without thought, and fetching a crossbow when women are screaming should be one of them."

Simon looked sheepish. "Well, I shall try and keep that in mind the next time a boar attacks you."

Emily exchanged a timid look with Alys as Draven went to fetch their bucket. He lingered over the spot, and when he didn't come right back, Emily moved to join him.

"Is something amiss, milord?" she asked.

Draven picked up the bucket and gave her a suspicious look. "You came to fetch water?"

"Aye."

"Then why were the two of you kneeling here so long that you made a deep indentation in the grass?"

She was caught!

"I . . . um . . ." She tried to think up a reasonable lie, but nothing would come to her mind.

"Well, you see . . . We . . ."

Oh, why couldn't she think up *something*?

"You what?" Draven asked.

A devilish light burned in his eyes as he watched her closely. Oh, he was enjoying her discomfort. Too much.

Lifting her chin, she decided to rob him of his torment. "Very well, we came to see you bathe, if you must know the truth of it."

He arched a brow at her. "I suppose I should be flattered."

Unable to meet his gaze any longer, she dropped her eyes to the necklace about his neck. It was a single golden rose blossom suspended on a leather cord that rested just between his hard, well-sculpted pectorals. But what caught her notice most was the vein beneath the leather that beat in time to his heart.

Draven felt her breath fall against his naked chest. It raised chills the length of his body.

He waited for her to speak, but she seemed entranced by his heraldic emblem that Queen Eleanor had given him when he won his first tournament.

"Have words finally failed you?" he asked.

Before she could answer, Simon and her maid joined them.

Simon tossed his tunic to him. "We should set up a watch to keep an eye out for that boar."

"Aye. As well as other things that might come upon a man when he least expects it."

That got her to look at him again. Her cheeks pink, she narrowed her dark green eyes on him.

An overwhelming urge to kiss her seized him, and if they were alone, he doubted he would have had the strength to deny it. Instead, he focused his attention on Simon and not her moistened lips.

So, she had come to spy upon him.

In truth, he *was* flattered, and most dreadfully aroused by the knowledge. What he truly wanted to know was, had she liked what she'd seen?

Never before had he cared what a woman thought of him. But for some reason, he wanted her to desire him as much as he desired her.

Are you mad?

Aye, he must be. There was no other explanation. The last thing he needed was for her to want him any more than she already did.

With that thought in mind, he grabbed his tunic, handed her the bucket, and quickly dressed himself.

"We'd best get back to camp before the boar returns," Draven said, then led the way.

Emily followed behind Draven with Simon by her side. As they walked back to camp, it dawned on her what she'd done while they faced the boar.

Without a moment's hesitation, she had trusted Draven with her life. Never before had she done such a thing. She'd always been adventurous, but never to the point of such foolishness as she had shown with the boar.

But in her heart she had known he wouldn't allow her to be harmed. And he had proved her right.

"Thank you, Lord Draven," she said.

He looked back at her over his shoulder. "For what?"

"For saving me."

His look softened. "I should say the same for you. Had you not distracted the beast, I'm sure I'd be tending a severe wound right now."

"Oh, Draven," Simon said in a falsetto as he clasped his hands together and held them to his shoulder. He gave Draven a worshipful look. "You're my hero too!"

Simon sniffed as if he were holding back tears and threw his arms about Draven's shoulders. "If not for you, that mean old boar would have eaten me alive."

Draven pushed Simon away from him. "Get off me, you nimble-pated gelding."

"But Draven," Simon said again in his falsetto, "You're my hero. Give me a kiss."

Draven ducked Simon's embrace and stepped behind Emily. "What are you? Moonstruck?"

"Fine then," Simon snapped. "Here, Emily, you kiss him for me."

And before either one knew what Simon was about, she found herself tossed into Draven's arms.

Their bodies collided.

Draven's arms encircled her, and for a moment she couldn't breathe as she stared up into those startled blue eyes. Heat sizzled between them, skipping along both their bodies. Stealing their breath and setting fire to their blood.

When Draven made no move to kiss her, Simon tsked.

"Fine then," Simon said, pulling her out of Draven's embrace and into his own. "Let me show you how a kiss is given."

Simon dipped his lips to hers, but before he could make contact, Draven caught his chin in one hand and pulled his face away from hers. "If your lips so much as pucker near hers, I *will* geld you, brother."

Simon gave her a wink. "Whatever you say, brother dearest. Whatever you say."

Simon let go of her and Draven let go of him.

"But I say this," Simon said as he straightened his tunic with a tug. "If such a tender maid had

saved my life, I think I could find a better way to
thank her than with mere words."

"I'm sure you could."

Simon ignored him and took Alys by the arm.
"Hey, Maid Alys, 'twould appear you forgot to get
your water. What say you that I accompany you
back to the pond lest the boar return?"

"I would thank you most kindly for your
chivalry, milord."

"Another thank-you with words." Simon sighed.
"Alas, what am I to do?"

Alys took the bucket from Emily, and by the glint
in her maid's eye, Emily had a good idea that Alys
would be thanking Simon with more than mere
words.

Blushing at the thought of what her maid was
about, Emily clasped her hands before her and
faced Draven.

"You might want to fetch your maid," Draven
warned her as Alys and Simon disappeared from
their sight. "I have a feeling my brother is after
more than just a mere drink."

"And I have a feeling Alys is as well."

An awkward silence fell between them as they
started back to camp.

"Oh, milord, what a large, hot lance you have!"

Emily stumbled at Alys's words.

Draven paused. "I'd best go—"

"Nay," she said, taking his arm. "Leave them to
their amusement."

He looked askance at her. "There aren't many
ladies who would be so understanding of their
maid's behavior."

"I should be mortified, I know. But Alys is a good friend to me, and though she has her faults, she has a good and generous heart."

"And is that all that matters to you?"

"Aye," she said. "People will always make mistakes, but in the end 'tis their heart that matters most."

"And if they have no heart?"

Emily hesitated at the strange note in his voice. "Everyone has a heart."

He shook his head. "Not everyone."

Emily pulled him to a stop. "Aye, Draven. Everyone. Do you know what I see when I look at you?"

Draven stared at her, wary of what she might say next. "I have no heart," he confessed. "It was ripped out long ago."

She placed her hand to his chest. Draven looked down. Her hand appeared so small and frail against his tunic as she touched him.

"For a man with no heart, you have a strong pounding in your chest."

"That is but an organ."

"Perhaps," she said, meeting his gaze, "but I know the truth of you."

"And that is?"

Emily reveled in the heat of his skin that traveled up her arm and to her body. How she wished she could make him see himself through her eyes. For just one moment.

He had been hurt. She knew it. And though he might be the most feared warrior in Christendom, she sensed there was still a part of him that was vulnerable. A part of himself he had closed off from the world and if she could ever reach it, then she would hold the key to the heart he claimed he lacked.

"One day, Draven," she whispered. "One day you will see the truth as I see it. You will come to know yourself."

His jaw flexed. "My only hope is that one day *you* don't come to know the truth of me."

And with those words, he stepped back from her touch and led her the rest of the way to the camp.

Emily tried several times to speak more with him, but he would have none of it.

Just before dusk, Alys and Simon returned.

Alys sauntered up to her with glowing eyes and a rosy hue about her face. She leaned over Emily, who sat before the fire, and whispered, "All I have to say, milady, is if Lord Draven is half as talented as his brother, you are in for one marvelous ride."

"Alys," Emily chided.

Her maid smiled. "Just you wait. You have no idea how—" Alys broke off as one of the knights walked by.

When they were alone again, Alys wrinkled her nose. "Just you wait," she whispered, then went to help serve dinner.

While they ate, the knights in the company exchanged tales of adventure, but Emily didn't listen. They spoke of the same timeless tales she had heard countless times.

Besides, she had other matters to attend. Such as making Draven laugh.

She'd spent the entire time thinking up ways to go about it. Chewing her roasted hare, she listened as Draven and Simon talked about the king's policies with the French and Scots. No wonder the man never laughed. Who could laugh over something so dry and boring as politics?

What Draven needed was a jest. Aye, that might bring a sparkle to his eyes.

She waited until they had finished their discussion, then leaned forward.

"Milord?" she asked Draven. "Know you how many Byzantines it takes to light a fire?"

His look hovered between boredom and skepticism as he reached for his goblet. "I cannot imagine."

"Two," she said simply. "One to start the fire and one to confuse the issue."

Simon burst out laughing, but Draven merely glanced sideways at her.

Failure.

Emily drummed her fingers as she thought of another. "Very well," she began again. "How many Norsemen does it take to light a fire?"

"Three?" he asked glibly.

"Nay, why bother with a fire when there's a monastery over the next hill."

Several knights joined Simon's laughter that time. But still Draven showed no sign of mirth. If anything it only served to make him more stoic.

"Come now, Draven," Simon said, "that was funny."

Draven said nothing as he took a draught of wine.

"Do you have another one, milady?" one of the other knights asked.

"Aye," she said, turning to look at him. "How many Romans to start a fire?"

Draven tried to block her voice out of his mind, but for some reason he couldn't. Indeed, he was attuned to everything about her. The way the breeze caressed the blond tendrils of her hair. The way the firelight played in the crevices of her face and added a rich sparkle to her eyes.

He knew what she was about. Still, he couldn't keep himself from being amused by her.

"I have no idea how many Romans it takes to start a fire," his knight Nicholas said.

"One thousand and one," she announced.

Draven cocked a brow at her answer. "One thousand and one?" he asked in spite of his intention to ignore her.

"Aye. It requires the emperor to order that the fire be set, nine hundred and ninety-nine Roman governors to pass down the order, and one slave to light it."

The rest of his company enjoyed it, and if he dared admit it, he found it humorous too. Had he been the type of man who laughed, he would join his men and brother, but too many years had passed.

He couldn't even remember how to laugh anymore.

Emily sighed and looked to Simon. "Your brother is a hard man."

Draven choked on his wine.

She frowned. "Milord, are you all right?" she asked, pounding her hand on his back.

"Fine," Draven said, then he shrugged off her touch. "Your choice of words just caught me off-guard."

Once more Simon burst into laughter.

"What?" she asked.

Simon shook his head. "I'll leave it to my brother to explain to you just how *hard* a man he is."

"Simon," he warned.

"Don't growl at me when you instigated it."

Confused, Emily looked back and forth between them until Draven got up and left.

Emily watched as Draven made his way to the outskirts of the camp.

"Did I say something wrong?" she asked Simon.

" 'Twas merely your choice of words."

She still didn't understand, and by the look on Simon's face she didn't think he would elaborate.

But then he didn't have to. Alys came up behind her and whispered the answer in her ear.

Heat exploded across her face as she refused to look at Simon or anyone else for that matter. Her embarrassment was just too great.

They finished eating in silence, and Draven took up a post just beyond the reach of the firelight.

The camp retired, and Emily and Alys went to their beds to sleep.

Hours later, Emily lay awake trying her best to sleep. She couldn't.

Alys lay on the cot beside her, snoring mightily. Emily threw back the covers and reached for her saddlebags. Giving up on sleep, she dug out the book Christina had given her, and took it outside the tent to where the fire burned low.

No one was about. She didn't even see Draven at his post.

Stifling a yawn, she opened the book, then immediately slammed it shut.

Heat scalded her face at what she'd seen. Surely she had been mistaken! Surely she hadn't seen what it was she thought she'd seen . . .

Timidly, Emily cracked open the book, and her eyes widened as she viewed pictures of men and women doing unspeakable things to one another.

Her face flamed as she opened the book a little wider.

"No wonder you bid me keep it for a private moment," she whispered, looking about hurriedly to make sure no one could see her. Luckily the camp was still vacant.

Embarrassed and amazed at Christina's gift, Emily saw the piece of parchment that had been tucked into the front of the book.

She pulled it out, saw it addressed to her, then read it.

Dearest Emily,

I know how curious you are about the matters of men and women. This is the book my mother gave me the night before my wedding. It is shocking, but you'll find the book very enlightening and helpful. And judging by the look of Lord Draven, I am quite certain you will have much more use of this than I have with Orrick.

My best advice, study position number seventy-three. That seems to be Orrick's favorite.

Love always,
Christina

Emily chewed the tip of her finger as she considered Christina's note. Dear heaven but her father would fall over dead if he ever knew she possessed such a thing!

She should cast it into the fire and be done with it. That's what a decent lady would do.

Too bad she was more brazen than that. For in the end, her curiosity rose high and she found herself looking to make sure no one was up and then opening the book again.

She tilted the book toward the fire and tried to study the way the man and woman were entwined in position seventy-three. With his hands cupping the woman's breasts, the man lay on his side, behind the woman, and appeared to be thrusting—

"What's that?"

Emily gasped at the sound of Draven's voice and slammed the book shut. She looked up to see him standing above her.

Lord in heaven! She was caught.

Could she be any more mortified?

" 'Tis nothing," she said quickly.

"Is that what Christina gave you as we left?"

She nodded and tucked the book up under her arm.

"May I see it?" he asked, reaching for it.

Her eyes flew wide at the very thought of him seeing what she had just seen. Whatever would he think of her if he did?

In truth, she didn't want to know or find out.

"Oh, nay!" Emily gasped, then moved it out of his reach.

He frowned at her. "What is the matter with you?"

"Nothing," she said, rising to her feet. "Absolutely nothing."

"Then let me—"

"Nay, nay. I needs go back to bed."

And before she could move, he grabbed the book from her hands and opened it wide.

Draven felt the breath leave his body as he stared aghast at the pictures of nude couples, and in some cases more than two were involved, in all manner of sexual positions.

He hadn't seen such a book in years. 'Twas the type of thing knights passed around on campaigns and bragged about doing with ladies of questionable virtue.

He'd never thought to see one in the possession of a well-born lady. And a maiden at that!

Closing his mouth, which had fallen open, he looked to Emily to see her face fully flushed as she gazed at the fire.

He didn't know what to say.

What *did* one say to a lady after this?

Slowly, he closed the book and handed it back to her.

Emily didn't say a word as she took it from him. She could feel his incredulous stare on her, and at the moment she wished she could jump into a great, big hole to escape having to face him after this.

Embarrassed and ashamed, Emily placed her forehead against the worn leather cover of the book. Could anything be worse? She could kill Christina for this! What had the woman been thinking?

If she lived to be two thousand years old she would never forget the look of shock on his face.

What must he think of her?

"Draven, I didn't know what the book . . ."

Nay, that wasn't what she should have said, she realized as he looked at her with an arched brow.

"I am a maiden, milord," she said even though the words were hard on her lips. "I don't know what possessed Christina to give me such a—"

He shook his head. "Speak no more of it. We shall forget the matter."

Emily drew a deep breath, grateful for his mercy.

"Don't you think you should go to bed now?" he asked, his voice strained.

"I can't sleep and I would rather stay here with you than toss in my bed, listening to Alys snore."

"Why?"

Emily tilted her head to look at the confusion on his face. "Is it that hard to believe someone could desire your company?"

"Aye," he said simply. "No one ever has before. What makes you so different?"

Emily set the book aside and rose to her feet to face him. "Perhaps because I am the only person you've ever had to be around. I would think your habit of being alone has pushed away even the most determined."

"But not you."

She smiled. "Not me. I am far more stubborn than most."

"I would concur."

Emily ached to touch him, but something in his

stance warned her not to. Instead, she stared into the dark forest.

Draven listened to the sound of her breathing. She was so close to him, yet not touching, and still he could feel her presence as a physical touch.

"There was a man," she said, breaking the silence, "who went to confession carrying a turkey."

Draven sighed wearily at yet another attempt to make him laugh.

Would she ever admit defeat?

"A turkey?" he asked, wondering why he bothered to encourage her and yet unable to stop himself.

"Aye. He begged the priest, 'Forgive me, Father, for I have sinned. I just stole this turkey to feed my starving children. Would you please take it from me so that I can be forgiven by Our Lord?'

" 'Certainly not,' said the priest. 'You must return it to the one you stole it from.'

" 'But Father, I tried and he refused, what should I do?'

"The priest replied, 'If what you say is true, then it is God's will you have the turkey. Go in peace.'

"The man thanked the Father, then hurried home.

"After the priest finished the rest of his confessions, he returned to his residence. When he walked into his pantry, he realized someone had stolen his turkey."

Without smiling or laughing, Draven looked at her. "And just how many jests does milady know?"

She beamed. "Quite a few, actually. My father loves jesters, and we entertain many in our hall."

His head ached at the thought of how many such tales she would subject him to. "Then I am to endure such for the rest of the year?"

"Unless you make it easy on yourself and laugh now."

That almost succeeded in making him smile, but he caught himself. "You should be aware that, like you, I never admit defeat."

She leaned toward him until the tip of her nose almost touched his own. "There's always a first time."

Pulling back ever so slightly, she spoke. "A daughter went to her father for advice. 'Tell me, Father, who should I marry, Harry or Stephen?'

" 'Stephen,' her father answered.

" 'Why?' she asked.

" 'Because I have been borrowing money from Stephen for the last six months and still he comes to see you.' "

Draven focused his stare back at the dark trees. "Not as good as the Norsemen."

She arched a brow. "So you did like one?"

"If I said aye, would you go back to bed?"

"If I could sleep, I would be delighted to return to my cot, but since I can't, I might as well stay out here and annoy the one who prevents me from sleeping."

Draven wasn't sure he liked the new venue their conversation was taking, "And how is it I prevent you from sleeping?"

"You haunt my dreams."

Nay, he didn't like this at all. "I don't want to hear this."

She reached out and touched his hand. "Then can you at least forget what I said about husband, and just treat me as a friend?"

Her touch was so very warm against his skin. Her long fingers pale against his tan. How could a hand so fragile shake him to his very core?

"I have no friends," he whispered, allowing her for some unknown reason to lace her fingers with his own.

"Not even Henry?"

"I am his vassal and I serve him as such. We are cordial, but hardly friends."

She stroked the backs of his knuckles with her fingers, sending waves of heat to his groin. "I never thought I'd ever meet someone even lonelier than I."

Draven cleared his throat. "I never said I was lonely."

"Aren't you?"

He didn't answer. He couldn't deny the truth.

Aye, he was lonely. Had always been so.

"Do you know what a friend is, milord?"

"An enemy in disguise."

Her jaw dropped and her hand froze its torturous assault on his own. "Do you believe that?"

He pulled his hand away. "I know it for fact. Without friendship, there can be no betrayal. Indeed, you never have heard someone say, 'He betrayed his enemy.' "

"And so you would trust no one?"

"I trust in the fact that sooner or later everyone betrays."

She shook her head. "Does that include you as well, milord? When you say everyone betrays, does this mean that in your heart you would betray the king you serve so zealously?"

"Haven't I?"

She frowned. "How do you mean?"

"I swore to him I would not touch you and yet twice now I have kissed you, not to mention what we did last night. Seems to me I have betrayed him, for he trusts me to keep my word. And here you are in the moonlight by my side attempting to seduce me yet again."

She stiffened. "Then forgive me for seducing you, milord, I had thought you shared my feelings. How silly of me. I think I shall go back to bed now and leave you to stew in your solitude."

Draven watched as she retrieved her book, then headed back to her tent.

How he wished he could just "stew in his solitude," as she so eloquently put it, but in truth the only thing he was stewing in was red-hot lust.

All these years, he'd lived his life in a comfortable cocoon of muted feelings. Nothing made him angry, nothing made him sad, and likewise nothing made him happy.

Not until the day he'd seen her with that damnable chicken. Now that had been funny.

He felt the edges of his lips twitch as he saw her in his mind holding the chicken to the man's lips.

Draven sobered.

"Get out of my head," he snarled, balling up his fist and pressing it against his forehead.

No wonder monks castrated themselves rather than be tempted by women. At present castration was looking like a very viable option.

Unbidden, his gaze drifted to her tent. He saw Emily's shadow illuminated from inside her tent as she removed her kirtle, and every curve of her body showed through the canvas.

His groin leaped to life, demanding he take her now while everyone slept.

Hissing, he shifted himself.

Aye, castration was a very viable option indeed.

Chapter 13

Emily rode the rest of the way to Ravenswood with Simon. Even though she tried repeatedly to engage Draven in conversation, he refused. The best she could get out of him were monosyllabic responses.

The man was an unscalable mountain of silence! But little did he know that she would find a way to scale him. Literally as well as figuratively.

Indeed, after she got over the shock of her book, she had come to look upon position seventy-three with a whole new interest. What would it feel like to have such a dark, forbidding man command her in that way?

To have such a strong, untamed champion surround her, fill her with himself as he claimed her in ways no man had, while she claimed him as no woman had before.

230

The mutualness of it held great possibilities and appeal to her.

Still, she couldn't imagine the feel of him inside her, even though Alys had assured her position seventy-three would definitely hold much pleasure for both of them.

Emily stared at Draven's strong back and again saw the sleek muscles in her mind's eye. Aye, she would lay bare that tawny skin and explore its bounty with her hands and lips. He would be hers.

If she could just get him to the altar!

Her mind wandered on. What would it take to make him laugh? Her jests had failed. There must be something she could do. Something he found amusing.

And she *would* find it.

They returned to Ravenswood with the setting of the sun. Exhausted and feeling daunted, she allowed Simon to help her down.

Draven didn't wait for them. He made his way up the steps to the donjon. Emily noted the way he stiffened as he paused in the doorway.

Climbing the steps, she stopped behind him and peered over his shoulder. "Gracious," she breathed as her gaze swept the interior. "Denys has been busy!"

New tables had been made and stacked in the corners. Fresh paint stung her nose and brightened the formerly drab walls. New tapestries had been hung, and the shutters had been thrown back to show off the brightly colored windows. Fresh rushes had been laid, and a pleasant, spicy scent greeted her nose.

"Am I in the right hall?" Draven said gruffly.

Emily laughed. "I believe so."

"Denys!" Draven bellowed, walking into the foyer.

Denys came running from a side door. "Milord!" he greeted.

Emily saw the trepidation on the steward's face as Denys rubbed his hands together in a nervous gesture. "Does it meet with your satisfaction?"

Draven looked to her. "Milady?"

She nodded. " 'Tis wondrous."

Denys smiled.

"Was there any money left over from your budget?" Draven asked.

"Aye, milord," Denys said, nodding. "Quite a bit, point of fact."

"Then keep it."

Denys looked shocked. "Are you certain, milord?"

"You've earned it. Take the sennight off and rest yourself."

"Oh, thank you," Denys said gratefully, before leaving them.

Draven started for the stairs when a stern voice called out, "Not with those muddy boots on your feet, you don't!"

Emily arched a brow at the daring tone as a plump woman around the age of five and two score entered the hall from Draven's antechamber. Her dark brown hair was laced liberally with gray, and she held her spine as though she could confront an army with nothing more than her wits to brandish.

"I'll not have you muck up my floor," she said,

her voice even sharper than before. "Even if this hall be yours, it gives you no right to lay waste to our handiwork. Now off with those boots."

The look on Draven's face would have scared the devil himself. But the woman merely came to a stop before him and met his gaze with an impertinent directness.

"Who are you?" he demanded, his voice lethal and sharp.

"Beatrix. Steward Denys hired me to keep this hall, and keep it I shall."

Draven opened his mouth, then frowned. "Beatrix?"

"Aye, your mother's maid. I swatted your backside when you were just a babe, and I can do it now as well."

Emily's eyes widened at the woman's audacity.

Draven showed no reaction whatsoever. "I was told you were dead."

A tenderness for him burned in the woman's dark brown eyes, and Emily sensed a longing in the woman to reach out and touch him. "If I am, then I'm back to haunt you," she said in a much gentler tone. "Now off with those boots."

To Emily's utter amazement, he obeyed.

"Thank you, milord," Beatrix said gratefully. "Your room is waiting for you above. Denys and me moved the lady's things to the guest chambers."

"You have guest chambers?" Emily asked.

Beatrix smiled kindly. "His Lordship does now."

"My gratitude for your service, Beatrix," Draven said gently, then walked up the stairs.

Emily stared at the strange sight. Who would

have thought the most feared man in England would walk up the stairs in his stockings to please his housekeeper?

Aye, there was much goodness in Draven's heart.

Smiling, she took a step toward the stairs, but Beatrix's tsking stopped her dead in her tracks.

"That goes for you as well, milady."

Emily bit her lip, then removed her shoes.

Beatrix nodded in approval. "I'll send food up to your chambers. I'm sure you'll want to rest. Now, if you'll follow me, I'll show you to your new bower."

Emily thanked her, then followed her up the stairs.

She paused as they passed Draven's room. The door was shut tightly, and she heard no sound from within.

Reaching out, she touched the hard wood that separated them and wondered what thoughts were on his mind. He'd been so withdrawn today. Much more so than usual, even for him.

"I will claim you," she vowed beneath her breath.

She pulled her hand back from the wood, then hurried to catch Beatrix, who led her to the end of the hallway. Beatrix pushed back the door and allowed Emily to enter.

Emily's eyes widened at the cheery room. The new bed beckoned with clean sheets and fur coverlets. Another set of tapestries hung against the walls, and a thick, woven rug covered the cobbled floor.

While she removed her cloak, Beatrix started the

fire. "If milady needs anything, please let me know."

Emily stood in silence for several minutes, watching her work. "Beatrix?"

She paused and looked up at Emily over her shoulder. "Aye, milady?"

"Have you any idea what might make Lord Draven smile?"

A dark sadness crossed Beatrix's face. "There is no power on this earth that could do that."

"But surely—"

"Nay, milady. I promise you, there is nothing that could *ever* bring a smile to His Lordship's lips. Not after . . ."

Emily waited, but Beatrix turned back to the fire and added more wood.

"Not after what?" she prompted.

" 'Tis not my place to say," she said, rising to her feet and brushing her hands off on her skirt. "But were I you, milady, I would avoid him at all costs."

"And why is that?"

"Because every lady who has ever lived beneath the roof of Ravenswood was murdered here."

A chill went up her spine as horror and dread stilled her heart. "Murdered?" she whispered. "How?"

"By the hand of her lord."

Emily was aghast. "Draven's mother?"

"Killed by the hand of his sire."

The room seemed to careen around her. She couldn't imagine anything more horrendous. "And Lord Draven, where was he when it happened?"

"Lying unconscious on the floor because he dared protect her."

Her chest constricted and her stomach shrank. Emily crossed herself at the thought of such horror. Dear heaven, no wonder he was so withdrawn.

At last she understood why he never smiled. How could he? How could anyone find humor after having seen something so horrific?

And in that instant she wanted to reach him even more.

"Is that why you left?" she asked the elder woman.

"Nay, I tried to stay to look after His Lordship, but his father would have none of it. Said Lord Draven had been coddled enough by women. 'Twas time he made a man of him."

From what she had heard, Emily had a good idea of just what that had entailed. "What made you return now?"

Beatrix frowned and studied the hearth as if debating what she should say. " 'Tis not easy to answer, milady. When Denys first asked me to come, I refused. I remembered all too well what the former earl was like, and I feared his son had grown to be just like him. But then I heard Her Ladyship's voice in my head begging me to look after him."

The woman looked up and met Emily's gaze. "She would do that almost every night when I would prepare her for bed. 'Beatrix,' she would say, 'if anything should ever happen to me, please watch over my boys.' " She took a deep breath, and Emily saw the tears in her eyes. "Lady Katherine was a blessed saint. She was as kind and dear as the Madonna herself, and so for her sake, I let Denys talk me into returning."

Her own eyes tearing, Emily cleared her throat. "I'm glad you're here, Beatrix."

Beatrix nodded, then excused herself.

Emily took a seat at the dressing table as her mind came to grips with what Beatrix had told her.

"Oh Draven," she whispered, her throat tight. Her heart ached for him. He must have hated his father for it. How could he not?

And she wondered what his mother had done to warrant his father's actions.

Simon, she thought with a start. It must have been when his father learned Simon was illegitimate.

Closing her eyes, she gave rein to the tears inside her. Tears for the boy who had seen what no child should ever witness, and tears for the man he had become who now refused to love.

For over a fortnight Emily tried to find a quiet moment with Draven, but he treated her as if she were a leper with St. Vitus' dance.

She'd finally come to the realization that any attempt to be alone with him was futile. He wouldn't even take his meals in the hall with the rest of them, but rather stayed bolted in his room or didn't bother to come home at all.

She didn't know what he found to occupy himself. If Simon knew, he told her nothing.

But at least Simon provided some entertainment for her.

"Why do I bother?" she asked herself as she sat in the great hall, breaking her fast.

Several of Draven's knights were around her, but none close enough to hear. She didn't know where Simon had gone this morning, and she had allowed Alys to sleep since her maid had been up late doing something she hadn't wanted to share with Emily. And knowing Alys, Emily was probably better off not knowing those details anyway.

Picking at her bread, Emily sighed.

A shuffle in the hallway caught her attention.

Emily looked up to see one of her trunks being brought down the stairs by two servants. She rose from her seat and followed them outside, where they placed it into a waiting wagon.

"What goes here?" she asked one of the servants.

"Are you not ready?"

She jumped at Draven's thunderous voice behind her. Turning around, she saw him in the doorway.

"Where did you come from?" she asked, amazed a man so large could move without sound.

"I was leaving orders with Denys."

She frowned. "Orders?"

"Your sister's wedding is on the morrow. I had assumed you wanted to go. Indeed, your maid told me you were all packed."

Joy burst through her at his words. That was what Alys had stayed up so late doing!

"I didn't think you'd allow me to attend."

"I'm a beast, Emily, not a bastard."

She threw her arms around him and hugged him tightly. She pressed her cheek against the prickly whiskers of his face and tried not to notice the way her breath left her lungs.

"At the moment, milord, you are neither, but rather a wonderfully sweet man," she whispered in his ear.

He tensed, but didn't move away. It was a small victory, but one she gladly took.

Emily bit her lip and pulled away. "Give me a moment and I shall be right back."

"A moment or an hour?"

"One moment," she said, laughing. "I promise."

He nodded, and she rushed up to her room to retrieve her cloak.

In her room, she saw Alys looking pleased. "Are you surprised?" her maid asked.

"Why did you not tell me?"

Alys helped her fasten her cloak. "I wanted you to know 'twas His Lordship's doing and not mine. He was the one who asked the date of the wedding when we returned from Lincoln."

"That's what you were doing last night?"

Alys smiled sheepishly.

"Thank you. Now grab your cloak and let us not keep him waiting."

Draven couldn't believe his eyes when Emily appeared just a few minutes after she had left. Happiness pinkened her cheeks, and there was a lightness to her step as she drew near him.

She was truly lovely. And though he knew he had no business going to her father's, he decided her happiness was well worth whatever discomfort he felt.

If there was anything in life he respected, it was those who loved their family.

"Help her mount," he said to Simon.

Simon frowned. "You are certain?"

He nodded.

Once they were mounted, Draven led his small group out of the bailey.

They would reach her father's just after sunset.

Oh, joy, he thought morosely.

But it would make Emily happy, and for some reason that didn't bear thinking on, her happiness was more important to him than his solitude.

The last few weeks had been torturous for him. Every time he saw her, he wanted her more. Even now, all he could do was imagine how it would feel to bury his face in the hollow of her throat and taste the salty sweetness of her skin.

Night after sleepless night, he had imagined the scent of her hair on his pillow. The feel of her breasts against his chest. The sound of her pleasurable sighs in his ear as she wrapped her legs about his waist and welcomed his body with her own.

He cursed beneath his breath as every pore of his body ached for her.

And if that weren't bad enough, there was Beatrix in his home as well. His heart heavy, he tried not to think about the last time he had seen her.

He shook his head. He didn't want to remember. It was easiest to banish all memories of kindness. To banish all memories of being loved and held. And most of all, he had to banish all thoughts of Emily before she drove him insane.

* * *

Emily kicked her horse forward as the walls of her father's home came within sight. She raced her horse up the hill to the gate.

For years those gray stone walls had been a cage, but even so, delight filled her at the sight of them.

She was home!

Thomas, the partisan, was standing watch. Laughing, she waved up to him as he shouted a happy greeting to her, then ordered the portcullis lifted.

Her heart singing, she led Draven and his five men into the barbican.

Shouts of welcome greeted her and she waved to the numerous people she had known all her life. Graham the baker, Evelyn the crofter's wife, Timothy the master-of-arms, on and on it went.

The door to the keep flew open just as she reached the stone steps.

"Em!" her father bellowed, running down the steps like a child.

She slid from her horse, into his arms.

He hugged her so tightly she feared for a moment he might break her ribs. "My precious Em," he breathed in her ear. "Why are you here?"

"Lord Draven brought me for Joanne's wedding."

Her father stiffened at the mention of Draven's name. Pulling back from her, he looked about until he saw Draven approaching on his white horse.

Hatred flared in his eyes. "Has he touched you?"

She shook her head, even though she could feel heat creeping over her face.

What they had shared had been her fault and she

would not see Draven harmed for it. "He is a good man, Father."

Her father curled his lip. "He is the devil."

"Back to that, are we?" Draven asked sardonically as he reined to a stop. "I would have thought by now you'd find another insult for me."

"Bastard!"

Draven turned a bored look to Simon. "Methinks, brother, you need counsel the earl on how to effectively curse his enemy. His attempts are feeble at best."

Her father took a step toward him, but Emily held him back. "Please, Father."

Her father paused and looked down at her, then nodded.

"Come, milord," she said to Draven. "I will see you settled."

"We'll camp out—"

"Nay," she said sharply, before Draven could leave. "You came for a wedding feast and I demand you attend it."

"You demand?" Draven asked, his tone incredulous.

"Aye," she said, setting her chin stubbornly. "Now dismount and let our stableboy have your horses."

Draven exchanged a wary look with Simon. "What think you?" he asked. "Has the maid completely lost her wits now that she's returned?"

Simon shrugged. "I will do whatever you decide. In or out, it makes little matter to me."

Draven looked to Hugh. "Do I have your oath that none of my men will be harmed?"

"You would take my word?"

"For their welfare, aye."

"Then you may sleep in safety. No harm will befall you within my walls."

Draven nodded, then signaled his men to dismount.

Emily took a deep breath in relief. Perhaps she could bring peace between them after all.

Still, she noted the way Draven kept his hand firmly on the hilt of his sword as he ascended the steps with Simon one step behind, and the stiffness of her father's body.

Well, perhaps peace was hoping for a bit much. At this point, she merely hoped to keep them from bloodshed.

Emily looped her arm in her father's and led the way into the keep.

Wedding guests crowded the great hall as they milled about, sampling food and chattering together in groups while musicians played. Never before had she seen such a crowd in her father's home, nor did she see either one of her sisters among the mass of people.

She noted the reservation that immediately settled over Draven's face, the tenseness of his body. She stopped in her tracks.

Her father hated crowds as much as Draven.

"Why so many, Father?"

His features darkened. "Niles wished it," he said simply. "I had no desire to start the marriage off any worse than it already has. I want only Joanne's happiness, so I thought it best I humor my new son."

Someone she didn't know called to her father.

Niles stood beside the stranger with that familiar, almost evil snarl on his lips as he waved her father over.

What was it about that man that unnerved her so?

And why did Joanne not see it?

She noted the reluctance in her father's eyes before he excused himself. Leaning down to kiss her cheek, he whispered, "I'll return as soon as I can."

Once he left, Emily turned to Draven. "I had no idea it would be thus."

She hadn't seen Draven so reserved and harsh since the day he first arrived at Warwick with the king's men.

"We will make camp out—"

"Nay," she said, taking his arm to keep him from leaving. "There is plenty of room here for you."

A tic started in his jaw.

"Emily!"

She turned just in time for Joanne to grab her by the waist and squeeze her tight. "You came! I can't believe it."

Emily laughed and held her sister close. But as she caught a look at Joanne, her laughter died. There was a pinched quality to her features, and she had lost quite a bit of weight.

"Are you ill?" she asked, worried over Joanne's appearance.

"Nay," Joanne said, her voice shaky. "I've just been busy with wedding preparations."

Joanne was hiding something. Every fiber of Emily's body knew it.

But this wasn't the time to confront her. Instead,

Emily forced a smile to her face and introduced Draven to her sister.

" 'Tis an honor to meet you," Draven said almost charmingly. "The Lady Emily speaks of you constantly, and I can see she is quite right. You will make a most beautiful bride."

Joanne blushed. "Thank you, milord."

"Joanne!"

Her sister cringed at the shout from Niles.

"I must be going," Joanne said to them. She took Emily's hand. "I shall see you later in my room?"

Emily nodded.

Once Joanne left, she looked to Draven. "So, you *do* know how to be charming."

"I am not completely lacking in manners."

Simon snorted. "Aye, I'm told even a monkey can be trained to—"

Draven gave a sharp elbow to Simon's stomach.

Simon sucked his breath in between his teeth and rubbed his belly.

Draven stepped away from Simon and gave her a pointed stare. "What troubles you?"

Emily looked about uneasily. "Who says I am troubled?"

"I can tell."

What good would it do to hide her feelings from him? Indeed, she suddenly felt a strange urge to confide in him.

"Did my sister act strangely to you?"

"Since I have never met her before, I would say she seemed fine to me."

"She didn't seem stressed, or nervous?" she asked.

"Her wedding is on the morrow. I would imagine nervousness is typical."

"Perhaps."

And yet . . .

Emily shook her head. "I'm no doubt being foolish. Come, milords," she said, taking Draven's arm and looking back at Simon. "Let me see you fed and then taken to your chambers."

Draven allowed her to lead him across the hall, all the while damning himself for not leaving. He should never have come here. Hugh was his mortal enemy, and everything about the man screamed unwelcome at Draven.

So much for his sense of chivalry. Better he be flogged than surrounded by so many who would see him fall.

Unlike Emily, he could well understand her sister's misgivings about such a crowd. Who wanted to be a spectacle?

After they were fed, Emily left them for a time to socialize with her family.

Simon handed him a goblet of ale, and Draven drained it in one gulp as he watched Emily shriek and grab a nun in a tight hug. No doubt that would be her sister Judith, he thought.

"Draven, earl of Ravenswood?"

Draven turned at the unfamiliar voice to see a knight only a few years older than himself standing behind his chair. The man was at least a head shorter with a thick black beard and hair, and treacherous eyes. He glanced down to the gray surcoat, but couldn't place the boar emblem emblazoned in red.

Draven was immediately on guard. "Aye?" he asked the stranger.

"Niles, baron of Montclef," he said, extending his arm. "Soon to be bridegroom. I heard from my betrothed that you were here and I wanted to shake the arm of the man so well famed."

Draven shook his arm reluctantly. Those who flattered him were most often those to be watched the most closely. Especially when his back was turned.

And there was something about this man that he liked not at all, though for his life he couldn't lay finger to what it was. But something about his demeanor set him on edge.

Emily and the nun walked past.

Unconsciously, Draven's gaze trailed after them.

Montclef laughed and clapped him on the back. Draven ground his teeth at the contact. He could barely tolerate Simon doing such, but a stranger . . .

His blood boiled.

"You have good taste, milord," Montclef said with a laugh as he too watched the sway of Emily's hips with more than just a passing interest. "Tell me, is there anything better in life than bloodying your sword on a virgin field?"

Draven's lip curled in anger. 'Twas the type of comment his father would have made. And the fact that it was directed at Emily added even more rage to him.

Like a fool, Niles continued, "As spirited as Emily is, I imagine she provides quite a ride. Tell me," he said, leaning in, his voice lowered in confidence, "has she taken you in her mouth yet?"

Blind rage darkened his sight, and before he could think, Draven slammed his fist straight into Niles's face. The baron spun about and fell to the floor.

Draven leaped over the table to seize the baron and strike him again.

Suddenly, Simon was there, pulling him back from Niles.

All the music and voices stopped instantly as the people around them turned to see what had happened.

Niles rose shakily from the floor with bloodlust burning in his eyes. He wiped the blood from his lips and glared at Draven.

" 'Tis a lady you speak of," Draven said, his tone a low growl as he pushed Simon away from him. "And I caution you to better counsel your tongue when it comes to her reputation lest you find that offending member ripped out."

"I had thought we could be allies," Niles snarled. "But this night, you just made a lethal mistake."

"What goes here?" Hugh demanded, pushing his way through the onlookers. "Niles?" he asked, looking at the bleeding baron.

Hugh lifted the baron's chin and examined the damage Draven had done to the man's nose and cheek, then patted him comfortingly on the back as he summoned a servant to see to the baron's needs.

They passed words between themselves, and then Hugh turned his outraged glare to Draven. Hatred flared his nostrils. "I want you out of my hall."

Simon took a step forward. "But Draven just—"

"Come, Simon," he said flatly, cutting his brother off. "I have no wish to stay where I'm not welcome."

Draven took a step and found Emily planted in front of him, hands on hips. Her eyes blazed with fury and he was certain he was the cause of her anger.

She looked to her father. "Do you still consider me a lady of this hall, Father?"

"Of course," he said emphatically.

"Then Lord Draven is welcome here."

"Emily," her father growled in warning.

"Father," she shot back. "If he leaves, I go with him."

Draven lifted a brow at her cheek. So he wasn't the only one she tested. In a way, it comforted him to know she held no fear of anyone.

Hugh's brows drew together in fury. "I curse the day I ever laughed at your spirit, Emily. Little did I know then that it would long haunt my old age."

Hugh narrowed his gaze on Draven. "Very well, he can stay, but if he strikes another guest, he's out the door on his arse. Do you understand me?"

She nodded.

Hugh cast one last furious glare to his daughter, then ordered the guests back to their merriment. The mood of all was subdued as conversations resumed and the musicians began playing once more. Joanne gave him a strange, almost grateful look, then vanished into the crowd with the nun by her side.

Niles continued to stare at Draven until the man Emily had attacked with the chicken came forward to get him. They walked off together.

Draven relaxed a tiny degree until he saw the condemnation on Emily's face.

"Why did you hit him?" she asked, her tone low and angry.

"He begged me to do it."

"Oh," she said, her face bitterly amused. "I see. He just walked up to you and said, 'Lord Draven, please strike me on the face and knock me to the floor in front of my guests.' "

"Something like that."

Emily rolled her eyes and left him to stand with Simon.

"Why didn't you tell her what he said?" Simon asked angrily.

"Why?"

Disbelief glowed in Simon's eyes. "Emily has a right to know, as does her father, just what kind of man her sister is marrying."

"Why should I do that?" Draven shot back, his body tense. "Montclef is welcome in this hall while I am not. Think you for an instant Hugh would listen to anything I had to say regarding his new *son*?"

At the mention of the baron and what he'd done, all the anger drained from his body.

"I didn't mean to strike him," Draven whispered as horror whipped through him. "I was just so angry that I acted without thinking."

He looked to Emily, who was again speaking with the nun and Joanne.

He clenched his hand as fear swept through him. "Had it been Emily I struck, the blow would have killed her."

Simon gave an exasperated sigh. "You wouldn't have hit Emily."

Draven couldn't take his gaze off of her. He had lost complete control of himself with Niles.

Dear God, what if it had been *her*?

What if one day . . .

He looked at Simon and remembered the time when they were children. The one time he had struck out at his brother.

They had been fighting verbally over something he no longer remembered when Simon had unexpectedly punched him in the jaw.

Angered by it, Draven had returned the blow. The strength of it caused Simon to reel backward and fall down the stairs.

Even now, he could see it in his mind as if it were happening right before him. Simon, his baby brother who had always meant more to him than his own life, falling to his rage. Draven had spent most of his childhood accepting his father's blows in Simon's stead.

How many times had he protected him?

Yet that day, *he* had been the one who had hurt Simon, his anger so great that he had struck out without any thought. If he lived to be a thousand years old, he would never forget the sight of his brother falling, the sound of Simon's body hitting the stairs, or the image of Simon's broken arm as he lay at the bottom of the stairs crying in pain.

Nay, he was his father's son, and though he might have a better rein on his temper than his father, Draven knew that once his rage took hold of him he was powerless against it.

If he could hit Simon, he could hit anyone.

His heart heavy, Draven rubbed a tired hand over his face. " 'Tis only a matter of her making me angry enough."

"Draven, you are not—"

"Nay, brother. 'Tis a chance I can never take. Like my father, my rage is too intense when unleashed. My strength too great."

He gave Simon a hard look. "Can you honestly say with perfect certainty that I would never harm her? Indeed, how many times have you yourself fled my presence when I lose my temper?"

Simon looked away, and Draven had his answer.

Even Simon knew it was a possibility. His own brother feared him.

With one last look at Emily, Draven felt the longing in his heart more profoundly than ever before.

But he could never take such a chance with her life. Never.

Chapter 14

❧

L ater that night, Emily sat upstairs with her sisters Joanne and Judith in Joanne's bower.
Everyone had retired long ago, and the three of
them remained awake, whispering late into the
night as they had done when they were little girls.
Back then, they would spend hours upon hours
together until the sun would rise or their father
would hear their chattering and chastise them into
their beds.

Judith had taken off her nun's habit, but her
shorn brown hair was a stark contrast to their long
blond braids. Even so, 'twas good to be sisters
again, if only for the night.

She and Judith rested on the bed while Joanne
took her usual seat in her chair before the window.

"Did you see the look of shock on Niles's face
when Lord Draven struck him?" Joanne asked in a
glee-filled voice.

Aghast, Emily and Judith exchanged puzzled looks. Joanne had never been one to condone violence of any sort.

How could she take such enjoyment from seeing her betrothed humiliated before their wedding guests?

Joanne sobered as she looked to Emily. "Lord Draven has never struck *you*, has he?"

"Nay," Emily said quickly. "He is normally so well controlled that I cannot imagine what possessed him to strike out at Niles."

Joanne stared out the window as if she pondered Emily's words.

Silence fell for several minutes while Emily and Judith watched Joanne's pensive face. Something wasn't right. Judith had confirmed her suspicions by telling Emily earlier she had noted the same peculiarities in Joanne.

"Tell me of your plans for Lord Draven," Joanne said, her voice startling in the quiet. "How goes it?"

Emily squirmed uneasily. She loved Judith, but speaking about seducing a man she wasn't married to in front of her religious sibling was not something she relished.

Judith patted her hand. "Judge not, lest ye be judged. Have no fear of my censure, little sister. I am here tonight as your blood confidante. Tomorrow you may confess your sins to Father Richard."

Emily smiled at Judith, grateful for her reprieve. Indeed, it hadn't been *that* long ago since Judith too had giggled with them about the prospect of marriage.

"There isn't much to report," Emily said with a

sigh. "In truth, Draven has proven to be most stubborn. He seems determined to remain unmarried."

"Perhaps you should leave the matter be then," Joanne whispered, her brow troubled.

Emily frowned. This wasn't the sister she knew.

"How does Lord Draven behave when you are alone with him?" Judith asked.

"He's courteous and kind, but part of the problem is that I am so very seldom alone with him, and while others are near, he won't come within three feet of me." Emily looked at Joanne. "How did you get Niles alone?"

"I didn't," Joanne said sheepishly. "Remember the night Father went to Cromby?"

Emily nodded.

"Niles came looking for him. You were abed with a headache, and he plied me with wine while we waited for Father to return."

Judith gasped. "Joanne—"

"Shh," Joanne said. She looked away as a dark regret settled in her eyes. "I never told either of you the whole truth. I was too afraid you would tell Father and trap me here forever. You two have no idea how much I hate this place. I want my own hall where I may come and go at my leisure." Her look turned hard. "I would say or do *anything* to leave Warwick."

A wave of apprehension went through Emily. She'd never heard such rancor from Joanne before. "I don't understand."

Joanne leaned her head back in the chair and looked up at the ceiling as if blinking away tears. "I didn't know what I was doing that night. All I could think was that Niles was interested in me and if I did what he said, mayhap he would take me away from here forever."

Joanne's voice shook from pent-up tears. "Niles led me to the pantry in the main hall. My head was spinning from the wine, and his kisses were unbelievably wondrous. I'd never been kissed before."

Emily swallowed at the memory of Draven's lips on hers. If Niles's kiss had been anything like that, she could imagine how her sister's head had been turned.

Joanne rubbed her brow with her hand. "And then he started touching me. Oh Em, Jude, I was scared and confused and I didn't know what to do. I told him nay, but he kept on, and I was too terrified to call out lest someone find us there and blame me for it."

"What are you saying, Joanne?" Judith asked.

"Did he force you?" Emily demanded.

Tears streamed down her face, but she wiped them away. "Not exactly. I was curious too, but . . ."

"But?" they asked in unison.

Joanne sobbed. "It hurts so much when a man takes you. It felt as though he was cleaving me in twain. At first I thought 'twas because I was a virgin, but since then he has taken me three more times and it hurt every bit as much. Now all I can think of is how many more times I shall have to tolerate that awful pain."

Judith leaned forward. "But you said—"

"I know what I said. I was afraid to tell you the truth."

Emily left the bed and gathered Joanne into a

tight hug. For several minutes she held on to her, letting her sob until she was spent.

Judith wet a cloth and brought it to them, then helped dry Joanne's tears.

When Joanne had regained some of her composure, she grabbed Emily's hand. "Please, Em," she whispered. "Don't make my mistake. I'm no longer sure if life with Niles would be better than life here with Father."

Emily squeezed her hand back.

"It's just jitters, isn't it?" Judith asked. "You're just afraid of leaving here tomorrow?"

Joanne swallowed. "Perhaps."

Emily knelt before her chair. "You don't have to marry him, Joanne. You know that."

"But the guests—"

"Won't care," Emily interrupted. "They came for free food and drink and they've been served amply."

"Emily!" Judith chastised. "How discourteous of you. I've never heard you say such before."

Emily inclined her head sharply to Joanne to let Judith know what she had said she had said for the benefit of their older sister.

Joanne pulled back and stared into Emily's eyes. "Promise me you won't let Lord Draven take your virginity."

Emily frowned.

"I don't want him to hurt you, Em. You can't imagine what it feels like when a man buries himself in you. And they don't stop until they're well sated, not even when you cry from the pain of it."

Emily sat stunned as Joanne's words sank into

her. Surely if Joanne were right Christina and Alys would have told her?

Wouldn't they?

And there certainly had been no pain when Draven had touched her in Lincoln. But then again, he hadn't finished the deed.

Not that any of that mattered at the moment. Something needed to be done about the coming wedding. "I don't want you to marry Niles."

Joanne looked at her aghast. "But—"

"Nay," Emily said firmly, "we shall go to Father and—"

"Em, I'm with child."

Emily closed her eyes and held her sister's hand tightly.

"Then let us pray," Judith whispered. "Surely God knows what is best."

Draven leaned against the crenelated wall and stared at the moonlight-dappled moat far below. The late-night wind blew a chill through the air, but he didn't feel it.

His thoughts were on a winsome maid, with hair of gold and eyes of dark green.

He heard footsteps to his right.

Glancing, he did a double-take as he saw Emily approach. "Emily?"

She offered him a timid smile as she paused by his side and imitated his pose by folding her hands and leaning on her arms against the stone wall. "I thought I would find you here."

Draven didn't bother making an excuse. She had

learned weeks ago that he haunted the parapets at night like a troubled spirit seeking redemption.

"I fear I couldn't sleep if I had to," he said quietly. "Simon snores like a charging boar."

She laughed, but he noted the hint of sadness in her eyes.

"What troubles you, milady?"

"I need someone to talk to and there's no other I can trust."

Her words surprised him. "You trust me?"

"Aye, I do."

For the first time in his life he actually felt gallant as a swell of pride beat through him. "What do you need?"

"Why did you hit Niles?"

The tenderness fled as anger took root in his heart. So, she didn't trust him after all. She would yet question his actions.

"Don't be angry," she said. "I am not fault-finding. My sister has told me things that make me doubt his character. From what I know of you, 'tis not like you to strike for no cause."

"Your father swears otherwise."

She gave him a peeved glare, the likes of which he'd not received since he lived with his own father, and he almost swore he could hear her call him beetle brain.

"I am not my father," she said coldly. "I have spent several months with you now and I think I can judge your mettle on my own. Now, tell me why you struck him."

Draven clenched his teeth. His first instinct was

to remain silent, but somehow he found the truth coming out. "Montclef insulted your family."

"My family?" she asked in disbelief. "I find it hard to imagine you would defend my father."

She paused, then looked at him. "Niles insulted *me*, didn't he?"

Draven didn't answer.

She reached out and touched his right hand where a large bruise marred his knuckles. A tremor shook him as her warm hand enclosed around his.

"You're hurt."

"Montclef has a hard head."

She gave a short laugh. And then he made the mistake of looking at her. Gentleness, warmth and concern met his gaze. He felt as though someone had just struck him in the gullet.

What would it be like to see that look for the rest of his life?

And then he noted her troubled brow. There was still something on her mind.

"Is there another matter?" he asked.

Releasing his hand, she looked away. "Can I ask you something that is awkward and embarrassing, but 'tis something I really need to know?"

Alarms went off in his head. He felt like a hare trapped by a pack of wolves. "If you must . . ."

She nodded. "Before I ask, I want you to know that this is not part of my attempt to get you to marry me. This is simply one friend to another."

He cocked his head. That voice was back in his head telling him to run as fast as his legs could carry him.

Like a fool, he didn't move.

"One friend to another. Very well, milady, ask away."

"Does it hurt when . . ."

Draven waited expectantly, but she said nothing more. Instead, she looked as if she might be blushing and she refused to look at him.

Draven tilted his head to catch her gaze, but she tucked her chin to her chest and studied her folded hands.

"Does it hurt when what?" he prompted.

She met his gaze for only an instant, then she looked up at the star-filled sky.

"Does it hurt when you—" and then her words were lost behind the hand she rubbed over her lips.

"I didn't understand that last bit."

She closed her eyes and took a deep breath, then blurted out, "Does it hurt when a man enters a woman?"

He couldn't have been more stunned had she reached out and slapped him. Worse was the image in his mind of him taking her in several different ways as he showed her the answer rather than told her.

"I think I liked the hand gibberish better."

"Draven, please," she begged, finally looking at him. "I am embarrassed enough. Please don't make it any worse. I didn't know whom else to ask. Alys is off doing who knows what, and this is not something one goes around asking strangers."

"I should say not."

"Well?" she asked.

"Why do you want to know?"

"I can't say, but it is important."

He rubbed his hand over his face. If he didn't know better, he'd swear she was after him again, but the concern in her eyes was proof she really needed an honest answer.

Disregarding the painful burning in his groin as his body strained against his tight laces, he shook his head. "Nay, milady. It doesn't hurt. 'Tis most pleasurable, point of fact."

And if it wasn't for his fear she would readily agree, he would offer to show her just *how* pleasurable.

"Have you ever had a woman cry when you . . . nay, wait," she said stopping herself. "I don't want you to answer that. I don't want to know of any women you've been with."

She looked up at him and smiled a smile that made him weak in the knees. "Thank you for your honesty. I knew I could count on you."

"You give me far too much credit."

"Have you ever thought that you give yourself too little?"

Draven couldn't answer, and at the moment he wasn't sure if he should.

"Oh, Draven," she breathed. "I wish you could see yourself through my eyes for just one instant."

He scoffed at her words. "You said yourself that you are a dreamer, milady. When you look at me, you see what you wish to see. And you think of me as some hero the likes of which foolish minstrels sing of in their chansons. I am not Accusain to prove my love by walking naked"—*why did that word keep coming up every time they spoke?*—"through the gates to prove my love to you. I am a man, Emily. 'Tis all I am."

"Aye, you are a man. In every sense of the word. And I am a woman who can feel every part of you when you're near me. Indeed, I can smell the warm manly scent of you and feel your presence with every sense and pore of my body."

His groin even hotter and harder than before, Draven's head swam with visions of kissing her in the moonlight, of stripping her kirtle from her shoulders and taking her there on the narrow walkway.

It would be so easy.

She lifted his hand to her lips and placed a gentle kiss over the bruise on his knuckles. "Thank you for defending my honor."

She released his hand and he felt the coldness of the night against his skin, the coldness of the solitude in his soul far more sharply than he ever had before.

The absence of her warmth was almost debilitating.

"I would wish you sweet dreams," she whispered, placing a butterfly touch to his lips, which burned from the tender caress, "but I know you won't sleep in my father's hall. I shall see you in the morning."

Draven watched her leave him. His heart and soul cried out for him to stop her flight. To call her back to his side, but his sense of honor refused.

She wasn't his.

She could never be his.

His heart weary, he turned back to stare at the water below. In that instant, he wished he had been the one to fall that fateful day in battle. Why had the sword not pierced *his* breast?

And as he had done almost every day of his life, he cursed his fate.

The next morning was a flurry of activity as everyone rushed about with last-minute preparations.

Emily tried several times to get Joanne alone again and talk her out of the marriage, but her sister would have none of it.

" 'Tis done," Joanne said dismissively. "I wanted to flee Father's hall, and now I have my wish."

But something wasn't right about it. Emily knew it in her heart and most definitely after what Draven had told her.

In the end, she had no choice save to wish her sister well and watch as Joanne bound herself to a man Emily didn't care for one little bit.

After Niles and Joanne exchanged vows at the door of the chapel, she went to the front of the chapel to stand with her father and Judith while the priest conducted the wedding mass.

Draven, Simon, and Draven's men stood at the back of the chapel. And when the matter was finished, and Joanne and Niles had led their guests out of the chapel, Emily went to Draven's side for the walk back to the hall where the wedding feast awaited them.

Most of the crowd walked ahead of them, and they followed at a subdued pace.

"I can't help but notice your discomfort," Draven said as they left.

"Tell me," she said, "what do you know of my brother-in-law?"

"He has a small demesne outside of York. I fought beside his father during Henry's ascension, but I know very little of his personal attributes."

"Oh," she said, disappointed in his answer. She had hoped he could relieve her fears.

"I've heard he has quite a number of debts," Simon chimed in. "And Ranulf the Black has little liking for him."

"Ranulf?" Emily asked. She'd never heard that name before.

"One of the king's advisers," Draven explained. "Much like you, Ranulf sees only the good in people. For him not to like you is quite a feat."

"Aye," Simon said. "He even likes Draven."

Draven cast a droll look at his brother.

No more words were spoken as they entered the hall, which had been decorated with flowers and white serge. The tables were filled to overflowing with food, flowers, and wedding gifts for both Niles and Joanne as well as little tidbits for all the guests.

Emily had a place reserved at the table with her father, but opted instead to stay by Draven's side at one of the lower tables.

Her father met her action with blatant disapproval.

"Why do you sit here?" he asked as he came up behind her.

"Lord Draven is my guardian and guest, Father, I

thought it appropriate, and I meant no disrespect to you."

Indeed, the appropriate thing would have been for her father to include Draven at the lord's table. Her father's slight was a heavy one that Draven had made no mention of. But as the king's champion and one of the highest-ranking nobles among them, Draven should never have been set at one of the lower tables like a common guest.

"Well, I am offended," her father said gruffly.

Draven rose slowly to his feet. "Hugh, I know we have our differences, but for the sake of your daughter, I propose we lay them aside."

Emily smiled at Draven's kindness. It was a wonderful thing he proposed on her behalf.

Her father raked him with a glare. "You offer peace?"

"I offer a truce."

Her father laughed coldly. "From the son of Harold? Tell me, will you too strike at my back when I turn it?"

She dropped her jaw at his insult to Draven.

"Nay," her father continued, "I'm not the fool Henry is. I know the blood in your veins, and I'd trust you no farther than I can see."

Rage darkened Draven's eyes.

"Father, please!" she begged, taking his arm. "He made an offer in good faith."

"And I declined it. As would anyone with sense. Only a fool would ever trust a Ravenswood under his roof or at his back."

For one tense minute, she feared Draven would

strike her father. Just as she was sure he would, he took a step back. "Come, Emily, Simon, we leave."

Her throat tight, she nodded.

"But the feast isn't over," her father snarled. "Emily said she would stay a few days. You can't take her yet."

"Aye, Father, he can."

The look of hurt on her father's face brought tears to her eyes, but she refused to cry. Or to try and change Draven's mind yet again. Her father had done naught but insult him, and on her behalf Draven had put up with it without even so much as a single complaint.

She would ask no more of him.

"I will have my cousin Godfried fetch my trunk," she said to Draven. "If you'll prepare the horses, I shall say good-bye to my sisters."

Draven nodded, then left her alone with her father.

"Why could you not give just a little, Father?" she asked him when they were alone.

His face hardened. "You would have me belittle myself to a man such as he?"

Her throat tightened. How could he be so dense?

"I won't argue the matter with you. I had hoped you would give him a chance to prove to you—"

"He murdered my people, Em. Have you forgotten that?"

She hesitated. "Nay, I don't believe it. Any more than I believe him when he says you attacked his village." She looked straight into her father's eyes. "Did you?"

"You know better. 'Twas a lie he told Henry to mask his treachery. How could you doubt me?"

She touched her father's arm. "I don't doubt you, Father. But I think the two of you should stop blaming each other long enough to consider that if you're both innocent, then someone else raided your lands, and perhaps you should join forces to find out who that someone is."

Her father curled his lips. "I *know* who the somebody is, girl, and if you were wise, you'd stay here under my protection."

Emily patted his arm. "You know I can't do that. The king has ordered otherwise." She rose on her tiptoes and kissed her father gently on the cheek. "Let me say farewell to Joanne and Judith."

Emily walked through the crowded room toward her sisters. A red flash dashed in front of her, and she instantly recognized her cousin's scarlet tunic.

"Godfried?" she called before he left earshot.

He doubled back to her side. "Aye?"

"Could you please see that my trunk is taken outside to Lord Draven's wagon?"

He nodded, then hesitated as his eyes fell to the door.

"Is something amiss?" she asked.

Godfried ran his hand through his short black hair. "I suppose not, it's just . . ."

When he didn't finish the thought, she asked, "Just?"

He drew his brows together into a deep frown. "Last night Joanne said the man who struck Niles was Draven de Montague."

"Aye."

He looked straight at her. "But that's not the man I fought the night of the village fire. I know it."

Emily's heart stopped. "What are you saying?"

"I fought him, Em," Godfried said, his voice certain and his gaze sincere. "I stood toe to toe in battle with the earl, or at least with a man dressed as he. I recognized the surcoat, but the man I fought was my height and wide of girth. Had I fought someone a full head and shoulders taller, I would have remembered it well."

"Did you tell my father?"

"I tried to last night, but he refused to believe it. He said I was mistaken."

"But you're certain?"

"Aye. I even wounded the man. A cut across his right forearm halfway between his wrist and elbow."

Chills erupted all over her. She had been right! There was someone else playing her father and Draven against each other. For she had no doubt that if Godfried had fought Draven he would now be lying in his grave.

But who could possibly have anything to gain by pitting them against each other?

Something strange was definitely afoot. And one way or another she would find out what.

Draven didn't begin to calm down until they were out the gates and headed across her father's property.

Emily had tried to speak to him before they left about some ridiculous notion of someone else perpetuating the hostilities between her father and him, but he didn't believe a word of it. 'Twas more of Hugh's lies.

And he had had enough of them.

But far be it from him to belittle her father to her. Let her have her delusions. He wasn't a fool.

Not soon enough to suit him, they approached his property. And as they rode over a sharp hill, a movement in the trees to his left caught his eye.

Draven glanced just in time to see the flash of sunlight glinting off a crossbow in the forest. Before he could give a word of warning, a bolt snapped from the bow, piercing his left thigh.

Hissing in pain, he wheeled his horse about. "Attack!" he shouted to Simon and the others as more bolts rained down upon them.

Draven moved his horse to shield Emily from the volley of arrows. "Get Emily to safety!"

Simon grabbed Emily's reins and pulled her toward a copse of trees while his men fell in by his side, drawing their weapons.

Grinding his teeth against the burning in his thigh, Draven unsheathed his sword and led his men toward his attackers who were hidden by the forest.

His horse reared as an arrow landed in its haunches. Draven struggled with his mount to keep the horse from bolting as his men continued on toward their assailants without waiting for him.

Just as he brought Goliath under control, a bolt buried itself deep within his chest, knocking him back. Agony coursed through his veins as the wound throbbed unmercifully.

Draven refused to be brought down by cowards lurking in the trees.

He locked his knees against Goliath's ribs, determined to keep his saddle. Another arrow hit him in the leg. Pain ripped through his limb until he could no longer feel his hold on Goliath.

Goliath shrieked and reared and Draven felt himself slipping.

He hit the ground with a solid thud that knocked the breath from his body.

Stunned, he lay on his back, trying to feel his arms or legs, but he felt nothing save throbbing pain, while arrows continued to rain down around him.

From her concealment in the trees, Emily saw Draven fall.

"Draven!" she screamed as she took her reins back and started to head toward him.

"Get back!" Simon snapped as he jerked the reins from her hands.

Emily launched herself from her horse and ran toward Draven while the arrows fell dangerously close to her.

She didn't think about the archers or anything else. All she could focus on was the still form in front of her.

Draven didn't move at all.

She fell to her knees by his side.

"Draven?" she whispered as she carefully removed his helm and touched his cold, whiskered cheek. Her hands trembled as terror wracked her body. He couldn't be dead. Not her champion. Not like this.

"Draven?" she cried.

He opened his eyes and looked up at her.

She sobbed in relief.

"Get down!" Draven said, but his voice had lost its thunder.

Tears streamed down her face as she saw the three crossbow bolts jutting out of his body. And the blood . . . There was so much of it.

Simon came up behind her and snatched her from the ground by her arm. "Get away from him," he snarled, shoving her in the opposite direction.

His unwarranted fury startled her. "He needs help."

"Not from you, he doesn't."

Stunned, she didn't move while he stooped to help Draven up from the ground. Draven hissed in pain as Simon draped his right arm over his shoulder and helped him to stand.

It was only then she realized the arrows had stopped falling.

"We need to get him back to my father's," she insisted.

Simon's hate-filled glare blistered her. "Why? So he might finish the deed?"

Her jaw dropped. "You can't think my father had anything to do with this?"

"I saw their colors. They were Warwick's."

"Nay," Draven rasped. " 'twas not her father."

"What? Are you mad?" Simon snarled as he helped him toward the wagon. "Who else?"

"I know not," Draven gasped as he staggered in

Simon's arms. "But Hugh would not have attacked me with archers who like as not might have hit Emily. He wouldn't have taken the chance."

"How do you know?" Simon asked.

"I know," he whispered. "Just get me home."

Emily hurried her steps to keep apace of them. "But my father's is closest."

Draven looked at her, his expression calm in spite of his pain. "A wounded hawk doesn't bed down in a fox's den."

When they reached the wagon, Simon let go of Draven who held himself upright by draping his uninjured arm over the wagon's side. Simon pushed her trunk aside, but Emily stopped him. "Take it from the wagon and leave it."

Simon frowned. "But your—"

"Leave it."

Simon nodded, then did as she ordered. Once the bed was cleared, he helped Draven into the wagon and carefully laid him down.

Emily opened her trunk and removed her jewelry case and pulled out a light saffron-colored kirtle, then joined Draven in the wagon.

"What are you doing?" Draven asked as she started ripping her gown.

"Making bandages for you," she said.

"Your dress—"

"Shh," she said, placing her fingers to her lips. "Save your strength."

The wagon lurched forward. Emily considered removing the bolts from him, but thought better of it. For one thing, they were in motion and it might maim him, and for another, she feared removing them would cause him to bleed even more. So she set about using her kirtle pieces to apply pressure to the bleeding to help slow it.

She kept checking his face, and as each minute passed he seemed to grow paler and paler. She took a piece of her dress and wiped the blood from his cheek.

The tenderness in his gaze stole her breath.

"You have such a gentle touch," he said softly.

She smiled sadly, remembering the first time he had said that to her.

And then he did the most unexpected thing, he reached out and took her hand in his. He laid her hand upon his chest, just over his heart, and closed his eyes.

Emily didn't know what startled her most. That he had finally reached out for her, or that he trusted her enough to close his eyes while she sat beside him. Both were such small gestures and with any other man they might have gone unnoticed, but for Draven they were monumental actions, and neither one was lost on her.

Emily stared at her hand. It looked so tiny in comparison to his. The darkness of his hand made hers appear all the more pale. His knuckles were scarred and she saw the purple bruise he'd gotten from hitting Niles when the man had insulted her.

And in that instant she realized she loved him.

She didn't know when it had happened, but it had.

Her lips trembled as she allowed her love for him to fill her. It was a truly powerful thing. Marvelously warm and completely intoxicating.

Impulsively, she brushed the hair back from his brow. The black silken strands caressed her fingertips as she ran several strands between her fingers. It surprised her that he didn't protest, but he said no more words to her while they made their way back to his home.

They reached the gates just after sunset. A fever had started, and he had shed so much blood that she had begun to fear even more for his life.

He'd lost consciousness as they rode, and Simon and one of his knights carried him to his room. Emily ordered Beatrix to fetch her sewing kit and wine, then ran to join Simon.

Simon's face was only a shade less pale than Draven's as he reached to grasp the bolt in Draven's shoulder. "This is going to wake him. Monty," he said to the knight who had assisted him, "stand ready to hold him when he strikes out."

The knight nodded.

Simon pulled at the bolt. Draven came awake with a curse that brought heat to her cheeks. As Simon had predicted, he swung out his arm to strike him, but Monty caught him before he could lay Simon low.

Draven threw his head back and groaned.

"I know," Simon whispered, then reached for the bolt in his leg.

Fully awake now, Draven locked his jaw and reached above his head with his uninjured arm to hold the headboard as Simon pulled.

She cringed as Draven's entire body drew taut while his brother struggled to pull the bolt out. How Draven could stand it without screaming, she didn't know. But at last Simon pulled the last two bolts free.

Simon held a bandage to Draven's shoulder and Emily rushed to hold one against his leg.

After several minutes, the blood flow slowed.

"Cauterize it," Draven rasped between panting breaths.

"What?" Emily asked in stunned surprise.

"Get her out of here, Simon," Draven snarled, "and do it."

Simon ordered Monty to escort her outside.

Emily shook her head. "But—"

"No time to argue," Simon said, drawing the dagger from his belt.

The last thing she saw was Simon planting the dagger in the coals of the fire as Monty slammed the door shut in her face.

But she didn't leave.

Her stomach twisted in knots from fear and uncertainty, she waited outside Draven's room.

After a few minutes, Simon opened the door. Sweat covered his face, and he looked as if he would be sick.

"I need a drink," he whispered, walking past her with Monty trailing in his wake.

Emily rushed inside the room to find Draven unconscious again. Simon had stripped his clothes from him and covered him with a fur before he left.

She paused by the bed and looked down upon his resting form.

Like Simon, he was covered in sweat. The skin on his shoulder was pink and blistered from where Simon had dragged his blade over the wound to seal it. And the stench of burning flesh still clung to the air.

Emily reached out, then stopped before she touched it. So much pain, and he hadn't even cried out.

How had he borne it in silence?

Beatrix came in behind her with a ewer of water and towels. Emily thanked her, then poured water into the basin and dampened a cloth.

"How does he?" Beatrix asked as she stoked the fire.

"I know not," Emily whispered. "All we can do is pray."

Beatrix nodded, then left her alone with him.

As carefully as she could, Emily bathed his fevered brow. His roughened whiskers scraped the palm of her hand as she tested the temperature of his skin.

His long eyelashes rested against his tan cheeks. Never before had she seen him look so peaceful. So at ease.

And he was so handsome it took her breath.

She traced the cloth down his hard, muscular chest, cleaning the blood away from his wound and arm. She paused over his heraldic emblem and took it in her hand. Made of fine gold, it shone in the faint light. The petals of the rose had been meticulously made, and on the back it read simply "The Rose of Chivalry."

She smiled as she traced the words. They fit him perfectly, and it was then she realized that though he wasn't the blond-haired man she had dreamed of, he was indeed all she had ever wanted. He was her rose come to fetch her off on the back of his white charger.

Instead of dimpled smiles and poetry, he wooed her with courage and honesty.

Brushing her lips across his forehead, she inhaled the spicy masculine scent of him. One day she would win his heart the same way he had captured her own.

You will be mine.

And as she cleaned his arm, she remembered Godfried's words.

Though numerous scars crossed his body, there was no sign of any wound on his forearm.

Emily went cold as she realized the significance. Who would dare such a scheme?

And why?

At least Draven wasn't as obtuse as her father. He had known her father wouldn't attack him so cravenly. Mayhap when he awoke he would look for the culprit and see justice finally met.

Consumed by her thoughts, she absently pushed the blanket down his chest to his waist.

Emily froze as she finally realized what she was doing. Almost the whole of his body was bare before her.

Swallowing, she trailed the wet cloth slowly over the mountainous terrain of his torso. His chest rose and fell with his deep, even breathing.

Draven's dark, tawny flesh called out to her, and she wondered what it would feel like to touch it.

Biting her lip, she laid the cloth aside. Grateful for her solitude, she traced her hand over his fevered skin, marveling at the texture, at the feel of his taut nipples beneath her hand. He felt like velvet stretched over steel. Never had she felt anything so marvelous.

Hungry to feel more of him, she traced one hand over his pectorals, delighting in the feel of his skin against her palm.

Draven moaned.

Emily paused her hand over the planes of his rippled stomach.

Draven heaved a heavy sigh, then shifted his body to the right. His movements caused the blanket to slip down, exposing him to her.

Her breath caught in her throat as she stared at his unadorned nakedness. Even unconscious there was a raw, masculine power that emanated from him that warned the world just how dangerous a man he could be.

She had seen most of him when he fought the boar, but fear had robbed her of the pleasure. Now there was nothing to distract her from his hard, lean body.

Nothing to cloud her thoughts except the red-hot desire burning through her.

He was magnificent.

Impulsively, she leaned over and touched her lips to his. He groaned as she kissed him while trailing her hand down his ribs and to his naked back. Desire coiled in the center of her stomach, aching for his touch, for any avowal of his affections for her.

"Emily," he breathed, her name a caress on his lips.

"I am here," she answered, only to realize he was still unconscious.

Pulling away from him, she reached for the covers and pulled them over him.

"I will always be here," she said to him. "And not even you will be able to drive me away."

At least she hoped she could live up to that. She still had to find some way to reach him. Some way for him to open up his heart to her.

She just hoped it was possible to get a man to open a heart he claimed he didn't have.

Chapter 15

For days Draven drifted in and out of consciousness. But with each awakening, he recalled glimpses of heaven. Of a blond angel sitting beside him urging him to drink water and broth. Of her singing to him as he lay there unable to move.

And when he finally came to his full senses, he found Emily sleeping in a chair beside his bed. She was curled into a small ball and her chest rose and fell ever so slightly with each breath.

The only light in the room came from the low-burning fire that flickered across the planes of her precious face. Dark circles marred her eyes even in slumber.

Her long blond braid trailed down to the floor only inches from him. Without conscious thought, Draven reached out and touched it. Her hair felt like fine silk in his palm.

She had stayed.

Draven blinked at the thought as unknown emotions swirled through him. Every time he awoke, she had been there.

He could even remember Simon and Beatrix begging her to leave, but she had steadfastly refused.

Why?

He couldn't fathom it. No one had ever been so diligent. No one.

Her arm fell from her lap and she jerked awake. Clearing her throat, she rubbed at her eyes.

Draven withdrew his hand from her hair, and it was that motion that drew her attention to him.

"You're awake," she said with a smile.

She left the chair and sat on the mattress next to him. Her touch gentle, she stroked his brow. "Your fever is gone."

"How long have I slept?"

"A sennight."

He frowned at the news. "A *full* sennight?"

She nodded.

Draven started to rise, but she stopped him by placing her hands on his chest and pushing him back toward the bed. " 'Tis the middle of the night. Where are you going?"

"The garderobe," he said gruffly. "And I suggest you let me."

She blushed, then released her hold of him. "Then let me assist you."

His head spinning from his effort, Draven sat up, and slowly put his injured leg on the cobbled floor.

He gathered the fur pelt around his waist to cover himself from her gaze.

She gave him her shoulder, and using her as a crutch, he slowly röse from the bed.

Draven was careful not to hurt her as he took a tentative step. Pain exploded through him at his first attempt to put weight on his leg. Grinding his teeth, he forced himself to ignore it.

"Are you all right?" she asked.

"Aye, and you?"

"Never better," she huffed as she helped him take another step.

Draven almost smiled at her bravado.

It was slow progress to the room across the hall, but they finally made it. Draven left her outside while he went to relieve himself.

When he opened the door a few minutes later, he found her still there waiting for him.

"You should take yourself to bed," he said gruffly, noting her look of exhaustion.

She waved his words away and again took him by the waist. "Are you hungry?"

Aye, but what he hungered for, mere food wouldn't sate. "Nay."

They worked their way back to his bed. Draven sat down and carefully lifted his legs back to the mattress.

Draven had never in his life had anyone take care of him. It was strange to watch her buzz around the room bringing him a cup of ale, checking his bandages, and tucking the covers in around him.

"What?" she asked as she caught him frowning.

"I'm just amazed," he said quietly. "I didn't expect you to do so much for me."

"Well, 'tis what people do when they care for each other."

"And do you care for me?"

"If I said aye, would you believe it?"

He thought it over. Did he dare believe a woman such as she could ever care for a man like him?

Or was it all just a ruse?

"Are you doing this in hopes of gaining a husband?"

"Nay, Draven," she said, her voice thick and chiding. "I do this for you as I would for any friend I care about. I told you the day you brought me here that I bore you no animosity, and I meant it."

He swallowed at the hurt he saw reflected in her eyes. He had been wrong to accuse her of deception, and he regretted his words. "Then I owe you an apology. You'll have to forgive me if I don't know how to treat a friend. Having never had one before I'm not sure how to behave."

Her smile took his breath. "You're forgiven."

She piled pillows up behind him and helped him lean back against them.

Draven sipped at the ale as she retook her seat and retrieved a small cloth she had been stitching.

A strange feeling came over him. It was such an intimate moment. One a lord might share with his lady wife. The type of moment he had never thought to experience.

And in that instant, he discovered that he liked it.

Nay, that he craved it more than he had ever craved anything in his life.

He closed his eyes against the wave of longing that crashed through him. This was not his to feel. She was not his to covet. He could *never* have her, and wishing for it was wrong.

Draining the ale, he set it aside and sought a way to drag his thoughts away from her.

"Did my men find the ones responsible?" he asked.

She shook her head as she made a tiny stitch. "They gave chase to two men, but they escaped."

She stretched the thread tight and bit it in twain with her teeth. "Simon still believes my father responsible. Have you changed your mind?"

"Nay. As I said, your father might hate me to the depth of his soul, but he'd never take a chance with your life."

By her face he could tell his words pleased her, and that gave him much more satisfaction than it should have.

"Have you any idea who else?" she asked as she picked up another color of thread, placed it in her mouth to moisten it, then threaded it through her needle.

Draven diverted his gaze from her perfectly white teeth and his mind from the thought of her sinking those teeth into his flesh in a tender lover's bite.

"Unfortunately my list of enemies is long and plentiful. It could have been most anyone."

"Aye, but it was someone who wanted you to blame my father." She set her sewing aside. "I think whoever it was is also the person who attacked your village and my father's."

"Emily—"

"Nay, hear me out. My cousin told me he fought someone wearing your surcoat on the night my father's village was attacked. He wounded the man he thought was you."

Draven frowned. "Why would someone do such a thing?"

She shook her head. "I know not, but my guess is it would be someone who could profit by both your deaths."

"There's no one who could do that."

"Then I'm out of ideas."

"That I find hard to believe, knowing you as I do."

She laughed as she retrieved her sewing from the floor and leaned back in the chair with it.

They were silent for several minutes while Draven enjoyed the peace of sharing the solitude with her.

"Know you how many knights it takes to extinguish a candle?" she asked at last.

Draven looked askance at her. "None, 'tis what squires are for."

She laughed at his answer. "That's good, but the answer is one. However, the candle must accept the blow."

Draven rolled his eyes.

Emily huffed at him. "Do you find nothing amusing?"

"Aye," he said in a whisper. "I find *you* very amusing."

By the shocked look on her face, he could tell he had caught her off-guard.

She leaned forward. "Draven—"

"Nay," he said, leaning his head back and closing his eyes. "Say nothing more and don't try your wiles on me for I am weak and in no condition to fight you."

"My father says that is the best time to press the advantage."

"But it wouldn't be very chivalrous of you."

She moved to sit next to him. And before he could move, she pressed her lips against his. Draven opened his mouth to taste her and balled his fist in her hair as he held her head to his.

Glory, but she tasted of heavenly delights and earthly desires. Her arms surrounded him with warmth and he pulled her fully against his chest. He was all too aware that he wore nothing more than a fur and that she would be more than willing to have him take her.

So easy . . .

And so very hard.

Her tongue stroked his an instant before she pulled back. "Tonight I will let you escape," she whispered against his lips before she took an impudent nip at them, "but on the morrow when your strength is back, I will again challenge you. And I *will* win."

He frowned at her words, not understanding why she didn't press her advantage. "Why would you leave knowing I can't fight you like this?"

The hungry look in her eyes was almost enough to undo him. "Because I want you to have no excuse to deny me later. I'll deal with you fairly."

He was so tempted to ask her to marry him anyway. But he couldn't. There was his oath to the king, the curse of his temper, and the little matter of the fact that her father despised the very ground he trod upon.

Even if Henry willed it, her father would never approve, and he refused to put her in the position of choosing between them.

"You need to sleep," he said to her, touching the dark circle beneath her eye.

She moved back to her chair.

"Not there!" he snapped. "Go to your bed. You've earned a good night's sleep."

"But if you need something?"

"I assure you I can shout down the walls if needs be."

She gave a short laugh. "I have no doubt about that."

"Then go."

"Aye, Lord Ogre. Your wish is my command."

Draven watched her leave, his chest tight. More than anything he wanted to call her back. To feel her against him once more.

But what was the use?

He leaned his head back and felt the pain swell inside him.

"God," he said quietly. "I beg you, give me peace. Please take this heart from me and kill it now before 'tis too late. I don't want to harm her, yet You of all people know what I would do to her. Please, give me strength."

Closing his eyes, Draven clenched the fur covering him in his fist. He would harden his heart to her. From this moment forward he would spend no

more time with her. He would make certain she
stayed far away from him. Forever.

Emily awoke just after the midday, but when she
tried to see Draven she found herself barred from
his room.

"What do you mean I cannot enter?" she asked
Simon.

" 'Tis on Draven's orders. I dare not cross him on
this."

"Simon," she said darkly, "you're supposed to be
my ally."

"I am, but I also want to keep all my teeth in my
head, and he was most explicit on what he would
do to me if I allowed you to cross this threshold."

Emily saw red. So he thought he could thwart
her so easily. Well, he would soon learn otherwise!

"Fine," she said angrily.

Then she raised her voice and addressed the
door. "You can't stay in there forever. Sooner or
later you will have to leave."

As expected, no answer came.

So be it.

She would win him in the end. She would!

Turning on her heel, Emily stalked down to the
hall below.

Days went by as she waited for Draven's appearance, but not once did he so much as crack open his
door. She was about to give up on him when one
morning found him coming down the stairs.

Emily's heart soared at the sight of him fully
clothed and heading out the door.

"Draven!" she called, rushing to his side.

He ignored her.

Miffed, Emily stepped in front of him to block his path.

"Out of my way, woman. I've no time for foolishness."

"Woman?" she asked in surprise. "What is wrong—"

"Nothing is wrong. Now go to your sewing or whatever it is you do all day."

Emily's jaw fell. "I beg your pardon?"

The look he gave her was so cold it froze her all the way to her toes. "Make yourself useful, but bother me not. I have duties to attend." He stepped around her and went on his way.

An urge to strangle him consumed her, and if she were a few inches taller and broader she might have actually attempted it.

"Fine," she said to his departing back. "I'll just go and do that."

Heading back into the hall, she summoned Denys to her. She had one more modification to the hall she wanted to make. One everyone had told her not to, but her vengeance was such that she wanted him to feel the angry betrayal that burned in her.

She had thought they had gained a friendship. But obviously she was wrong.

Fine, she didn't need him anyway.

And if he wanted to be so bullish, she would give it right back.

"Milady," Beatrix begged. "Do not do this! Have them remove it before His Lordship returns."

As she'd done all afternoon, Emily ignored the housekeeper as she studied the carpenters finishing the dais. The men hammered in the last nail and moved back so that she could inspect it.

Emily ran her hand over the rough wood. It needed painting, but that could wait until the morrow. Satisfied with their work, she told Denys to pay them.

He reluctantly did so, but muttered beneath his breath the entire time. "Were I you, I'd order it destroyed before Lord Draven returns," he grunted.

Emily stood her ground. "Unless someone gives me reason, it stays." She looked to Denys.

Denys shook his head and studied the floor.

Beatrix opened her mouth, then clamped it shut.

"Is there anything else, milady?" the master carpenter asked.

"If you'll have your men place the table upon it, I would be most grateful."

"Aye, milady."

She didn't care if it angered Draven. In truth, she hoped it did. For if he were angry, then he wouldn't ignore her, and as she had so plainly said, better to be annoying than to be ignored.

The men had barely finished placing the table in the center of the dais when the door to the donjon opened.

A sudden hush fell upon everyone in the hall.

Emily turned her head to see Draven and Simon standing in the open doorway.

Simon's face grew as pale as a ghost. Draven's, on the other hand, flushed to deep crimson. He let out a fierce battle cry as he rushed into the room.

His servants and the carpenters fled the room at a dead run. Emily stood frozen. Never had she seen such rage as Draven rushed across the room and seized an axe from the wall above the hearth.

Her eyes widened as he brought it down upon the table and split it in twain with one forceful blow.

Suddenly Simon was behind her pulling her back. "Get out, Emily."

"But—"

"He knows not what he's doing," Simon said, urging her to leave. "Get out before he hurts you!"

She shrugged off Simon's hold as Draven continued to shred the table and dais with his axe.

What on earth was wrong with him?

What could there possibly be about a table that would so enrage him?

She didn't know, but she had to find out. Rushing to his side, she ducked the axe as it came within inches of her head.

"Draven?" she called, reaching for his arm.

He turned on her with his arm raised as if to strike her.

Emily gasped in terror as she tensed for the blow.

But the blow never came.

As soon as his gaze fell to her face, he froze. And then she saw not the fierce countenance of a warrior, but the tormented eyes of a man in pain. Unbridled agony laced his brow, and he looked as if some dark phantom haunted him to the core of his very soul.

The axe slid from his hands and fell against the floor with a sharp clatter.

He looked at the shredded table, then the hall as

if waking from a bad dream, and she noted Simon had left them alone.

"Draven, what is it?"

His gaze went back to the table. "My mother," he whispered. "She was killed . . . on the table in this hall."

Emily covered her lips with her hand.

What had she done?

Why hadn't anyone told her *that*?

No wonder they had all acted so strangely this afternoon.

His entire body rigid, Draven kicked at the remnants of the table.

She took a step toward him and he threw his head back and bellowed, "I hate you, you evil bastard! And I pray God you are burning in hell for eternity."

Tears filled her eyes as she heard his misery. Emily went to stand in front of him and took his face in her hands. "Tell me what happened," she begged.

She saw the torment in his eyes. "We were eating," he said hoarsely. "My mother leaned over and told me a jest and I laughed."

His gaze held hers in thrall as he repeated. "I *laughed*."

Emily felt the room careen at his words and the agony she saw on his face.

He swallowed. "My father became enraged. The earls of Ravenswood never laugh. We are warriors, not jongleurs or jesters. And so he grabbed her to punish her for my slight. I tried to stop him, but he knocked me away. And then he threw her across the table and started choking her. I drew my dagger to stop him, and he turned on me with his own drawn. We fought and he did this," Draven dragged his hand over the scar on his neck. "By the time I regained my feet 'twas too late. She lay dead upon the table."

"Oh, Draven," she breathed as her tears fell. "I'm so sorry."

He wiped at her tears, his hands warm as they lingered on her cheeks. "I knew it to be the curse."

"What curse?"

"Our rage," he whispered. "Every lady who has ever lived here fell victim to the rage of her lord. Every one has died by the hand of her husband."

At last she understood his distance. Why he had never married.

And in that moment she loved him more than she ever had before.

"But you didn't hit me," she said, hoping to make him realize that he had mastered his rage. That he would never harm her.

"Emily, I—"

"Nay, Draven," she said, interrupting him. "Listen to me. Just now when I grabbed you, you were out of control. But you didn't strike me. You came to your senses as soon as you saw me and you stopped, just as you stopped when your knight hit you the first day I was here."

Draven blinked as her words sank into his mind. He hadn't struck her. Even in his blind rage he had recognized her and he had stopped himself.

"You are not your father," she whispered.

And for the first time in his life he believed that. "I didn't hit you," he repeated.

"Nay."

Draven pulled her to him, wrapped his arms tightly about her, and laid his cheek against the top of her head. "I didn't hurt you."

"Nay, but you're squeezing me to death now," she said.

Draven released her ribs and cupped her face in his hands. He stared into her eyes as if seeing her for the first time. There was wonderment there and a fire so hot it scorched him.

Draven couldn't catch his breath as emotions tore through him. It felt as if a tremendous weight had lifted from his soul. He had been furious and he had stopped himself. All these years he had been terrified of what he might do, and Simon had been right.

He was not his father.

Relief and gratitude overwhelmed him. And in that instant he knew he would have her. Now, this instant while the taste of victory was strong within him.

No matter what Henry might do to him on the morrow, for this one moment in time, he would live.

And he would love.

Even if the cost of it was his life, he would gladly pay it in full. To have her, he would give up anything.

Everything.

Draven pulled Emily to him and kissed her with all the fierce longing and desire he had kept caged inside. He turned it all loose and basked in the pure, basic elements of life.

She would be his.

Emily's head swam at the contact of his lips on her own. No gentle savoring kiss, this was one of pure possession. A ravishing, demanding kiss that took her breath as his untamed, masculine scent filled her senses. She laced her fingers through his hair as he nibbled her lips with his teeth and clasped her body against his.

She felt him from her lips to her toes as a raw, fiery need consumed her.

With a groan, he pulled back from her, then scooped her up into his arms and headed for the stairs.

"Draven, your chest. Your leg!"

"I don't care," he said, his voice hoarse.

"Where are you taking me?"

"Wherever and as many times as it suits me to."

Heat crept over her face at his words, but her body tingled with anticipation. At last she would have him, and he would possess her completely.

She knew she should be afraid or shamed, and yet all she felt was a strange sense of rightness. As if they were meant to have this moment, whatever the consequences.

Draven carried her up the stairs, into his room, and slammed the door shut behind them. He set her down before him, slowly as if savoring the feel of her body sliding against his, then dropped the bolt into place.

Emily stood on shaky limbs as he turned to face her.

"I give you this one chance to leave while I'm able," he said as he pulled his surcoat over his head. "If you stay, you are mine."

"I am yours," she whispered.

And this time when he took her into his arms, his hold was rough and demanding. His lips tasted of passion and delivered sweet promises to her as his hands reached behind her to unlace her kirtle.

Boldly, she unlaced his black tunic and pulled it over his head, exposing his hard, corded chest to her eager hands. He sucked his breath between his teeth as she touched skin so hot it felt as though it could scorch her.

Emily gave in to all the yearning she had felt for him since the moment she first glimpsed him on his white stallion, so commanding, so powerful. So very masculine.

This day, she would let loose her fantasies and find out once and for all what it felt like to be a woman. To be taken by this warrior as nature had intended woman to know man.

Gingerly, she traced a line over the healing burn on his shoulder as she remembered the way he had looked lying wounded in the meadow. She had come so close to losing him, and fear gripped her.

"Are you certain you can do this?" she asked, fearing the pain it might cause him.

He cupped her face in his hands and looked at her fiercely as the pad of his left thumb traced her passion-swollen lips. "At this moment, lady, I could fly."

Emily smiled.

Draven curled his hand against her cheek, then

buried his lips against her throat. A thousand ribbons of pleasure tore through her as he nibbled a fiery trail around her neck, his warm breath tickling as his tongue gently, sensually twirled on her skin.

She encircled him with her arms and ran her hand down his naked spine.

Draven shuddered in pleasure. Never in his life had he felt this way. Never had he been with a woman where he felt so free. All he could taste was this moment and all he could feel was her love.

Her warm acceptance.

He trembled from the force of it and from the need he had to possess this woman who was the closest thing to heaven he would ever know. Today he would savor every inch of her body, claim her in ways no one ever had.

Draven pulled back and stared into her passion-dulled eyes. "You are beautiful," he whispered.

She answered his words with a possessive kiss of her own. And for the first time in his life he allowed someone to claim him. Indeed, he took pleasure in the claiming as he gladly gave himself over to her touch.

Her boldness amazed and thrilled him. He leaned his head back as she placed her lips to his jaw and stroked his skin gently with her tongue. Ultimate pleasure consumed him.

Everything in the world shattered and all he knew was Emily. All he felt was her touch, her breath, her warmth.

Her feminine essence consumed him. Filled him. Completed him.

He had no life save her. And in that instant he

banished every bad memory of his life. There was no past he would ever remember save that to which she belonged.

Emily was his past, his present, and his future—whatever it might be.

She was his.

Emily gasped as he pulled her gown from her and stared hungrily at her fevered body. Never before had anyone seen her unclothed. The sensation was titillating, exciting, and it left her breathless. Self-consciously, she tried to cover herself with her arms.

"Look at me," he commanded.

She did as he ordered.

He took her arms in his hands and spread them wide while holding her gaze with his eyes. "I don't want you to hide from me. Ever," he said as he reached out and cupped her swollen breast with his hand. Her nipple hardened to his touch as it became heavy and full against his warm palm. "I've waited far too long to see you for you to cover yourself now."

She licked her dry lips. "It seems to my memory you were the one who did the running, milord."

"Draven," he corrected her as he dipped his head down to nuzzle her neck. His breath fell like fire against her skin, and she let it consume her. "I never want to hear you call me anything but that, and I am through running from you, Emily."

He kissed a trail up her neck until he nipped playfully at her earlobe, sending chills the length of her body.

Her head swam as he backed her up against the

wall and shed the rest of his clothes. He seized her in his arms and she moaned as her bare flesh collided with his. The hard planes of his chest pressed against her breasts, which hardened even more as they brushed against his soft curls.

Never had she felt the like as his naked flesh touched hers from shoulder to foot. Instinctively, she arched herself against the searing heat of his body, needing to feel closer to him.

His swollen shaft pushed against her stomach and a moan came from deep within him. It reverberated through her until she could feel his pleasure as if it were her own.

Draven's eyes darkened as he reached out and cupped her breasts in both his hands. He dipped his head and took her right breast into his mouth. Emily moaned as he twirled his tongue over the tautness of it, causing it to contract until it became a tiny sensitive bud.

She hissed as tendrils of pleasure shot through her. Still, he was relentless in his tasting of her. He trailed kisses to her other breast, where he gave it the same deliberate, scorching attention.

"Draven," she moaned, marveling at the mixture of pleasure and desire he stoked.

He returned to her lips as his hands ran the length of her body, stroking and exploring everywhere they went. She ached for his touch. Craved the endless pleasure they supplied her.

He ran his hand down her stomach and touched the center of her body.

Emily jerked at the unexpected contact.

"Shh," he breathed in her ear. " 'Tis fine, trust me."

She relaxed as his fingers separated her tender folds and began to stroke her in an intimate caress. Never had she felt anything like it as all the heat in her body pooled where his fingers stroked and teased. Instinctively, she rubbed her body against his hand, seeking even more of the ecstasy he provided.

Draven's body stiffened and he pulled away from her with a curse.

"Did I do something wrong?" she asked.

He shook his head. "I can't wait for you, Emily," he whispered. "I want you too badly."

She didn't understand his words as her gaze ran down his naked body. Heat flooded her face at the sight of him jutting out like a lance.

Then he returned to her. His eyes were apologetic as he pressed her back against the wall.

"Draven?"

He kissed her, then separated her thighs with his knee. Emily moaned at the feeling of his hard thigh pressing against the part of her that ached for him, and instinctively she rubbed herself against the hard muscles of his thigh, wringing a deep moan from him.

Her body afire, Emily delighted in the feel of his body completely against hers.

Until he drove himself into her.

She gasped as pain overrode her pleasure. "You lied to me," she whispered as her body throbbed from the strange fullness of having him inside her. "You said it wouldn't hurt."

He kissed her cheek tenderly. " 'Tis your maiden-head giving way, Emily. I promise once you get used to me, it won't hurt anymore."

She didn't know if she could believe him. Over and over, she heard her sister's voice warning her of the pain.

He lifted her legs up from the floor and had her place them about his waist. He tilted her head up to where he could stare down into her eyes.

"Look at me," he commanded.

She did.

"If you will suffer me for the next few minutes, I swear to you when you leave here, you won't be afraid."

"I don't understand."

"You will." And then he started moving against her hips.

Emily clenched her teeth, trying not to cry out from the pain of him thrusting inside her.

Draven buried his lips against her throat, hating the way she remained tense.

"Relax," he breathed in her ear. But she didn't. If anything, his words seemed to distress her more.

He cursed himself for not knowing what to do to alleviate her discomfort, but he'd never before taken a virgin.

With a frustrated curse, he pulled out of her.

Her legs fell to the floor as she took her weight back on her own feet. She didn't say a single word as she retrieved her kirtle from the floor and clutched it to her breasts.

It was then he saw the tears in her eyes.

"Oh, Emily." He sighed. "I didn't mean to hurt you."

"Joanne was right," she whispered. "It hurts terribly."

Draven pulled her against him. His body still needed hers, and it was all he could do not to cry out from the pain of his pent-up desire, but he wouldn't hurt her again.

He would never be that selfish.

"It doesn't hurt," he whispered, then kissed her.

At first she tensed and after several heartbeats she relaxed. Draven breathed a sigh of relief. He would help her through this if it was the last thing he did.

Emily didn't know what to think as he buried his lips against her throat and his tongue returned to work its magic on her flesh.

This felt so delightful, so wondrous.

But with that thought came the knowledge he would enter her again. She cringed at the thought. Wasn't it supposed to be over once a man did that?

Yet the feel of his lips on her was pleasurable enough. If only it didn't lead to the other.

He breathed in her ear and then ran his tongue over her lobe. Dropping her kirtle, Emily moaned in pleasure, then ran her hands over his ribs. Draven pulled back and carried her to the bed.

Still uncertain, she tensed as he laid her upon the rose-scented mattress.

His gaze traveled from the top of her head to her breasts, which burned from the intensity of his look, then down to the juncture of her thighs.

The aching hunger on his face haunted her.

Then, he joined her on the bed.

Like a large, sinewy beast, he crawled up her body and hovered above her. His gaze captured hers as he looked down upon her as if he could devour here where she lay.

Even though he didn't touch her, she could feel the heat from his body.

And then the most wondrous thing of all happened. He looked upon her face and smiled.

Emily's heart leaped at the gesture.

"You have never feared me before," he whispered roughly. "And by all the saints above you'll not fear me now. Not when I have you as I have dreamed of having you."

With those words spoken, he dipped his body down in a gentle caress from her head to her toes, then he lifted himself up. She moaned at the feel of his hot flesh touching hers.

He trailed his hands up over her body to her breasts and up to her face to cup it gently, possessively.

"You are mine," he said fiercely.

"Aye, Draven, I am yours."

Draven stared at her as he heard the most precious words on earth to him. He could feel her supple form against him as she surrendered herself once more to his touch.

His body burned with need, but having so botched his earlier attempt with her, he made himself move more slowly lest he hurt her again.

The storm of his passion crashed around him,

through him, and into him. She would be his, and he would treat her accordingly.

Emily moaned as he deepened his kiss and stroked her breast with his thumb. To her dismay, he left her lips, then nibbled a trail down her cheek to her neck, then up to her ear. She writhed in pleasure as her body shook in response to his tongue as it swirled and darted around the tender flesh.

His warm breath tickled her. "Like that, do you?" he asked.

"Aye," she breathed.

Then he moved lower with his kisses. To her breasts, her stomach. His whiskers gently scraped her skin as he licked her all over.

Emily closed her eyes and savored the feel of him while he moved to nibble her hip. She was his. She had given herself over to him and she promised herself she wouldn't revoke her body from him ever again.

Even if it did hurt, he meant more to her than any discomfort.

His pleasure would be hers. Now and forever.

She buried her hands in his hair and moaned as he nibbled the sensitive flesh over her hipbone.

He pulled back from her and placed his body between her thighs.

"Draven—"

"Shh," he whispered against her thigh. "I promise you it won't hurt."

Reticently, she opened her legs wider and allowed him access to her. He shifted his body, and she tensed, expecting him to enter her again. But he didn't. Instead, he gently parted her tender folds and took her into his mouth.

Emily cried out as sheer pleasure ripped through her. Never had she felt anything more wondrous than the sensation of his tongue doing the most wicked things imaginable to her body.

Her head spun.

Relentlessly, he teased her with his tongue, his breath, his whiskers, making her body hotter and hotter, her pleasure greater and greater.

And to think she had been fearful of pain!

She reached down and buried her hands in his hair, and still he pleased her. Her rapture mounted until she was sure she'd perish from it, and just as she was certain she would, her ravishment coalesced into something so profound and deep that it felt as if her very body was being ripped asunder by pure ecstasy.

Throwing her head back, she cried out in release as her entire body shook from a force unimaginable.

Her body still quivering, Draven crawled up her and then slid back inside her with one strong, masterful stroke. She moaned at the foreign sensation of him deep inside her.

There was no pain this time, only a sense of fullness.

An overwhelming sense of completeness.

"Are you all right?" he whispered.

"Aye," she breathed, wrapping her body around his.

Draven closed his eyes to better savor the feel of her.

Relieved he wasn't hurting her, he moved slowly

against her hips, delighting in the tight heat of her around him. Her sighs of pleasure thrilled him, and when she began to move her hips against his, he feared he might very well perish from it.

She dug her nails into his back as he buried himself deep inside her again and again. Over and over while her hands and moans urged him on.

And when his release came, he thought he'd go blind from it.

Emily smiled as she felt him shudder and collapse on top of her. She wrapped her legs around his hips, and just enjoyed the feel of his skin against hers. The feel of him still inside her. Oh, but his weight felt so good on her. She never wanted him to leave.

For the longest time he didn't move, but simply lay there until she feared he had fallen asleep.

Draven clutched the golden strands splayed across the pillows in his fist. He could feel her chest rise and fall against his as she breathed easily.

If he could, he would make this moment last forever.

But sooner or later, they would have to leave the room, and then . . .

He closed his eyes and sighed.

"I am going to die for this," he whispered, not realizing he had spoken aloud until he felt Emily move.

"You are being overly dramatic."

Nay, he wasn't. He knew Henry well. There was nothing or no one the king valued over his laws. Since the day he'd ascended the throne, Henry had fought for peace in his kingdom, and with what

Draven had done this day, her father would not be appeased until he was dead.

She pulled back to look at him. "If you married me—"

"Marry how?" he asked as he rolled off her. "What priest would dare marry us without your father's approval?"

"People marry in secret every day."

"And those marriages are quickly annulled without the guardian's approval. Not to mention my oath to Henry. The king doesn't take betrayal easily."

"That's not always true," she argued. "My father recanted his oath to Henry, yet he retains his lands."

"Your father retains his lands only because your grandfather fought with Henry and died from a blow he received protecting Henry's back. In payment, he asked Henry to swear to him that he would forgive your father and not leave him homeless."

She blinked as if unsure whether to believe his words. "I never knew that," she whispered. "How do you know of it?"

"I was there."

"But you saved the king's life as well," she insisted. "Will he not forgive you?"

He considered her words. But he knew the truth. Henry would take his betrayal as a personal slight and as such he would react emotionally to it.

Nay, there was no hope for a future.

But unwilling to hurt her, he said quietly, "Perhaps he might."

All of a sudden, her face lit up and she raised

herself to look down at him. "I am the king's ward, correct?"

"Aye."

"Then as such can he not give permission for my hand?"

"Aye."

"Then my father would have no choice but to allow our marriage." Emily smiled and laid her head down on his chest. "All will be fine. You will see. The king shall forgive you, and my father will learn to accept our union."

Draven stroked her soft hair. What he failed to tell her was Henry's departing words to him.

"Mar her maidenhead, Draven, and we will see you hunged, drawn, and quartered for it. 'Tis our honor you represent. Tarnish it and you will suffer the consequences."

He didn't delude himself for a moment that Henry would forgive him. He knew better. He had known better the moment he swept her up in his arms and carried her to his room. But that hadn't mattered to him. He had wanted her, and so he had taken her.

But his one moment of pleasure with her would come at a high price indeed.

Chapter 16

Draven wanted to spend the rest of the day in her arms, but didn't dare. There were too many people around who could easily get word to her father. Not that he feared for himself; far from it. He had accepted the possibility of dying young the first day he held a sword in his hand.

But he refused to see Emily harmed for his actions.

He left her with a kiss, then dressed and went to find Simon.

And find him, he did. Simon was waiting for him in the hall with a look on his face as if Draven were the angel of death come to claim his unrepentant soul.

"You took her, didn't you?" he asked as soon as Draven drew near.

"Is that not what you wanted?"

Simon looked away sheepishly. "Since when have you ever listened to me?"

"It appears today."

Anguish contorted Simon's face. "I didn't mean for you to take her like this. I thought you would marry her first. 'Twas my intent. Now what are you to do?"

"She wants me to send word to Henry and ask if he'll sanction a wedding."

"Will he?"

Draven looked at him. It would do no good to lie, besides he had never done such to his brother. "What think you?"

"Henry can be reasonable at times."

Draven snorted. "You mean capricious. If I catch him in the right mood, 'tis possible he might forget what he said."

"And how likely is that?" Simon asked.

Draven heaved a weary sigh. "Not, I'm afraid. He will see my actions as a personal betrayal against him since I am his champion."

Simon hung his head. "I'm sorry I got you into this."

"Easy, Simon," he said, placing a comforting hand on Simon's shoulder. "You didn't get me into this. I did. I knew the repercussions and I made the choice."

Draven smiled at the memory of her in his arms. "If it makes you feel better though, she is well worth it."

Simon gave him a hard stare. "I hope you can still say that when they're scooping your entrails out and you're still alive to feel it."

"I've had worse."

"Such as?"

"The day my heart was ripped out of me. I assure you the king's executioner could never equal the pain I felt the day I saw our mother die." He stared at the far wall where his father's table had once stood. "I never faced all of it until today. And now . . ."

"Now?" Simon prompted.

"I can't say 'tis all better, for I still ache, but that hollow part of me has somehow been filled."

Simon frowned. "What hollow part?"

It suddenly dawned on Draven just what he was saying. It had been years since he shared such confidences with Simon.

What had Emily done to him?

Stiffening at the thought, he looked at Simon drolly. "The hollow part between my ears. Now go and leave me."

Emily went downstairs to wait for Draven, but he never showed himself. The servants had cleaned away the remnants of the dais, and when she had tried to speak with Simon, he had offered a feeble excuse and vanished.

She felt like a pariah as she sat before the burning fire in the darkened hall waiting for Draven's return. One of Draven's hounds sat by her side, and she idly stroked his ears as she stared into the hearth. Most of the castle's occupants had retired, and she wondered if Draven had any intention of returning to the hall this night.

"What are you doing here?"

She jumped at Draven's voice behind her. "Do you never make a sound?" she snapped as her heart pounded.

"I thought you heard my footsteps on the stairs." He moved to stand behind her chair.

Emily looked up at him over her shoulder. "I would ask what brings you here, but I assume 'tis time for you to start your nightly vigil."

"Aye."

She reached up and took his hand. He squeezed hers gently, then lifted it to his lips and kissed her knuckles. Warmth filled her at the tender gesture.

He released her hand and fished in his purse for a minute. Emily frowned.

"Close your eyes," he said.

She did as he commanded. He placed something cold and heavy around her neck. Emily stroked the object with her fingers and knew it for a necklace.

Opening her eyes, she looked down to see the emerald necklace the merchant had tried to talk her into at the fair in Lincoln.

"Draven?" she asked in disbelief.

"I saw the way you looked at it at the fair and I wanted you to have it."

"But how?"

"I sent Druce for it the night before we left."

Warmth filled her at his thoughtfulness. "Thank you."

He nodded.

Emily rose from her seat and kissed him gently on his cheek.

Draven closed his eyes to savor the feel of her lips on his skin.

"Come upstairs with me," she whispered in his ear.

God help him, but he followed. After all, what did it matter at this point? Henry couldn't hang him twice for the same offense.

Besides, 'twas infinitely better to spend the night in her arms than walking the parapets.

She led him to her room where the fire had burned low in the hearth and a single tallow candle lit the room. It smelled of roses and apples, and the smell instantly warmed him.

Draven stopped in the center of the room and pulled her into his arms. He leaned his face down into the hollow of her throat and inhaled the precious scent that was his Emily.

She cupped his elbows in her hands and nuzzled her head against his neck. Draven swallowed. She had seen him in ways no one ever had. When he looked into her eyes he didn't see the bastard demon born of hell, he saw himself as he wanted to be. Kind, heroic, noble, and most of all lovable.

He touched her lips with his fingertips. "Thank you," he breathed.

"For what?"

"For seeing the best inside of me."

She smiled at him. "I only see what is there."

Not believing it for a minute, he leaned forward and kissed her.

Emily surrendered herself to him with a gentle moan of pleasure.

"I have never seen anything more wondrous than you," he said softly.

She smiled at him. He enveloped her with his arms and held her close to the heat of his body.

Emily trembled. For some reason, she felt as though she'd come home after a long absence. Something about being with this man just felt so very right.

She looked up to see if he felt it as well. She didn't know, but his gaze burned into hers.

He dipped his head toward her lips, and she welcomed his kiss. Emily moaned deep in her throat as their lips met. This was what she had been aching for. Time alone with a man she loved as he rained kisses on her.

With a boldness that astounded her, she took his lips between her teeth and tugged gently. She wanted to devour this man, to feel every inch of him against her and never, ever to let him go.

Draven's head swam as he tasted the sweetness of her mouth. She clutched at his back with her hands, pulling him so close to her that he feared he might actually hurt her.

In her innocence, she rubbed her breasts against his chest, searing him with heat. Draven moaned as she shifted her weight in his arms and her hip brushed against his swollen groin.

"Emily," he groaned, trying to pull back from her.

Instead, she leaned forward, recapturing his lips with her own.

His will shredded by her touch, Draven was past the point of rational thought. All he could focus on was the manifestation of his dreams. The pleasure of her smell, the feel of her hip grinding against the part of him he had longed to give her.

"Make love to me, Draven, for the rest of the night," Emily begged as she buried her hands in his hair.

She felt his hands tugging at the hem of her gown, lifting it up so that he was able to touch the bare flesh of her buttocks as he kissed her fiercely, demandingly.

She reveled in the feel of him, in the knowledge that she would never want another man the way she wanted Draven.

Never.

Ecstasy tore through her as chills erupted the length of her body. She wasn't sure what thrilled her more, the feel of his tongue stroking her neck or the strong hands that touched her in places no other man had ever touched.

Draven cupped her face in his hands and kissed her deeply.

Emily closed her eyes.

"Here," he said, his voice a ragged whisper in her ear. "Touch me here." He took her hand and placed it on the bulge of his breeches.

She widened her eyes at the feel of him throbbing in her palm. Her first instinct was to pull away, but the look of pleasure on his face was so great that it spurred her on. She lifted her hand up to the waist-band of his breeches, then boldly plunged her hand down through the tangled curls between his legs to touch the flesh of him with her hand.

He shook all over. Emily smiled in satisfaction at

the thought of the power she had over this man who claimed he needed no one.

He laid her down then, against the hard floor, and pulled her gown from her. Exposed to his gaze, she trembled in uncertainty. Her face warmed as his gaze ran over her.

"My Emily," he whispered. "I want to see you, to touch you, but most of all, I want to *taste* you."

He dipped his head to her breast. Emily arched her back at the sensation of his tongue playing across the taut peak. Moaning, she cupped his head in her hands and held him close as his hot breath scorched her skin.

He ran his hand down her stomach and over her hip. Her entire body ached with need. Bittersweet pleasure tore through her.

And then he trailed his hand around her thigh and touched the center of her body. Emily gasped as ecstasy whipped through her while his fingers caressed the tender folds of her body.

Draven groaned deep in his throat as he pulled back to look down at her. Over and over his fingers stroked her, teasing her with a promise of more pleasure, until he pulled away.

Emily whimpered in disappointment as he rose to his feet and pulled off his breeches.

Draven held his hand out to her. Emily took it and allowed him to pull her to her feet. He led her to the edge of the bed.

"What are you doing?" she asked.

He made a deep, throaty sound that warmed her. "You haven't been reading your book lately," he teased as he placed a kiss on the back of her neck.

Emily shivered.

Draven stood behind her then. He pulled her back against his chest and ran his hands over her breasts, down her waist, and to her hips.

Emily arched her back against him and reached up over her head to bury her hands in his hair.

He wrapped one arm about her waist, then trailed his hand back to the juncture of her thighs. Emily moaned in pleasure.

"That's it," he breathed against her neck. "Surrender your weight to me."

She did, and he rained kisses over her shoulders. She could feel the tip of his shaft pressing against her buttocks.

He sucked his breath in sharply between his teeth, then lifted his head. His fingers returned to the center of her body to torture her with pleasure. Emily couldn't stand it. She writhed in his arms as his fingers slid in and out of her, heightening her pleasure.

And as the ache in her built, he nudged her thighs wider apart and plunged himself into her body.

Emily moaned in bliss as she lowered her hips to draw him deeper into her.

Draven closed his eyes, savoring her sighs as he buried himself up to his hilt. Never had he felt anything more incredible than the tightness of her heat surrounding him as he thrust himself back inside her.

Heaven help him for what he was doing. But this was all he had ever wanted in his life. Someone who could accept him.

She was a part of him he hadn't realized was missing until she had stumbled into his life, holding that damned red chicken in her hands.

Emily clenched her teeth as exquisite torture wracked her body. Her head spun as he drove himself into her again and again, deeper than before. It was incredible, this feeling of him behind her and in her.

His fingers quickened to a rhythm to match the strokes of his hips. Her body became possessed of its own free will as it met him stroke for stroke, building her pleasure until she could barely stand it.

And then she exploded into ribbons of sheer, unadulterated ecstasy. Emily cried out as a pleasure more profound than anything she had ever imagined tore through her. She tightened her hand in his hair as her body was turned inside out by his touch.

Draven closed his eyes as he felt her shuddering in his arms, and then he filled her with his own release.

Sated to a depth he had never known existed, Draven sank to his knees.

Emily turned around slowly. A sheen of sweat covered Draven's body as he looked up at her in awe. Smiling, she knelt down by his side and pulled his lips to hers.

His kiss was deep and possessive as he toyed with her lips. "You were incredible, milady."

She ran her hand over his brow, then through his hair as she stared at those multicolored blue eyes. "I had no idea it could be like that," she said in awe.

"Neither did I." He reached for his tunic and

wiped the sweat from his face before he returned to her.

Draven sat cross-legged on the floor, then pulled her to his lap. Emily bit her lip as he wrapped her legs about his waist and held her tight against him.

She quivered at the sensation of his muscled stomach touching the sensitive flesh between her legs. Smiling, she brushed his hair from his eyes and planted a quick kiss on his cheek.

Draven nuzzled at her neck, sending waves of chills over her. Pulling back, he toyed with her necklace. Emily groaned as he picked up the large tear-shaped emerald, and his knuckles brushed against her breast. He gave her a hard look before seizing her breast with his teeth.

Hissing in pleasure, she leaned back. Draven laid her gently against the floor and she lay exposed to him with her buttocks still resting in his lap.

"You know," he said, staring at her. "I have wanted you since the moment I first saw you with that chicken."

"Truly?"

"Aye," he said, moving his thumb to gently stroke her between her legs. "I can still see you there tormenting that poor man."

She moaned as she again writhed to his touch. "That *poor* man was accosting me, Sir Knight."

By the look of his face, she could tell he didn't care for that thought one little bit. He stopped his torturous assault on her body.

"Accosting you how?"

Emily frowned at him. "Now don't be angry,

Draven. If not for Theodore's inept attempts, I would not appreciate you."

His face softened as he again returned to his careful ministrations.

Emily could scarce think straight as he touched her. There was so much magic in his touch. It was strong yet gentle, and it amazed her that he could be so giving.

His eyes darkened again and she felt him grow hard once more.

"Are you *never* sated?" she asked in awe.

She arched a questioning brow at him, and then he did the most unexpected thing of all.

He laughed.

Stunned, she sat upright as the musical sound filled her ears. "Draven?"

He shook his head. "I couldn't help myself," he whispered. "You make me happy, Emily."

And then he shifted her hips until he filled *her* with pleasure.

She moaned at the sensation of him hot and hard inside her again. Biting her lip, she lifted herself up, then brought herself down upon him.

He hissed and tightened his hold on her waist. She opened her eyes to meet his hungry gaze.

"I am yours, milady. Do with me as you please."

And she did. Over and over again until some time in the wee hours when she became too tired.

Draven picked her up and laid her in the bed. She fell asleep almost as soon as he covered her with the blanket.

He marveled at the way she slept so soundly. He

couldn't recall a time in his life when he had felt as happy as he did just then with her nestled by his side.

He would sell his soul to keep the dawn from breaking. To be able to hold on to her like this forever. But he of all men knew the futility of dreams and wants.

The morning would come.

And eventually the truth of them would be known to all, and he would have to face Henry's wrath.

A few short hours later, Draven watched the sun rise through the open window. Birds began to chirp, and he heard the servants waking and going about their business in the hall below.

Emily whispered in her sleep of dragons and roses.

Smiling at her honeyed voice, he felt himself stir.

He shook his head, amazed at the fact he could still want her after the night they had shared.

But want her, he did.

Brushing her hair from her shoulder, he placed a tender kiss on the bare flesh as he cupped her supple breast in his hand. She lay on her side facing away from him. Draven moved beneath the sheets, tilting her leg up ever so slightly so that he could gain access to her.

With his body afire, he drove himself back into the paradise that was her.

Emily came awake instantly to the warm fullness of Draven inside her again. Moaning in pleasure, she arched her back toward him. "What are you doing?" she asked.

He brought his hand around to gently stroke her breast as he leaned over to whisper in her ear. "Position number seventy-three."

Heat crept over her face. "And how do you know it?"

His laughter filled her ears. "Know it? It has done naught but haunt me since the night I saw it in your hands."

Her own laughter caught in her throat as he trailed his hand from her breast to slide his fingers into her wet cleft. His stroking fingers stoked the fire inside her as he drove himself into her even deeper.

All thoughts fled her mind as she focused on the pure pleasure of his hot body behind her, while his hand played in time to his thrusting.

And when her release came, it was all consuming. All satisfying. With three more forceful thrusts he joined her in heaven.

He was hers and she was his. She smiled at the knowledge. They were united in more than just body; they were united in their souls and in their hearts.

United for eternity.

Her love overwhelming her, she turned to face him.

Draven placed a tender kiss on the tip of her nose and he stared in wonderment. He had no intention of leaving this bed today. Not even for an instant.

A gentle breeze ruffled the burgundy bed hangings and it carried on it a most unexpected sound.

At first he thought he was imagining it, but as the minutes ticked by it grew closer and more clear.

An army? Draven frowned, then shot out of the bed.

"Draven?" Emily asked as she sat up and clutched the sheet to her breasts. "What is it?"

"Someone marches on Ravenswood." He scrambled to pull his clothes on.

"What?" she asked in disbelief. "Are you certain?"

Draven picked his sword up and belted it to his waist. "As many campaigns as I've been on, aye. I know the sound all too well."

Emily watched as he deserted her room. She too heard the sound of horses drawing near. Scrambling for her clothes, she quickly dressed and went to join Draven on the parapet.

At first Emily thought she must be dreaming as she focused her gaze on her father's yellow and white pennant drawing closer.

But it wasn't her imagination, she realized as her father halted his army just outside of Draven's walls.

"What means this, Hugh?" Draven called down once her father came within hearing range.

"I've come for my daughter, you bastard!"

Emily went cold. "He couldn't have found out, could he?" she asked Draven.

"Nay," he said, then shouted to her father, "She is under my protection. You've no right to come here to claim her."

"Not after last night, she's not. Now send her out or I shall tear down your walls to fetch her."

Emily gasped at his words.

Her father knew! But how?

Draven put his hand on her arm to steady her.

"Father?" she called. "Why do you come for me?"

"He raided Keswyk in the night. I've sent word to Henry, and I will have you back now or else I will see his walls collapse. Release her, Ravenswood, and I might speak in your favor to Henry."

Emily frowned. "You didn't raid last night."

He gave her a droll look. "I know well enough where I spent the night, Emily, but should we tell your father where I was, he'll want to raze more than just my walls."

Draven was right. And she gulped at the thought of what her father would do if he ever found out what they had done.

"Father, you're wrong!" she shouted, hoping he might be swayed to reason.

Draven grabbed her. "What are you doing?"

"I'm going to explain to him that you didn't do it."

"Think you he'll listen?"

"A . . . nay," she finished. "He'll hear none of it."

"Prepare our defenses," Draven called to his men. "Man the walls and—"

"Nay," she gasped, grabbing his arm. " 'Tis my father you would fight."

"Would you have me surrender my castle?" he asked, his face hardened, his eyes determined.

Frustrated, upset, and terrified beyond thought,

she snapped sarcastically, "Hmm, let me think. Surrender your castle to my father or kill him. I believe my answer is aye, surrender your hall!"

"Nay," he shot back angrily. "I hold Ravenswood in the name of Henry, king of England, and I will not throw back my gates in surrender to a man Henry trusts not at all."

She heard her father call to his men to prepare for battle. Emily trembled in fear.

What should she do?

What *could* she do?

Draven took a bow from one of the men-at-arms and prepared the arrow. As he tested the string, he caught sight of Emily's ashen face.

Her eyes wide with panic, she stared at her father, and he saw the love in her for her sire.

He lowered the bow and glanced out to Hugh. The man knew he stood no chance whatsoever. No one had ever taken Ravenswood, and no one ever could.

Yet for the love of his daughter, Hugh prepared his men to die.

His own father would have thrown him over the battlements to ward off an army. Harold would never have sacrificed himself to see his son safe.

Draven raised the bow again and aimed it straight at Hugh's heart. He could end it all with one shot. Hugh was too stupid even to hide himself, and Draven had clear vision straight to the yellow surcoat.

All he had to do was let fly the arrow . . .

Do it!

He could hear his father's voice in his head as he did every time he faced an enemy. *Give a man the chance and he'll be at your back, sword drawn, and plunge it straight through you. Always kill before he has a chance to strike the first blow.*

Draven pulled back the arrow.

One shot and it would end.

One shot and she would be his forevermore.

Aiming, Draven let go the arrow, and as he intended, it flew wide of its mark.

He couldn't do it.

Good or bad, right or wrong, Hugh was her father. And she loved him.

"Emily," Draven called to her, his tone empty, his body cold. "I give you a choice. You can stay with me, and I will protect you, or you can return with your father."

She blinked at him as if she didn't understand his words.

Draven approached her, his body numb in fear of what she would decide. "If you leave me now, know your father will never allow you to return here. You'll be lost to me forever. But the choice is yours. I will not make it for you."

Emily couldn't believe her ears as she stared at his stoic face.

Draven would let her go?

He would give her a choice?

In that instant she realized the full depth of her love for him. Few, if any, men would ever allow a woman to voice her opinion over her life or welfare.

He was her guardian and had full sovereignty over her. Yet he left the matter entirely up to her.

She reached up to lay her hand against his cheek. She felt his jaw flex beneath her hand as he stared at her with those icy blue eyes awaiting her answer.

How she hated having to make this decision, but there was only one decision she *could* make.

"You know I must go with him."

The hurt in his eyes burned her, but his face showed nothing.

"Draven, listen."

He shrugged her touch off as he gave her his back. "Go!" he shouted.

"But Draven, hear me out, I—"

"Nicholas," he said as he walked away from her, "get her off the wall and escort her out the partisan gate."

"Aye, milord."

She fought Nicholas's hold on her arm. "Draven!" she called, but he didn't stop or turn around.

Nicholas didn't break his stride as he pulled her down the stairs. Desperate, she tried to get free, but it was useless.

"Hugh," she heard Draven shout. "Hold your attack. Your daughter is coming out to you."

Against her will, Emily found herself forced out the small gate to the side of the main door of Ravenswood.

She turned to open the door, but they had bolted it the instant she'd been shoved through it.

"Draven!" she cried desperately, banging on the solid wood until her entire arm ached.

But it was too late. He had finally succeeded in closing her out of his life.

Emily sank to her knees and wept at the door, wishing she could have five more minutes to explain herself to him.

"You stubborn fool," she sobbed. "How could you?"

"How could you?" Draven whispered as he watched Hugh approach his gate and collect his daughter.

The vacuous hole in his chest returned tenfold as he saw her mount a horse and ride off.

She didn't even look back.

Draven stood at the wall until he could see no trace of her. She was gone.

His heart breaking, he ripped the damned stupid brooch from his cloak and clenched it tightly in his fist. Rage and pain shredded his soul and he drew back to toss the piece.

"I thought you might have more need of a happy memory than I." Her words echoed in his mind.

He tightened his grip on the brooch, digging the pin so deep into his palm that he bled from it.

"Damn you," he cursed beneath his breath. "I wish I had never laid eyes on you."

Indeed, she had taught him to love when he had thought himself incapable of it. Gave him wings to fly, and in one instant she had ripped them off his shoulders and sent him back into hell.

Only this time he knew the face and name of heaven, and the comparison made his damnation all the more unbearable.

His chest tight, he turned on his heel and made his way slowly back to the hall.

"Denys," he called as soon as he entered the donjon. "Gather the lady's maid and her things and send them to Warwick, godspeed."

"Aye, milord."

Unclenching the brooch from his bleeding hand, he gave it over to Denys. "And see to it that goes with it."

Denys frowned as he noted the blood. "Aye, milord," he said hesitantly.

Simon entered the hall behind him. "Draven?"

"Leave me."

"But—"

"Leave me!" he shouted, taking an angry step toward Simon.

Simon locked his jaw, spun on his heel, and did as Draven ordered.

As Draven made his way to his room, he swore he could hear the echo of Emily's laughter on the turret stairs. Smell the fresh honeysuckle of her hair.

He slammed his fist against the wall, leaving a bloody smear from where the pin had dug into his palm.

"I banish you from my thoughts," he hissed. "It will be as if you never were."

But even as he spoke the words, he knew he would never be capable of the feat. She had branded him with her pure essence and he would never be the same.

Chapter 17

"**W**hy do you weep?" Hugh asked as Emily wiped at her cheeks, but 'twas useless. She couldn't seem to *stop* crying.

They had been home only a few hours, and she had headed straightaway to her room. Now she sat before her dressing table with her head lying on her folded arms as she wept while her father sought to comfort her.

"I have freed you from your captor," her father said as he placed a gentle hand on her shoulder. "You should be happy."

"I didn't want to leave, Father."

"What!" he roared.

"I love him."

"Are you mad?"

Unable to look at him as she felt the heat of his glare upon her, she shook her head. "He didn't raid Keswyk."

" 'Tis a lie he told you. I saw his colors myself. He was even riding that damned white horse of his. Think you I don't know my enemy when I see him?"

"It wasn't Draven," she insisted.

Then, she made the mistake of turning to face him.

His look of hatred burned her. "And how do you know where he was in the middle of the night?"

"I—" Emily stopped herself just in time. It wouldn't do to tell her father the truth. He needed time to calm.

In a day or two she would make him see the truth.

She had to, for the thought of living without Draven was too bleak to contemplate.

Two days later, Emily went to seek her father. His manservant halted her at the door of his chambers. "Forgive me, milady, but a messenger just came from the king and they are together."

Her heart stopped beating as she stared at the closed door. Dread consumed her.

"What did you say!" her father roared, his voice carrying with ease through the thick oak and stone.

She jumped in alarm.

"How can he be in Normandy?" her father demanded. "Send for him forthwith."

Emily moved to the door and placed her ear to it.

"Word has been sent, milord," she heard the messenger say. "But 'twill not likely reach King Henry for several weeks. The matter will be brought to his attention and you can rest assured he will deal with it."

Several more angry words were passed between them before she heard the messenger approach the door. Emily stepped back as he swung it wide.

The messenger muttered something foul about her father beneath his breath as he swept past her, and Emily decided this might not be the best time to convince her father Draven wasn't responsible.

Stepping backward, she returned to her room to wait out his distemper.

Days turned into weeks as she waited for her father to calm, but as each day passed with no word of Henry, he grew more and more incensed.

Worse, he began fortifying the hall by hiring knights and soldiers. No matter how much she tried to say otherwise, her father was convinced Draven was after his lands.

"He'll be coming to take us while Henry gallivants about," he said over and over. "Damn them both."

Emily barely spoke to her father. She didn't dare. In his present state of mind she knew not what he might do.

And worse, as her first month home passed and she had no flow, she began to suspect something that was guaranteed to cause war between her father and Draven.

That night, Emily sent her own messenger to the king, and she prayed that this time Henry might actually bother to show himself.

* * *

"Draven?"

Draven didn't move as Simon entered his chambers. He sat in his chair before the hearth and stared blankly at the fire.

"There's a messenger come from the king."

Draven nodded. He had been expecting as much. In truth, he was amazed it had taken the king six months to summon him.

He couldn't count how many times over the last few months he had thought to go after Emily and force her to return to his home. But she had made her decision that day. And even though he knew she'd had no choice in the matter, he refused to defy the king further.

Nay, he would accept his fate as a man.

"Send him in."

The herald entered wearing the red and gold lion of the crown.

"Draven de Montague, earl of Ravenswood, the king bids thee come to his counsel. He will be in Warwick a fortnight from Saturday. Your attendance is mandatory."

"Tell His Majesty I will be there."

The herald nodded, then left.

Draven still hadn't moved. He merely stared at nothing as he had done much of late. It was as if all his energy had left him and he had no strength to move.

No will, no desire.

Nothing.

For days following Emily's departure, Simon had tried to engage him in conversation. But as the weeks passed and Draven spoke no words to him whatsoever, Simon had finally learned to just leave him be.

Draven wanted no one near him.

In fact, he didn't want anything anymore.

He couldn't wait for Henry's arrival and the imminent death the king's presence would demand.

That would be the only thing he would welcome.

Chapter 18

"Milady, the king requests an audience with you."

Emily trembled in fear as Alys held the door open for her. The king had arrived just that morning, and she had known it would only be a matter of time before he made the request.

Still, she was terrified of facing him.

"Courage, milady," Alys whispered, placing a comforting hand on her shoulder.

Emily thanked her and patted Alys's strong grip.

Taking a deep breath for courage, she forced herself to leave her solar and descend the stairs that would take her to her father's great hall where Henry waited.

The king's guards and courtiers milled about at the foot of the stairs. Her servants struggled to bring them food and drink while the hounds milled between their legs.

To her horror, all eyes turned to her as she descended the steps and a hush fell over them.

Emily reached to touch Draven's brooch, which she wore on her mantle, seeking some of his courage from it. It had crushed her when Alys had returned the brooch to her. But as the months passed, she had started wearing it for the memory it provided of a wonderful day.

Now more than ever, she needed that memory.

As she drew nearer the group, the courtiers' heads came together and she could hear them whispering dreadful things.

"Hardly pretty enough to warrant the death of a champion," one of the crueler ladies-in-waiting said as she passed.

"And all this time I thought Ravenswood preferred the company of his squire," one of the men said.

"Better than me, I thought he preferred his brother!" Laughter erupted.

Her face flooded with heat as she cast a bold, angry stare at the ones mocking her and her lord.

They turned away, their faces filled with shame.

Never one to be intimidated, Emily lifted her head high. "Laugh if you must," she said to them. "But the tip of Lord Draven's finger be worth more than the lot of you combined. Were he here, I daresay there would be none of you brave enough to even look upon him, let alone mock him with your words."

They exchanged looks with one another that told her she had guessed rightly.

Her father emerged from the subdued crowd and

nodded his approval to her as he joined her. He kissed her brow and tucked her hand into the crook of his arm. "Never let it be said my daughter is not the bravest woman in Christendom," he whispered to her.

Easy for him to say since he had no idea of the way her knees knocked or of the tight lump she had in her stomach.

Patting her hand in comfort, he led her into the great hall where the king waited.

Emily saw Henry at once. A tall man with red hair, he was hard to miss. She had expected him to be seated, but instead he paced the room with his hands clasped behind his back.

She dropped into a deep curtsy as he finally took notice of her.

"See what he has done," her father snapped, gesturing to her rounded belly.

Henry's gaze narrowed on her stomach, which had only recently begun to show her condition. Emily straightened and touched her belly protectively.

"Leave us," Henry commanded. "We wish to address the lady in private."

Her father nodded, then left her alone with the king.

Emily clasped her cold hands together and kept her gaze on the floor.

Henry drew near, stopping just in front of her. "You are a fetching maid. Perhaps we were thoughtless in handing you over to Draven's protection?"

"Majesty, I—"

"Did we command you to speak?" he snapped.

Emily swallowed in fear and quickly clamped her lips together.

"So," Henry said, "you can follow orders."

She nodded as she studied the king's gilded shoes.

"Good." He fell silent for several minutes as her heart thundered in her breast.

When he spoke again his voice was harsh and angry, and his eyes branded her with malice. "Now tell us, aye or nay, is Draven the father of your babe?"

She bit her lips, refusing to answer. If she couldn't explain, then she would say nothing to damn the man she loved.

His glower made her breath catch. "Are you testing our patience?" Henry asked, his voice even more menacing than before.

"Nay, Majesty."

"Then answer our question."

Emily thought she might faint from her nerves as the quiet stretched out interminably.

His glare intensified. "Why do you refuse to answer?"

Tears fell from her cheeks as she lifted her head. "I cannot."

Henry frowned. "Here now, none of that. We despise tears." He handed her a cloth. "For Peter's sake, dry your eyes."

She did as he ordered.

His look kinder, he said, "Now tell us what happened while you were in Draven's custody."

Emily took a deep breath and slowly began telling Henry the whole story from how she had felt the moment she first saw Draven to the moment he had taken her virginity.

She did her best not to be embarrassed, but she wanted to be frank with the king. To make him forgive Draven for his actions.

"So you see, Majesty, it wasn't his fault," she said, looking up at him. "Draven tried to resist, but I wouldn't let him. If anyone is to blame, it is I."

Henry's stare would rival the winter for coldness. "Draven knows better than anyone what we do to those who betray us."

"But Majesty, please, he is your loyal servant. He has served you the whole of his life."

"Enough," he said, cutting her off and making her jump in terror of his harsh tone. "You speak of his service as if you have much knowledge. And knowing Draven as we do, we find *that* hard to believe. Tell us, has Draven ever told you how he came to be in service to the crown?"

She shook her head.

The coldness faded from his eyes as he spoke of Draven. "He was no more than four and ten when we met him. Did you know that?"

"Nay, Majesty."

Henry paced a small path before her as he continued his story, "We had been gathering troops in France to fight Stephen when we happened upon his training."

He paused in the tale as if remembering the event.

"Draven fought like a lion, and we watched in amazement as he disarmed his lord. I knew in that instant that I was witnessing a boy who would grow to be invincible in battle."

Emily arched a brow as she noted Henry's slip in referring to himself singularly. But she wisely held her tongue as he spoke.

"Knowing the boy would one day grow into a knight to be reckoned with, I accepted the oath of Miles de Poitiers for the service of himself and his squire. Miles served us well and in the battle for Arundel, he fell."

Henry's face looked haunted as he recalled the event.

"I shall never forget that moment," he said, his voice calm and reflective. "I turned just in time to see Harold of Ravenswood charge me with his sword raised. They say you can see your life flash before your eyes when you are about to die. 'Tis truth. I saw it clearly. And just as I prepared myself for the death blow, out of nowhere came Miles's squire."

Henry shook his head as if finding it hard to imagine even on this day so many years later. "Draven caught Harold by the waist and the two tumbled away from me. They fought each other with such hatred and skill that I couldn't tear my eyes from them.

"Harold wounded the boy and moved in for the coup de grace, but somehow Draven gained his feet even though the boy had a wound in his gut that would have killed most men."

Emily clenched her teeth as she recalled the long scar that ran beside his navel.

Henry frowned. "As Harold extended his sword, Draven made an upper cut and plunged his sword through Harold's body. Harold laughed cruelly as he stumbled back. He actually patted Draven on the shoulder." Henry met her gaze. "Do you know what he said to Draven then?"

Emily shook her head.

" 'At last you have done me proud, beetle brain. On this day, I finally admit that you are the blood of my blood. For only my son could have killed me.' "

A chill went through her as she tried to imagine what Draven must have felt.

"I have never forgotten that moment," Henry whispered, his eyes dark and tormented. "Nor the look on Draven's face. He accepted the words as if they came as no surprise. I, on the other hand, was stunned, for I couldn't conceive of a father saying such a brutal thing in parting to his son.

"Then Draven turned and handed me the sword of his father, and swore his unyielding loyalty to my service. I knighted him on the spot, and not once since that day has he *ever* done anything to cause me to question his loyalty."

His glower held all the wrath of hell in it. "Until now."

Emily felt the tears prickle the backs of her eyes, but she withheld them.

He raked her with a cold glare. "We cannot help but wonder what it was that made a man so loyal to us forget his oath. What say you, lady? Can you give us *one* reason why we might spare his life?"

"Aye," she answered, meeting Henry's gaze. "The most important reason of all, sire . . . Love."

He blinked in disbelief. "Love?"

"Aye, Majesty. We love each other."

He snorted incredulously. "Draven in love? Do you *honestly* expect us to believe such? As you pointed out, we have known him most of his life. Never have we witnessed him do anything without calm, *deliberate* contemplation. Now you offer up some misshapen excuse for his betrayal?"

"But 'tis true, Majesty."

Henry laughed bitterly. "We believe you love him, for women are prone to such romantic notions. But Draven is a warrior through and through. We find it impossible that he could feel such. Nay," he said decisively. "We will see him punished in the manner in which we promised him should he touch you."

"And his punishment, sire?"

Henry cocked a surprised brow at her. "Did he not tell you the price of your virginity?"

"Nay."

"When he comes on the morrow he is to be hanged, drawn, and quartered for treason."

Emily felt as though she had been struck. Indeed, she wasn't even sure how she continued to stand, for her knees were weak and her legs trembled in fear.

"Nay!" she gasped. "You cannot be serious."

His face stoic, he nodded. "Draven knew the consequences," Henry said coldly.

Emily closed her eyes and gulped for air.

"Please, Majesty," she implored him. "Do as you will with me, but harm him not. I beg you. You cannot do this to him. Not when it was all *my* fault."

But he didn't speak.

Emily sobbed out her misery as she sank to her knees in despair.

"What have I done?" she asked, wishing she had never contemplated Draven's seduction.

"On your feet, lady."

Emily wiped her tears away and bit her trembling lip, then rose slowly to her feet.

This time, she saw a very subtle softening to Henry's features as he regarded her carefully. "You truly love him?"

"Aye, Majesty. More than my life."

Henry considered her words for a minute as he again paced before her. "You are aware of your father's accusations regarding Draven's activities?"

"Aye, Majesty, but I know Draven didn't do it."

"And how do you know it?"

"I was with him the night Keswyk was attacked."

"Have you proof?"

She looked to her belly.

Henry laughed bitterly. "Aye, we believe you do."

For several minutes he paced in silence as she clenched her hands together, terrified of what he might say to her, or do to Draven.

Just when she was certain her nerves could take no more of the sound of Henry's shoes clip-clopping on the cobblestones, he spoke. "Very well, milady, we say this to you, your love of Draven is plain. If on the morrow we see proof that he loves you as well, and that his love was what motivated him to betray us, we *might* be swayed to mercy."

Emily looked up as her spirit lifted.

"But," Henry cautioned, his face stern, "if we see none of it and Draven shows himself to have done nothing more than use you while you were in his care, we will see his punishment met fully and swiftly. Is that understood?"

"Aye, Majesty."

"Now leave us."

Emily curtsied and walked backward from the king.

Once the doors to the hall were closed, she breathed a sigh of relief.

There was a chance! 'Twas small, but it was enough for her to grasp.

Surely Draven would—

Emily stopped the thought as reality came crashing down.

Oh, who was she fooling? Draven was a man forged of iron. Never had he shown his emotions, and in all likelihood he would march through the gates stoically to take his punishment without so much as a sideways glance to her.

Emily placed her hand on her stomach and the life that was growing there.

"Please," she prayed under her breath. "I would have a father for my babe."

Chapter 19

Morning came too slowly to Draven, who met it with relief. At last it was over. Soon he would have the peace he craved, and all his misery would end.

Gathering his brother and a handful of men, he left for Warwick. With every league that brought him closer to his destiny, he had but one hope.

He wanted to see Emily's face one last time before he died. Draven could die in peace if he could have that one request. It was the only thing he focused on as he rode.

By late afternoon, they approached the castle. Draven arched one brow as he stared up the bleak, stone walls ahead. From the distance, it appeared as if a thousand men were manning the parapets. Hugh had gone to quite some effort to fortify his home.

"Halt!" Hugh cried as they approached the gate.

"Your men are to stay outside, and only *you* will be admitted."

"Nay," Simon said to Draven as he reined his horse by Draven's side. "I don't trust him."

Draven stared blankly at his brother. "Trust him to do what, Simon? 'Tis my execution I go to."

"Draven—"

"Nay, brother, stay here. I don't want you to witness it."

They dismounted in unison and as Draven took a step, he found Simon's arms wrapped about him in a tight hug.

"Don't go," Simon whispered in his ear. "We can hold the king's army. You know we could."

Draven pushed him away harshly, and then seeing the hurt in Simon's eyes, he patted his shoulder to comfort him. "Take care, little brother. I would say that someday we shall share eternity together, but I pray you'll be off to a better place than that which awaits me."

His eyes shining bright, Simon swallowed hard, patted his arm, then looked away.

Draven took a deep breath and started toward the castle gate on foot. Looking up at the parapets, he paused.

For an instant, he thought he might be dreaming as he saw the sunlight shining on hair of pure gold. But he would know that slight form anywhere.

Indeed, her essence was branded into his very soul.

His Emily.

Her father pulled at her, and he knew Hugh was

demanding she leave. He could just imagine the stubborn tilt of her chin, the fire in her eyes as she refused.

Draven's throat tight, a thousand and one emotions ripped through him simultaneously as he stared at her while she struggled against her father's grip.

Most of all he felt gratitude that he saw her again.

Her presence gave him strength.

And Draven wanted desperately to tell her what he felt in his heart. But such tender words had never come easily to him. In truth, he knew no tender words at all.

Nay, he was a man of action, and in that instant he wanted her to know he had no regrets. He wanted her to understand just how much love he held for her.

For this one moment in time, he would be her Accusain. Her champion. Her Rose of Chivalry.

Aye, there was only one way to show her the depth of his love. His spine stiff with pride, he pulled the mail gauntlets from his hands and tossed them to the ground.

"What is he doing?" Henry asked.

Her father paused and looked down to where Draven stood. Emily took advantage of his distraction to twist from his arms and run back to the wall. She drew alongside the king and peered over.

Draven stood below the gate disrobing. Slowly, and piece by piece, he removed his sword, his surcoat, his mail armor, and then his padded aketon—

until there was nothing left but the wealth of tawny skin gleaming in the sunlight.

Stark naked, he walked toward the gate.

Emily bit back her tears as she understood. "You asked me for proof of his feelings, Majesty. You now have it!"

Henry turned to her with a frown. "What say you?"

"Does Your Majesty know the troubadour tale of Accusain and Laurette?"

"With Eleanor for a queen, we know all such insipid tales by memory."

"Then Your Majesty recalls the part where Accusain walks naked through Laurette's father's troops to prove his love for her."

"Aye, but that is just a fable."

"Aye," she said with a laugh as joy swept through her, "a fable. And when Draven heard it he told me that no man worthy of the name would ever do such a thing for a woman, and yet he does it now. What madness other than love could possess him to do such a thing?"

Henry considered her words.

He looked back at Draven skeptically for several heart-wrenching minutes.

Draven approached the door while Emily prayed Henry would see the truth.

The king took one last look, then motioned to her. "Come with us, lady."

Emily followed Henry and her father off the wall and into the keep.

Once they were in the hall, Henry turned to her,

his face blank and empty. "Go hide yourself while we speak to Draven. Do not show yourself until you are called. Hugh," he directed to her father, " 'tis your life if she disobeys."

Her father nodded and took her to stand in the small pantry behind the dais.

Emily's heart pounded in fear and uncertainty as she waited.

Eternity seemed to have passed before she heard the familiar baritone of Draven's voice greeting his king.

"What is the meaning of this?" Henry demanded as he raked Draven's nude body with a sneer. "Is this another insult you feel the need to deal us?"

Draven shook his head. "Nay, sire. I would never insult you, by word or by deed."

"And yet you show yourself naked to us?" Angrily, Henry removed his cloak and tossed it to him.

Draven caught the garment with one hand.

"Cover yourself."

"Thank you, sire," he said, doing as the king commanded.

Henry's cold glare pierced him. "Now explain your actions to us."

Draven stared at the far wall as he conjured up an image of Emily's face. Taking strength from it, he spoke, "I didn't want anyone to mistake my intentions, sire. I am here to accept my punishment."

A look of disappointment darkened the king's eyes. "So, you're ready to die?"

Draven met Henry's gaze without flinching. "Aye, sire."

"And have you any regrets?"

Draven shook his head.

"None?" Henry asked incredulously.

He paused. Aye, he had a regret. He was sorry that he had never told Emily how he felt about her.

And most of all he was sorry he had given her the chance to flee his hall.

But he would never tell that to Henry.

"None, sire."

Henry stroked his beard thoughtfully as he paced before him. "So, the wench was so good a bedmate that you can actually suffer torture and death without regret. We shall have to try her—"

"Do not touch—" Draven broke off his warning as he realized he'd taken two steps toward Henry in anger.

Henry stopped his pacing and arched a royal brow in censure. "By God's law, Draven, that be the first time we have ever heard you raise your voice to anyone. Least of all us. And you actually approached us recklessly."

"Forgive me, Majesty," he said, lowering his gaze to the floor. "I forgot myself."

"Then the lady was correct. You do love her?"

Draven's throat tightened, and he refused to meet Henry's gaze lest he see the truth of the matter.

"Was she also right that it was love of her that made you shed your clothes?"

Draven said nothing.

What could he say?

Henry moved to stand before him. "Speak up, boy, your life depends upon your answer."

Still Draven said nothing.

The king waited impatiently before he spoke again, "When you came to London with Hugh, we asked you then what you valued most on this earth. Simon told us 'twas your honor you held dearest, that you would die to protect it. Were we to ask you this day what you valued most, what you would die to protect, what answer would you give?"

Draven locked gazes with Henry. "Emily," he said simply.

To his surprise, Henry nodded in approval.

"Emily?" the king called.

Draven looked past the king's shoulder to see a door open. Emily came out, her eyes shining as she led her father toward him.

Elation tore through him at the sight of her as he squelched his overwhelming urge to run to her and sweep her up in his arms.

Only Henry's presence kept him from it.

Hungrily, he drank in the sight of her glorious face and blond curls. His gaze dipped lower and shock jolted him as he saw her rounded stomach.

"Did you hear his words?" Henry asked her as she came to stand by Draven's side.

"Aye, Majesty," she breathed.

"Hugh?" the king asked her father.

"What of my lands he destroyed?" Hugh asked.

Henry folded his arms over his chest. "Tell us what you worry over more, your precious lands or the fact your grandchild will be born the bastard child of a man executed for treason?"

Hugh approached Draven with his lips curled. "I still have no use for you."

Draven held his tongue.

"What?" Hugh asked in disbelief, "No clever retort, Ravenswood? Never have I known you to not return insult with insult."

Draven didn't look at Hugh; his gaze was held in thrall by the woman he loved who carried his child. "I would not hurt Emily by insulting you, Hugh. For whatever reason she loves me, she loves you as well, and that is enough for me to respect you."

Hugh snorted. "I can't say I approve of this match, but for the sake of my daughter, I shall abide with whatever terms His Majesty decrees."

Henry nodded. " 'Tis good then. Hugh, fetch his brother and his clothes from outside your walls, and a priest. Let us see these two wed before the day ends."

"Thank you, Majesty," Emily said, her eyes bright and happy.

Henry's face turned sharp and forbidding. "Do not thank us yet, milady, for there is still the matter of his punishment."

Draven looked back at Henry.

He saw the sadness in Henry's eyes, but Draven expected little in the way of mercy.

"You have always been a loyal servant to us," Henry said, "and so we trust you understand why it is we cannot give you full immunity."

"Aye, sire. I didn't expect clemency of any sort."

Emily gasped at his side. "But—"

Draven shook his head at her, cutting her words off.

Henry smiled as she held her tongue. " 'Tis good to know you can command her," he said to Draven, then the smile faded from his face. "After the wedding, Draven is to be given twenty lashes for his disobedience."

Emily opened her mouth to speak, but Draven placed a finger over her lips.

Henry walked toward Hugh. "Come and let us find that priest."

At the door, Henry turned back to face them. "Draven?"

"Aye, sire?"

"We hope this time when you swear a holy oath you have better luck keeping your vow."

"I shall have no trouble whatsoever, sire."

Henry smiled. "We didn't think so."

When they were left alone, Emily looked up at him. "Twenty lashes. Draven, I am so sorry."

"Believe me, twenty lashes is much better than the alternative." Tenderly, he placed his hand against her stomach, marveling at what he saw. "Why did you not tell me?"

She smiled up at him. "I wanted to, but there was no one who would take a bribe to deliver the news. They feared my father's wrath."

Then he pulled her into his arms. Emily felt so wonderful there, especially the rounded part of her that rubbed against his bare stomach.

"Come, wench," he whispered in her ear. "While they are occupied elsewhere, what say we find a quiet place where I can show you how much I've missed you."

She dipped her gaze down to his swollen shaft. "I can see that for myself."

He nuzzled her neck, inhaling her warm scent. "Just call me Priapus."

She laughed as she hugged him close. "Then come, Priapus, and let me show you to our bridal chambers."

Emily led him upstairs to her room, where Alys waited. Her maid's eyes widened as she saw Draven's state of undress.

Without a word, Alys made a quick departure and left the two of them alone.

Draven dropped the king's cloak and pulled her into his arms. Finally, Emily could give him the kiss she had wanted to give him the instant she had seen him naked outside.

"You are my hero," she breathed against his lips.

"Aye, lady," he agreed. "Yours and no other."

Emily smiled as he unlaced her kirtle and pulled it from her shoulders. She felt shy and timid as he stared at her. It had been months since she last saw him and her extended belly didn't help her self-esteem any.

"Don't look at me," she said, stepping back into a shadowed corner. "I'm as huge as a swollen sow."

Draven placed his fingers against her lips. "Nay, milady. 'Tis my babe you carry there," he said, touching her stomach tenderly. "And that makes you all the more beautiful to my eyes."

His words thrilled her. "I have missed you so much," she said, wrapping her arms around him.

"And I promise you, Emily, you'll never again have cause to miss me."

"My sweet Draven," she whispered against his lips. "I'll never again let you leave me."

They made love slowly that afternoon, savoring each other until Alys returned to prepare her for the wedding.

Draven dressed quickly, then reluctantly withdrew from her and went below to sign the papers.

Unlike the day her sister married, Hugh's mood was somber and dark. Draven wished he could find a way to lay aside their differences for the sake of Emily and their child.

Their child.

He paused at the thought. She had given him more than he had ever expected to have. And he loved her for it.

"Ah, she comes," Henry said.

With Simon standing to his right, Draven turned to see Emily entering the small room where they stood with a priest. Instead of her father's colors, she wore a gown of bright red and a mantle of black held in place by the brooch she had given him. His colors, he noted as a surge of pride swept through him.

She was his and no one would ever take her from him again.

The ceremony was brief, with Hugh hesitating before he finally gave his approval.

Draven had no more kissed her than Henry called for his guards to escort him outside to the yard.

"Nay," Emily said as she reached out for him.

Draven kissed her hand reassuringly, and let go of her. "It is all right, Emily," he whispered.

He gently pushed her back into her father's arms.

Emily watched as Draven and Simon calmly followed the guards outside to the courtyard reserved for punishing wrongdoers.

Twisting away from her father, she went after them. She came to a stop as her gaze fell to the king's executioner, who waited with a barbed whip in his hand.

Her father stopped by her side and tried to pull her back inside. "You shouldn't see this."

She set her jaw stubbornly. "He is my husband, and my place is by his side."

But the words were hard in her throat, and she prayed she had the strength to stand by and watch him hurt.

Casting her a tender glance, Draven unlaced his tunic and bared his back. Emily looked to the king, hoping against hope that he might yet put a stop to this. By Henry's face she could tell he enjoyed the event even less than she did.

But he held his tongue, and her hope and heart withered.

The executioner used the frame of the gallows to tie Draven's hands above his head. When Draven was prepared, the executioner looked to the king.

"Begin," Henry commanded.

Simon turned to face the wall. Emily cringed as the hooded man brought the whip down across Draven's back. Blood dappled the man's clothes, but Draven made no sound whatsoever as his body tensed and strained from the blow.

"My God," her father breathed. "Does he not feel it?"

"Aye, he feels it," she said as another blow was dealt him in silence.

Her throat tight, she felt her tears fall down her cheeks. She clamped her jaw to keep from screaming out for them to stop this madness, and she could look no more. Mimicking Simon, she turned to face the wall and wait it out.

When all twenty lashes had been given, the executioner cut him down. Draven stood an instant on his feet before he staggered.

Simon caught him against his chest. "I've got you," he breathed.

Draven nodded as Simon draped Draven's arm over his shoulders and helped him walk toward her.

"Like old times, eh?" Draven whispered to his brother.

The look Simon gave her father was the most hate-filled glare she had ever beheld.

Emily touched Draven's face as they passed by her.

"Simon," Draven said hoarsely. "Tell her I'll be all right."

"I think she knows," he said as he walked Draven toward the castle.

Halfway across the yard, Draven lost consciousness.

Emily led Simon up to her room and helped him lay Draven facedown on the bed to keep his back from being hurt any more than was necessary.

As gently as she could, she washed the blood

from him. She frowned at the marred and puckered
skin left behind by the beating.   •

"What did he mean, 'twas like old times?" she
asked Simon.

Simon placed Draven's tunic by the bed. "His
father used to beat him like this on a regular basis.
When it was over, Sin would help him back to his
bed."

"Is that why he didn't cry out?"

"Aye. His father would add five lashes for every
sound he made."

Her heart lurched.

A knock sounded on the door. "Enter," Emily
called.

To her surprise, her father joined them with a
small vial in his hand. " 'Tis a linseed salve. It will
help take the sting from his back."

"Thank you," she said, amazed by his gift. Could
it be he was softening toward Draven?

She seized that hope and prayed for it to be so.

Her father took one last stony look at Draven's
unconscious form, then left them.

As carefully as she could, she spread the thick,
pungent ointment over his wounds, then draped a
light cloth over him.

Wiping her hands clean on a cloth, she looked to
Simon, who stood against the far wall, his face
beleaguered and pinched.

"How long will it take to heal?" she asked him.

"He'll be back on his feet by the morrow."

"Nay!" she gasped in disbelief.

Simon nodded. "He won't be swift, but he will be

up and about." With one last look at his brother's sleeping form, he moved for the door.

"Simon?" she asked as he reached for the latch. "Tell me, if you are the one who is illegitimate, why did his father abuse him and not you?"

"He never knew I wasn't his while I lived in his hall." Simon cast a look back at the bed. "And it wasn't from his father's lack of effort as much as it was from Draven constantly putting himself between us."

Simon took a deep breath and looked at her. "You know his limp?"

She nodded.

"I was but five and tilting the quintain when I fell from my horse. His father tried to run me down on his horse as punishment for my incompetence. One moment all I saw was his massive warhorse bearing down on me, and the next moment I was lying to the side of the field with Draven beneath the stallion, his leg broken in four places."

Emily closed her eyes at the horror. She couldn't imagine how either one of them had borne it.

"How did you learn of your birth?" she asked.

Simon shrugged. "Our mother told it to Draven not long before she died. She wasn't able to contact my father, but she knew Draven traveled enough with his father that he could find someone to send word to my father to come for me."

"Did he?"

"Aye. My father came for me the day after she died and reared me in Normandy."

In an instant everything made sense to her. "Miles de Poitiers?"

He nodded. "He was my father."

Now she knew how Draven had come to serve his king. "Draven went to Normandy to find you. That was how he became your father's squire?"

"And we have been together ever since. I owe my brother my life in more ways than one."

"You're a good man, Simon."

Simon shook his head. "I pale significantly in comparison, for he was the one who faced his father while I was always the one who ran away in fear."

"You're too hard on yourself."

"Perhaps, but I am truly grateful to you for reaching him when I couldn't."

"I could never have done it without you."

"Then we are eternal allies."

Emily smiled as he left her alone with her husband.

This was not the way she had imagined her wedding night. But she wasn't about to complain, for she had what she had always wanted. A husband she could love, and even more than she had dared dream, he was a man who loved her back.

Hours later, the king sent his physician to check on Draven. And once the castle had quieted, she curled up next to him and watched him sleep while she brushed her hand over his handsome face.

"You are mine forever," she whispered, then closed her eyes and slept.

* * *

In the morning, Henry took his entourage and left.

And true to Simon's prediction, Draven was on his feet.

Emily cringed as she helped him to dress. Surely the clothing had to hurt as it rubbed against the massive cuts and welts on his back. Yet he said not a word about it.

"I can't lie abed all day," he said as he rose.

"You need to," she insisted.

He shook his head, took her hand, then led her to the hall below. Her father looked up at their entrance and gave Draven a hard glare.

Emily sighed. After he had brought the salve she had hoped her father might be softening, but by the frown on his face, she could tell her father was a long way from ever accepting his new son-in-law.

Draven went to greet Simon, and she made her way to her father's side at the table.

"If you could accept Niles as your son after you found him in Joanne's bed, why can you not at least spare a smile for my husband?"

"Because I know his mettle," her father snarled as he cast another menacing glare to Draven. " 'Tis far beyond your ken, Em, for you see the good in people. I know the truth of him and his kith."

Shaking her head, she took a seat at the opposite end of the table, far away from him while she broke her fast. She could feel her father's stare on her, but she gave him her back as she ate bread and cheese.

Draven came to her side at about the same time she realized she shouldn't have eaten anything.

Her stomach heaved.

"Emily?" Draven asked, his face concerned.

She tried to leave the dais, but stumbled. Draven caught her against him and she heard him suck his breath in as she inadvertently touched his back. Still, he said nothing to her as he helped her toward the rear of the room.

"Are you better?"

She nodded as her stomach settled a degree. " 'Tis the babe."

Draven nodded. "How many more mornings should I prepare myself for this type of greeting?"

"I know not," she answered truthfully. "My mother's sickness lasted throughout all her pregnancies."

They had just rejoined her father in the hall when a cloaked form entered through the door. Emily frowned until the newcomer dropped the cowl from her head and showed a weary Joanne, whose body was so swollen with child that Emily couldn't believe she hadn't given birth. But what shocked her was the sight of Joanne's battered face.

Her father's curse rang out as he shot across the room to her side.

"Child, what happened?" he asked, gently cupping her bruised chin in his hand.

Emily rushed to her side as well.

Joanne sobbed. " 'Tis Niles," she gasped. "He has gone mad." She looked to her father as tears fell down her bruised cheeks. "He wants to kill you and inherit your lands through me."

Her father's nostrils flared in anger. "So help me, I'll see him dead for—"

"My Lord Warwick?" a boy shouted as he came

running through the door Joanne had left ajar. He gasped for breath, his brow split and bleeding. "My lord," he said as he paused before her father. "You must come quickly. Falswyth is under attack."

Her father released Joanne. "Who dares such?"

" 'Tis the earl of Ravenswood."

Every eye in the hall turned to Draven, who sat beside Simon at one of the lower tables.

Her father looked back at the messenger. "And how do you know?"

"I heard one of his men address him as such right before I was struck."

"What treachery is this?" her father snarled. "Both my in-laws attack simultaneously?"

"Father I must—" Joanne spoke, but her father cut off her words with a shake of his head.

"Em, take her above and see to her." Then he cast a menacing frown to Draven.

"Prepare my troops," he called, seizing his sword from its resting place above the mantel behind him. "We will put a stop to this once and for all."

As her father's men scurried from the hall, Draven gathered his own knights.

"Wait," Emily said to him, seizing his arm. "You can't go. You're hurt."

Draven shook his head, his face grim. "I will not stay here while someone mars my name. I will have the villain's head for this. Now go and tend your sister."

Emily wanted to argue, but the stubborn set of his jaw told her it would be a waste of breath.

Instead, she went to her father. "My husband rides with you. I pray you to guard his back."

Her father nodded, his eyes still filled with mistrust, and touched her arm.

Side by side, the two men she loved most strode from the hall, leaving her alone with her sobbing sister.

Draven felt Hugh's mistrust as they neared their horses. "You still think me responsible?"

"Until I see otherwise with my own eyes, aye."

Draven clenched his teeth. Her father would never accept him. So be it. He'd never been one to ask for acceptance.

To the devil with Hugh.

Draven pulled himself up carefully into his saddle. His back throbbed in protest, but he had fought with worse wounds than this.

Setting his heels to the flanks of his horse, Draven led his men to Falswyth.

When they reached the small village, the wasteful sight made him curl his lip in disgust. Most of the homes and buildings were burning while people ran away from soldiers bent on robbery, rape, and murder.

Draven heard a woman screaming. As Hugh and their men attacked the brigands, he leaped from his horse and kicked open the door to one of the few buildings still intact.

The woman had been tossed onto the table and was being held by four men as a fifth lifted her skirt and forced her knees apart.

Unsheathing his sword, he set upon her attackers with a vengeance. The frightened woman took refuge in a corner while he dispatched the men.

As he killed the last of them a shadow fell over him from behind. He turned, sword raised, to find Hugh standing in the doorway.

Hugh nodded in approval, then turned about and left.

Draven lowered his sword and took a moment to make sure the woman was still intact.

"Thank you, milord," she sobbed as she forced herself to stand.

Draven said nothing, then went to join the men fighting outside.

It was then he saw Hugh facing a man wearing a surcoat that bore a striking resemblance to his own. But worse than the fact that someone dared impersonate him was the fact that the imposter was about to kill Emily's father.

Hugh fought hard, but he was no match for the younger, more agile knight who twisted around Hugh, hammering blow after blow upon his sword and shield. Hugh staggered back from the assault.

Draven ran toward them, his sword raised. He reached them just in time to deflect a blow that would have surely separated Hugh's head from his shoulders.

Hugh stumbled back as Draven engaged the knight. The man was strong, but if Draven had been well, the man would have been no match for him.

As it was now, though, Draven felt himself weakening with every blow that fell upon his sword. He could feel the wounds of his back opening up and blood oozing down his spine.

His attacker caught him an upward blow to his shield that caused him to stagger back. Before he

could recover, another blow to his right sent him
hurtling to the ground.

Draven landed hard on his back. He gasped as
pain exploded throughout his entire body. He could
scarce draw a breath, let alone move his limbs.

This was it.

His opponent lifted his sword straight up.
Draven prepared himself for the death blow, but
just as the knight plunged the sword down, Hugh
caught him about his waist and knocked him away.

Awkwardly, painfully, Draven rolled to his side
and forced himself to stand. Yet it was hard. Every
part of him ached.

He staggered toward his horse, where he
grabbed on to his saddle to keep himself upright.

He glanced over to where Hugh still fought the
imposter and saw the second attacker moving for
Hugh's back.

Draven grabbed his dagger from his girdle and
hurled it with fatal precision into the attacker's
chest. Hugh saw the man fall, then with renewed
strength he finished off the man he fought with one
fatal sword stroke.

His strength gone, Draven tried to pull himself
into his saddle. It was no use.

He sank to his knees.

"Ravenswood?"

He heard Hugh's voice as if it came from a great
distance. Someone removed his helm, but Draven
couldn't be sure who it was. The pain was too great.

He looked up into Hugh's face as it swam above
him.

"Boy, don't you die like this. You hear me?"

Draven couldn't respond. Closing his eyes, he let the darkness take him.

Emily ran to the steps as soon as she heard the men returning. Joanne joined her.

As her gaze fell to her husband draped over his horse, Emily felt the blood drain from her face as terror consumed her. But even worse than the site of Draven was the fact her father refused to meet her gaze.

"Oh, mercy, nay," Emily choked.

If not for the support of her sister's arms, she would have collapsed.

Simon and her father pulled Draven from the horse and carried him toward her.

"Move, daughters," her father snapped. "We needs get him inside before he dies."

Emily closed her eyes in relief. "He's not dead?"

"Nay, child," her father said in a more tender voice. "Now move."

Still trembling, she opened the door for them, offered a prayer of thanks, then followed them up the stairs.

Hours later, Emily sat beside Draven on the bed in her room. He had only just awakened.

"You scared me," she scolded him.

His look bore into her. "I scared myself."

"How do you mean?"

Draven reached out and took her hand in his. "Until today, I never cared in battle whether I lived. Today, I learned that I care. When I hit the ground, my only thoughts were of you and of the babe. For the first time in my life, I didn't want to die. I wanted to return here to see you. I wanted to be here to see our babe born."

She cupped his cheek in her hand. "I love you, Draven."

"I love you," he said back to her.

The door to the room opened. Emily looked up to see her father hesitating in the doorway.

Never before had she seen him look so uncertain.

"Father?" she asked.

He cleared his throat and stepped into the room. "I didn't expect you to be awake," he said to Draven.

"Haven't you ever heard the devil never sleeps?" Draven asked bitterly.

She saw the shame in her father's eyes as he approached the bed. "You're not going to make this easy on me, are you?"

Draven frowned. "Make what easy on you?"

"My apology."

Emily sat in shock. Her father had never apologized to anyone in his life.

"I'm a prideful man," he said to Draven. "I admit that, but I'm not so prideful that I can't admit when I'm wrong. And I was terribly wrong about you . . ."

Her father paused, then gave him the largest compliment she knew him capable of when he said, "My lord."

And then she noted the softening of Draven's face, the relaxing of his taut muscles.

Her father swallowed. "All I can say in my defense is that I knew your father well, and I know I don't have to tell you what kind of man he was."

He met Draven's gaze levelly. "I don't know why you saved my life today. I wouldn't have done it for you."

"I wouldn't have expected you to."

Her father nodded as a muscle flexed in his jaw. "I think that might be the most painful part of all this. But I want you to know that had I been blessed with a son, I would want him to be just like you."

Draven gave a bitter laugh. "Then you should be grateful you had daughters. If you recall, I killed my father."

Her father's gaze gentled. "And today you saved his life. For whether you acknowledge me or not, from this day forward I will always claim you as my son."

Emily smiled at her father. Never had she been more proud of him, and by the look on Draven's face she could tell how much her father's words meant to him.

"My thanks, Hugh."

"Father," he corrected.

Draven gave a halfhearted laugh. "My thanks, Father."

Her father turned to leave.

"Hugh?"

Her father turned back with an exasperated sigh. "I can see you'll have to practice the father address, eh?"

"I shall work on it," Draven promised. "But I was wondering who it was you killed in my colors."

Her father looked to her, his gaze troubled. "You didn't tell him?"

"I didn't have the chance."

He nodded and looked back at Draven. " 'Twas Niles who wore your surcoat. The man you threw your dagger into was his cousin, Theodore."

Draven looked back and forth between them. "But why?"

"According to Joanne, he married her wanting my property," her father said. "His finances were such that he needed my entire wealth, and he couldn't wait for me to die of natural causes. Since he couldn't kill me for it without being hanged for murder, he devised a scheme to set us at odds so that you would do it for him."

Draven frowned. "Why did he not marry a rich heiress or widow?"

"He tried, but since he was out of favor with the crown, he could never get Henry's approval." Her father clenched his teeth, and she saw the sorrow on his face. "I've been such a fool. I welcomed the son who was unworthy and turned my back on the one who was decent."

"You're being too hard on yourself, Hugh."

"Father!" he snapped.

Draven's gaze mellowed. "Father."

"Good boy, now rest yourself. My grandson needs a father of his own."

Emily couldn't resist teasing her father. "How do you know it's a boy?"

"After having nothing save daughters, I figure the good Lord owes me a boy."

Emily laughed.

Her father bid them a good night, then left them alone.

She turned back to Draven and gasped as she felt a slight stirring in her belly.

"What?" he asked.

Joy filled her. " 'Tis the quickening. I just felt the babe for the first time."

And to her even greater delight, Draven smiled.

Epilogue

Ravenswood
Nine years later

"**E**mily, help!"

Emily came running into the rose courtyard behind the keep at Draven's frantic shout. She
stopped as she caught sight of him surrounded by
four boys who pummeled him with wooden
swords while another hung on to his left leg and yet
another hung precariously about his neck.

Emily laughed at the sight. " 'Tis your own
fault," she said to Draven.

"How so?"

"Out of six, could you not have given me a single
daughter?"

Draven laughed as Jace climbed further up his
back and wrapped one spindly arm around his
father's head, over his eyes.

"Mama!" six-year-old Christopher shouted, stamping his foot. "You're not supposed to make the dragon laugh. It makes him less fierce."

"Less fierce?" Draven asked as he gently flipped Jace over his head to land on his feet, then scooped Christopher up in his arms and tickled him. "I'll give you fierce, you scamp."

Emily shook her head at their play. Their eldest, Henry, looked up and shouted to his brothers, "Look, Grandpa's here with cousin Harry!"

Emily turned to see her father entering the yard with Joanne's son by his side. It never failed to amaze her how much Harry favored Joanne, with his blond hair and blue eyes, while none of her own boys held any of her features, except for Christopher, who had her green eyes.

But then the entire lot of them were her father's pride and joy. And in spite of the fear that had once ruled him for his daughters' safety, her father took great pleasure in his grandsons, and especially in the one granddaughter Joanne had gifted him with three years ago after her marriage to a Scottish nobleman.

Though they didn't see Joanne much these days, Harry, who was being fostered by her father, was an almost constant addition to their household.

Before she could blink, her sons set upon the two newcomers with the same vigor they had used to attack their father. Jumping up and down and hugging them, they all talked at once, making understanding any one of them impossible.

Draven whistled loudly.

They quieted down.

"All right, boys," Draven said. "Go easy on your grandfather, or he'll not take you hunting."

"Sorry," they said almost in unison.

"All right," Hugh said with a smile. "Are the lot of you ready?"

"Aye."

"Then let us be off. I saw a perfect doe just over yon hill!"

As they left, Emily joined Draven and wrapped her arms about his waist in a tight hug.

"Listen," she whispered. "Do you hear that?"

Draven frowned. "Hear what?"

"The silence," she said in a low tone. "Is it not truly eerie?"

He draped his arm over her shoulder. "Indeed. I can't recall the last time I heard such."

"So tell me, milord," she said as they walked arm in arm toward the donjon, "what are we to do this afternoon with no children about?"

He considered the possibilities. "We could try for that daughter. I believe there may yet be a position in your book that we haven't tried . . . ten times."

Emily laughed. "You know, that reminds me of a jest."

He rolled his eyes. "Not another."

"Aye. Do you know the one about the king and his knight?"

"Nay," he said with a sigh of resignation.

"They were having a discussion about bedding wenches. The king looked to the knight and said, 'In our opinion bedding a wench is fifty percent pleasure and fifty percent work.' The knight responded, 'Sire, forgive me, but I respectfully disagree. In my opinion 'tis seventy percent work and thirty percent pleasure.' For hours they argued and could come to no agreement. Finally the knight turned to his squire and asked him to settle the matter. The squire spoke up to say, 'Milord, and Majesty, 'tis my opinion that it must be one hundred percent pleasure, for if any work were involved, His Lordship would bid me do it in his stead.' "

Draven laughed. "Wherever did you hear such?"

"Your eldest son, milord. It appears your brother told it to him on his last visit."

Draven frowned. "I shall have a word with Simon about what he's teaching them. But come, wench," he said, his face instantly softening as he looked down at her, "let me see for myself how much pleasure there is to be had for the work involved."

"Aye, milord, I think I shall most definitely have to try and make you work off a few of those extra pounds."

"Extra pounds?" he asked offended.

"Aye, I believe Christopher called them your dragon's horns."

Draven snorted. "I'll show you my dragon's horn, wench."

Emily bit her lip as she looked up at him hungrily. "And I shall gladly make use of it, knave."